# Macramé Murder

# Macramé Murder

## Mollie Cox Bryan

KENSINGTON PUBLISHING CORP.

http://www.kensingtonbooks.com

KENSINGTON BOOKS are published by

Kensington Publishing Corp.
119 West 40th Street
New York, NY 10018

All Kensington Titles, Imprints, and Distributed Lines are available at special quantity discounts for bulk purchases for sales promotions, premiums, fund-raising, and educational or institutional use. Special book excerpts or customized printings can also be created to fit specific needs. For details, write or phone the office of the Kensington special sales manager: Kensington Publishing Corp., 119 West 40th Street, New York, NY 10018, attn: Special Sales Department, Phone: 1-800-221-2647.

Kensington and the K logo Reg. U.S. Pat & TM Off.

ISBN-13: 978-1-4967-0468-9
ISBN-10: 1-4967-0468-1
First Kensington Mass Market Edition: September 2017

eISBN-13: 978-1-4967-0469-6
eISBN-10: 1-4967-0469-X
First Kensington Electronic Edition: September 2017

10 9 8 7 6 5 4 3 2

Printed in the United States of America

*Dedicated to my daughters, Emma and Tess—*
*Emma at the beginning of a new chapter,*
*Tess at the start of a new passion.*
*Bravehearts, both.*
*I'm so honored to be your mom.*

# Acknowledgments

Readers: Thanks so much for welcoming Cora Chevalier and Jane Starr into your reading lives. I'm thrilled you love them as much as I do.

Special thanks to my editor, Martin Biro, and my publicist, Morgan Elwell, both of whom go above and beyond the call of duty. Much gratitude goes to the whole Kensington team. From the gorgeous covers to the fun social media graphics, your hard work is so appreciated. Thank you!

A heartfelt thanks goes to my beta readers, Amber Benson, Jennifer Feller, and Mary Sproles Martin, who give their time, energy, and opinions freely to read my early drafts.

I'd like to thank a few bookstore owners who have been extremely supportive of both my series. Mary Katherine Froelich, owner of the beloved Stone Soup Books and Café in my hometown of Waynesboro, Virginia (now an online concern), and event planner extraordinaire, and Kelly Justice of Fountain Books in Richmond, who always includes me in signings and watches for my books. Both women are so supportive to writers and the book community. Thank you, ladies!

A special nod to my new agent, Jill Marsal. Here's to many years of a great partnership.

To the loves of my life, my husband and daughters, thank you seems hardly enough, but there it is.

Yours,
Mollie

# Chapter 1

The bride resembled a mermaid princess in her sparkling white-blue outfit. The dress fit her curves down to right above her knees, tumbling out onto the sand in a splay of tulle, with lace cut to imitate scales.

A small but rapt gathering of people encircled the couple, and not far from the group stood Cora Chevalier and Adrian Brisbane. The sun hung low in the sky, displaying great streams of colors—brazen orange and crimson, melting into the sea. Torches planted in a circle around them lit the area softly, and distracted the mosquitoes, always a problem for Cora.

Cora and Adrian had arrived at the Big Island Craft Retreat that morning, planning to make time for themselves before the official launch of the retreat the next day. They had decided to go for a stroll when they happened upon the intimate wedding.

Adrian slipped his arm around Cora.

"A beach wedding," Cora whispered. So stunning. So intimate there wasn't even a bridal party.

As the bride turned her head to kiss the groom, Adrian stumbled on the sand.

"Are you okay?" Cora asked.

"Um, yeah, I guess. Sorry," he said, red faced, flummoxed.

She turned back around to the bride and groom and spotted the most gorgeous tiara she had ever seen perched on the bride's head.

Crafted from sea glass, rhinestones, and a few seashells, the tiara fit her head as if she were born with it. Seized with a longing to find out all about that tiara, Cora wondered who made it. Was it created with real sea glass? She'd read about the rarity of authentic sea glass. People used fake sea glass in their crafts because it was cheaper and easier to find. She stepped forward but Adrian held her back.

"Whoa," he said. "Where are you going?"

"I just wanted a closer view of the tiara," she said. "It's stunning."

"We better head back," Adrian said. "Our dinner reservation—"

"Oh yes, sure, that's right," Cora said. But she hated to leave the scene, a tableau straight out of a bridal magazine, except for the lack of a large wedding party.

"C'mon," Adrian said, and grabbed her by the hand.

He pulled her away from the wedding and whisked her back to the resort. The place had one fine-dining restaurant and they were going to make the most of it this first night away from Indigo Gap, North Carolina, where they both lived.

Adrian, a school librarian, and Cora, the proprietor of the Kildare House Craft Retreat, had met only a few months ago. Their relationship was moving along at a snail's pace, according to Cora's best friend and business partner, Jane Starr. But both Cora and Adrian were comfortable with how it was progressing.

Before they reentered the resort, Adrian grabbed Cora and kissed her.

"Well," she said, after they finished kissing. "I don't know what brought that on, but I'm all for it."

He grinned and slipped his arm around her once more as they walked down the path to the resort. They were interrupted by a loud voice coming from behind a clump of spiky beach shrubs and small trees.

"Honestly, I don't know what you were thinking! That tiara is priceless! One of a kind! Why would you simply let her have it?"

*Tiara?* Cora and Adrian stilled.

"You don't need the money, for God's sake. I was hoping for publicity. She's got the connections," another voice said.

Cora's and Adrian's eyes locked. He grimaced.

"Connections?" the female speaker said, and made a noise of exasperation. "Are you that gullible? She's a rich girl from this island. She's modeled a few times. She's written a few books. But she's never going anywhere, especially now, since she married that trash."

Cora's eyebrows lifted as she glanced at Adrian, whose face was reddening, again.

"I'm not necessarily talking about that. She's a scholar, too, you know," the male voice replied. "She's got publishing connections."

"Unbelievable! She's published a few books on mermaids and now she's a scholar! Mermaids!"

"Now, now . . ." the voice said, quieter and moving away from Adrian and Cora.

"Wow," Cora said. "Do you think they were talking about our bride?"

"Um, well, I . . ." Adrian stammered and shoved his hands in his pockets.

What was wrong with Adrian? Normally he was a bit more articulate. This evening all he could do was stammer . . . and kiss. *More of the kissing, less of the stammering,* Cora thought.

Cora's empty, gurgling stomach prompted her to pull Adrian further along the path.

Later, her mood softened by wine and a satisfying meal, Cora slipped into her king-size bed, covered in luxurious, plush bedding. Maybe Jane was right. Should she have invited Adrian to stay in the same room with her? But then again, Cora wasn't exactly ready for that step—and Adrian hadn't pushed her. He'd gotten his own room. No questions asked.

As she rolled over to her side, she thought of her own quilt-covered bed in her attic apartment, and her cat Luna, whose purr usually lulled her to sleep. Luna was being well-tended by Zora, her new friend and the owner of the Blue Note B & B. Cora closed her eyes and found sleep, even without Luna.

A siren rudely awakened her several hours later. She listened to the siren, not a police siren, but more like a warning signal. A fire alarm? Or a boat out on the ocean? She leapt up out of bed at the same time the phone rang. She picked up the phone.

She was greeted with a recording. "Please stay in your rooms. The warning siren is a notice for beach security. There is an emergency on the beach. Please stay in your rooms until further notice."

*Emergency on the beach? What could it be?*

Cora mentally sifted through the possibilities. Beach emergency—that could mean almost anything. Not a hurricane. The weather was perfect. Could some sea animal be beached? Or had someone had a heart attack, stroke, or gotten hurt on the beach? Paramedics were probably working on someone. She walked over to her window and strained to see. Flashing lights came into view, though she could barely see them. But the police and the paramedics were on it. This emergency was none of her concern.

Not this time.

# Chapter 2

The next morning, the 8 A.M. "teacher breakfast" loomed, a time to go over the schedule and a few "housekeeping" items for the retreat. When Cora found herself stressing because the retreat wasn't as organized as she'd like, she reminded herself she was here to teach. This was not her retreat to run.

She met Jane and Ruby near the elevators. They were all on the fifth floor with incredible views of Sea Glass Beach. The small island, named after the large amounts of sea glass it was blessed with, gave rise to the Big Island Craft Retreat, part of the island's establishment for fifteen years.

"Good morning, ladies," Cora said to them. "Where's London?"

"She's outside with the day care people," Jane said. "They'll be keeping her busy. They have all sorts of activities for the kids. Best retreat ever," she said, and smiled.

Ruby pressed the elevator button. "Sounds like an awesome arrangement. What the hell went on last night?" Ruby, a slightly stooped woman of a certain age, who had lived her whole life in Indigo Gap, was like a fish out of water in this high-tech, swanky resort. She lived in the gardener's cottage on the property Cora had purchased for her own craft retreats and was grandfathered in to the purchase. When Jane and Cora found out she was an herbalist and crafter, they invited her to join them in their craft retreat business.

"Some kind of emergency on the beach. Didn't you pick up the phone?" Cora asked.

"No, I didn't reach it in time," Ruby said. "And I couldn't figure out how to use the bloody voice mail system."

"It cleared early this morning," Jane said. "A lot of people were on the beach already when I took London to the day care."

As the elevator door opened and the three of them entered, the two women already inside nodded a good morning. As the door closed, one of them said, "Are you Jane Starr?"

Jane smiled. "Yes," she said. "And you are . . . ?"

"I'm Jessica and this is May," she said. "I'm so pleased to meet you. We've signed up for all your classes this weekend."

"Great!" Jane said. "I look forward to it."

"I have about twelve of your pieces at home," May blurted. "Big fan here."

Jane, an award-winning potter, was gathering quite a growing fan base. She could hardly keep up with her orders, especially for her goddess-mythology-themed pieces, and had been talking about hiring someone to help. Cora beamed. Jane had come a long way from the little girl she knew who loved to play in the mud—and the woman who'd married a troubled man. Jane was now her own woman.

Ruby caught Cora's prideful expression and she grinned at her. Ruby hadn't known them long, but she knew both of their stories, of course. Cora wasn't sure, but she thought Ruby considered herself Jane's patron saint of single motherhood. But what Ruby didn't realize was Jane had it all figured out.

The elevator door opened and everybody exited. Each group went their own direction.

Jane, Ruby, and Cora found the restaurant down a plush carpeted hall with several hanging, glittering chandeliers and huge paintings. Chloe's was one of the many eateries at the resort.

Mathilde Mayhue welcomed them to the table and made introductions. She was one of the first organizers of craft retreats. Fifteen years ago, she saw the market and the need for these retreats. It had become a measure of success to receive an invitation to teach.

Along with Cora, who was teaching a blogging-for-crafters class, Jane, who was leading a pottery class, and Ruby, instructing several classes including one on seashell candles, two other teachers were on the program. The headliner was Zooey, the macramé artist. Just Zooey. Complete with a limp handshake, Zooey seemed a type Cora often ran into at these retreats. She was manageable. Cora could get along with anybody, but she didn't have to become friends with her. The other teacher was Ryan Anderson, a crochet expert. Cora liked him immediately.

Mathilde's assistant, Hank Simmons, also sat at the large table, smiling at them with his gleaming white teeth on display. Cora wasn't sure how she felt about him. All those teeth made her nervous.

"What happened on the beach last night?" Ruby asked after they were all settled in, each with plates heaped high with breakfast food from the buffet.

"Oh." Mathilde waved her hand. "Who knows? I hate when that happens during the retreat. It startles people. I kind of wish they'd give me a heads-up so I could warn the retreaters before the alarm goes off. But most of the guests aren't in yet. They will be arriving throughout the day."

"Do you mean they never tell you what the emergency is?" Ruby asked, with a note of incredulity.

"They will eventually," Mathilde said, and took a bite of her whipped cream and strawberry-topped pancake.

Cora was pleased she and her crew were here, but she hadn't made up her mind about Mathilde yet, either.

But as she went over the rules for the craft teachers, Cora leaned more toward not liking her—especially with Mathilde's "no socializing with students" rule. What was that about? Cora didn't like that one bit. Nor the policy about extra craft supplies—if a crafter messed up, he or she was allowed one more try, with supplies covered by the cost of the event. After the limit, it was their responsibility to buy supplies. Cheap, Cora thought, especially at such an expensive retreat.

A server came up and whispered something into Mathilde's ear.

Mathilde's face turned ghastly white and her mouth dropped open.

*What is wrong?* Cora wondered, becoming concerned.

"Are you okay?" Ruby said, reaching for Mathilde. She was the closest one to her.

"I'm fine," Mathilde managed to say. "I've just gotten some horrible news."

"Drink some water," Ruby said.

The group quieted. The sound of others' voices in the place took on a louder quality. Plates and utensils clanging. Someone laughed.

Mathilde blinked. Her eyes watered. "I'm sorry." She dabbed her eyes with a napkin.

*My goodness. What is the problem?* Cora thought.

"This has never happened before," Mathilde said, stiffening. "But I might as well give you the news myself."

Cora's heart raced. What was going on? What had happened? Mathilde was falling apart right in front of them.

"There was a body found on the beach last night," Mathilde said with a hushed tone.

"A body," Jane said, her eyes wide. "What kind of body? What do you mean?"

"A human body," Mathilde said.

They sat stunned.

"A drowning?" Cora managed to say.

"They're not sure what happened," Mathilde said, her voice cracking. "The poor woman was just married yesterday. The evidence suggests she died from a jellyfish sting."

Cora coughed as she tried to swallow her coffee. "Was she married here? On the beach?"

Jane and Ruby turned to look at Cora.

"Yes," Mathilde said. "Marcy grew up on the island and came back home to marry here. So sad."

"Do you mean to tell me she was married yesterday and then murdered later the same day?" Ruby exclaimed. "How horrible!"

Mathilde nodded and took a sip of her cranberry juice before saying, "Tragic."

Jane sat with her mouth hanging open, as if she wanted to find words but couldn't.

The image of the beautiful bride still fresh in her mind, Cora's appetite dwindled and she pushed away her plate.

# Chapter 3

Cora tried to ignore the crime scene tape on the sectioned-off part of the beach. But she was a bit distracted by it as she, Jane, and Adrian walked around it. They didn't speak about it, even as it flapped in the breeze, an unspoken pact among them.

"There!" Jane said, pointing to a cluster of sparkly sea glass caught in the sand.

Cora's attention moved from ignoring the crime scene to the gleaming glass nuggets half buried in the sand.

"Ah-ha!" Cora said.

They crouched and scooped up the sea glass. Enamored, Cora had studied up on sea glass in preparation for the trip. After viewing Mathilde's sea glass creations, she became even more thrilled about being here and trying her hand at crafting with the glass.

"So lovely." Jane splayed her hand out, revealing her treasure. Aqua and cobalt glass stones tumbled around on her hand. "I'm going to use this in some of my pottery." Her eyebrows lifted as she grinned. Jane's deep blue eyes were filled with inspiration.

"This island is magical," Cora said. "The way it attracts sea glass and seashells. It's like a crafter's fantasy come true."

"Yeah," Adrian said. "I've always found sea glass fascinating. It's like a reverse gemstone."

Jane laughed. "What do you mean?"

"Gemstones are made by nature and refined by people. Sea glass is made by people and refined by the sea. You know, after years of our discarded bottles and jars rolling around in the sea, we find these beautiful pieces of glass," he said.

"Exactly," Cora said, placing her glass treasures in her bag. "And Mathilde crafts some lovely jewelry from sea glass. She's made quite a career from it."

"I'm looking forward to her sea craft class," Jane said after a moment. "Hey, your nose is getting pink."

"Darn," Cora said. She wore a big floppy hat and plenty of sunscreen and yet an hour on the beach gave her a pink nose. "I should be moving inside anyway. I need to check the classroom out and make sure they have enough outlets and so on. The last time I guested, the class had to share outlets and it was so disruptive."

"I'll go with you," Jane said.

"Me too," Adrian said. "I'm going to head back and get my book. I think I may sit on the beach for a while and read."

A gentle, warm breeze blew up, ruffling Adrian's dark hair. His sunglasses prevented Cora from seeing and admiring those jade eyes of his.

"Gee, sounds like fun," Jane teased. "Sounds like something Cora would do. Go to the beach and read."

"What's wrong with that?" Cora asked as Jane walked off toward the resort. She looked at Adrian and pulled a face as they followed Jane.

"What time is our tour of the island scheduled?" Adrian asked, after they'd gotten to the vast lobby of the resort.

"We'll see you at two," Cora said, and kissed his cheek.

"You two are so much fun I can't stand it," Jane said, after he left them. "A kiss on the cheek?" She rolled her eyes. "You can do better than that."

"What? Right here in the lobby? I don't think so," Cora said.

"Let's find our classrooms," Jane said.

Cora pulled out her map and instruction sheet. "Okay. It looks like we are down this hallway. Over there." She pointed. "And out that door."

"A separate building?"

"Attached by a long hallway."

"I haven't been over there yet. C'mon, let's go."

They walked past the main indoor fountain and down one of the many long corridors, called Mermaid Hall, for obvious reasons. There were mermaid paintings, mermaids on the carpet, and even mermaids drawn on the ceiling. Cora and Jane stopped in front of the centrally located stained-glass window of a mermaid. The color of the mermaid's dress was the exact shade of blue the bride had worn the day before.

"I'm trying not to think of that poor woman," Cora said.

"Who?" Jane asked.

"Marcy, the woman who died on the beach last

night," Cora said. "Adrian and I saw her wedding. It was so gorgeous. She wore a dress just this color."

"London calls it mermaid blue," Jane said.

"But isn't it more of a green?"

Jane stood back and considered it. "I think it's a blue-green."

"What do you think happened to her?" Cora said after a minute.

"Who? Oh. Marcy? Who knows? It's devastating. She was just married yesterday and then died," Jane said, and walked over to a mermaid painting. "I love this. It's sort of Pre-Raphaelite with the color choices."

"I see what you mean," Cora said.

They continued walking down the hallway.

"I think it's kind of suspicious—what happened to Marcy. You know?" Cora said after a few moments.

"Don't become involved, Cora. You have no reason to. You didn't know her. We are guests of this resort and island. We don't know any of these people," Jane said.

"I don't plan on getting involved," Cora said.

"How many times have I heard that before?"

"I'm observing the curious circumstances. That's all," Cora said. After all, what could she do? She planned to be busy with her classes. And Jane was right; she didn't know any of these people. It wasn't anything like recent situations back home in Indigo Gap, where she was compelled to involve herself in police business.

When she thought about Indigo Gap, a surprising wave of homesickness rolled through her. She'd been there less than a year and already thinking of it as home, which was a good sign.

"Well, isn't this grand?" Jane said as she stood in

front of a new section of hallway—smaller and all glass. As they strolled, it felt almost as if they were outside.

"This must be built on the the tiny peninsula Ruby told us tabout," Cora said.

"It feels kind of more private here. I like it," Jane said. They walked into a round room with several smaller rooms jutting off.

WELCOME TO THE BIG ISLAND CRAFT RETREAT, a sign proclaimed.

Everything looked lovely. Everything seemed right. But Cora couldn't shake her ominous feelings about the bride who'd died. Was it because she had glimpsed a part of the wedding? She tried to ignore the creeping sensation along her spine and resolved to set her emotions aside. She was here to teach everything she had learned and practiced about craft blogging. She needed to be on top of it. When she found the room where she'd be teaching, she saw that everything was in perfect order.

So why did that make her so nervous?

# Chapter 4

Cora's group gathered together for the 2:00 P.M.—Cora, Jane, Ruby, her son, Cashel, and Adrian. Cora was surprised Cashel had come along for the retreat. He was a busy attorney, one of the few in Indigo Gap. But he had mentioned that another lawyer had been recently hired at his practice and he needed a break. So he joined his mother. Ruby was only too happy to spend time with him.

"I can't believe all the beautiful shells and sea glass I found this morning," Ruby said.

Their guide smiled, fiddling with his name tag. His hair was silver blond and face rugged with lines that spoke of years in the sun. "Do we have everybody?"

"I think so." Cora checked the group. "All here."

"Follow me," he said, and led them to his truck. Or was it a Jeep? Or some kind of strange combination of the two? They filed into the back of the vehicle, like an old-fashioned hayride.

"This ought to be fun," Jane muttered.

After they were situated, Frank, the tour guide, went over the rules. *This island is full of rules,* mused Cora.

"As you know, you're officially in Low County," he said. "Sea Glass Island is the smallest of the islands. When folks think of our islands, they usually think of Edisto or Hilton Head. We are barely a blip on the map compared to them. But because of the geography of our island and the way the currents enter, we have an unusual amount of driftwood, sea glass, and seashells."

"Hence the name Sea Glass Island," Cashel said with a sarcastic note.

Adrian looked at Cora as if to say "Didn't everybody know that?"

A grinning Cashel winked at Cora. She made a mental note to ask him to stop winking at her. It was something he did frequently. Once or twice was one thing, but now he was coming off like an old, creepy uncle.

She didn't quite understand Cashel. He was *GQ* gorgeous and when she first met him she was quite attracted to him—but his mother worked for her. She made it a policy to not date her employee's sons. Her policies were in flux, admittedly. But just now, in her head, it became a policy. She created policies as the business went along.

No male teachers.

No sleeping with retreaters.

No dating the sons of mothers who worked for her.

Always do background checks of her guest teachers.

The guide, Frank, explained about Sea Glass Island's booming tourism industry, but said that it was experiencing difficulties staying afloat during the off season. Plus, it was dealing with some damage from recent hurricanes, which had destroyed part of a public beach. He stopped the truck.

"Over there," he said. "It used to be a huge beach." He pointed to a small beach, full of huge rocks. "It's an area designated as unsafe for visitors, which on a small island like this, is too bad."

"Are there any restoration efforts in place?" Adrian asked.

"There's a group here trying to raise awareness and money. I can give you their card at the end of the tour."

Adrian nodded. "Sounds good."

Not only was Adrian attractive and smart, but he was just plain nice. You had to like that in a man. Some women, of course, didn't like nice guys, which was something Cora had never understood. Many of the women she used to work with at the Sunny Street Women's Shelter in Pittsburgh fell only for "bad" guys—and it never led to anything good.

She turned her face as she adjusted her hat and saw Cashel peering at her. He looked away.

"From this angle," Frank said, after driving further into the island forest and explaining about the plants and trees around them, "you can see our famous hook."

A piece of the island jutted out, forming a hook shape, and part of the resort was built onto it. The Mermaid Hall was built on it, connecting the crafting area attached to the older resort with the new crafting area.

"Wow," Jane said. "We were right there, almost at the tip of the hook this morning, right?"

Cora nodded. From here they viewed the long Mermaid Hall from a different vantage point.

"What's that?" Ruby said, pointing to a huge building on the side of one of the hills.

"That would be the home of one the island's biggest families, the Grimms," he said. "You'll see roads named after them and so on."

Adrian coughed.

"They were one of the founding families. Recently, they've been fighting to keep their property, though," he said, and drove off.

"What do you mean?" Ruby said.

"Well, developers are always wanting a piece of them. We hope they never sell. Of course the other big family on the island did sell, which is how the resort started. But it's never enough, you know?"

Ruby grunted. "One resort on this beautiful island is enough."

"I'd have to agree," Jane said.

Cora kept her opinion to herself. Of course she agreed with them. But she realized several sides to stories like this existed.

They turned a corner and the landscape changed. Smaller, tidy homes painted in bright colors sat clustered together in a straight line.

"This is Gator Corner," he said, laughing a little when Ruby gasped. "We don't have alligators anymore, but we used to. Behind that clump of trees is the swamp. I'll drive over there. But be prepared. It's different."

Different it was. Gone were the tidy homes. The places lining the swamps resembled nothing more than shacks. A glittering mobile or chime hung in the window of one of the homes. It caught Cora's eye.

"Don't be fooled," Frank said. "Some of these folks have more money than God. They just like to keep it simple."

Simple or not, the chimes currently catching her attention were gorgeous. Cora wanted to exit the car and find out who had crafted them. Who lived in such a place, with such beautiful chimes in the window?

But Frank kept moving.

When they returned to the main resort, the island police surrounded the area. They appeared to be waiting for them. Odd.

As they exited the van, the police took a special interest, watching each person. Several officers came up to the group.

"We're looking for Adrian Brisbane."

"Um, yeah, that's me," Adrian said.

"Please come with us to the station," one of the cops said.

"What? What for?"

"We need to ask you some questions about Marcy Grimm."

Adrian's face reddened.

"Adrian? What's going on?" Cora said. "Who's Marcy Grimm?"

"Marcy Grimm is the woman whose body was found last night," Ruby said.

"I thought her last name was Dupres," Cora said.

"Not officially yet," Ruby said. "According to the paper."

"Can you please come with us?" The officer held out his arm and gestured for Adrian to follow him.

Cora's heart thudded against her ribs. What was going on here?

Adrian began to follow the police and then turned around. "Cora, we'll talk about this later. I—"

She held up her hand. "Okay," she found the courage to say.

As he left, she caught Cashel's smirk.

"Don't just stand there," Ruby said to him. "Follow him. I didn't put you through law school for you to stand around with that stupid look on your face."

# Chapter 5

Jane grabbed Cora's hand.

"I don't know what's going on, but I can tell you Adrian had nothing to do with any of it," Jane said, trying to reassure Cora. It had been a long time since Cora was interested in anybody, and Jane herself had brought them together, thinking they were perfect for one another.

Cora paled and sucked in air. Jane hoped she wasn't having a panic attack—they were one of the main reasons they'd created their new life together. Cora couldn't handle her social work in a women's shelter in Pittsburgh.

"It must be some kind of mistake," Ruby said, coming alongside them. "Cashel will get to the bottom of it."

Cora said nothing, just squeezed Jane's hand.

"What do they want with him?" Jane said almost to herself.

"They're probably asking him the usual questions," Ruby said. "Who knows? Cops! Anyway, we'll find out the scoop when my Cashel returns."

Her belief in her son bordered on either sweet or ridiculous. Jane couldn't decide which right at this moment.

"Cora! Jane! Ruby!" A voice startled all three of them. It was Mathilde, the woman in charge of the retreat. "There you are!"

Mathilde came racing over to them, with a small woman next to her.

"Yes," Jane said, forcing cheerfulness. "We've just returned from our tour of Sea Glass Island. What a lovely place!"

"Stunning," Ruby said.

"I want to introduce you to Sherry Miller," Mathilde said. "She came all the way from California to take your class, Cora."

Cora perked up and smiled. She held out her hand. "Lovely to meet you, Sherry."

"Thanks," Sherry said. "I've been a big fan of your blog for such a long time. I can't wait for your class."

"What's your craft?" Ruby said.

"A little of everything," she replied. "But basically I love to crochet. I was thrilled to see Ryan Anderson is teaching here and I'll be able to take your class and his."

"Well," Mathilde interrupted. "We were on our way for drinks over at the café. Care to join us?"

"I don't know about anybody else, but the tour wore me out. I'm going to take a nap," Ruby said.

Jane agreed, but she was more worried about Cora than she was tired herself.

"I need a bit of a rest, too," Cora said. "We'll catch you later."

After the three of them entered the elevator and

went up to their floor, they stood in awkward silence. Jane shifted her weight. Ruby cleared her throat.

"How could the island police possibly think Adrian had anything to do with Marcy's murder?" Cora finally said.

"It's bizarre," Jane said. "He's one of the nicest guys I ever met."

Ruby harrumphed. "He's a man, ain't he?"

"What's that supposed to mean?" Jane said.

"Not all men are evil," Cora said.

"No, but a lot of them are not ruled by their heads, if you know what I mean," Ruby said. "And I think you do."

"Yes, but what could Adrian possibly have done? He's a visitor here. He doesn't know anybody," Jane said. "Let alone the woman who died."

"I think he did say something about having been here before," Cora said.

"What? When?" Ruby asked.

Cora waved her hands, as if trying to make the conversation go away. "I can't remember. Only that he'd been here before and it was a beautiful island. That's it."

"Will you let us know when you hear from Cashel? I need to take a bit of a rest. The heat is doing a number on me," Jane said.

"I hear ya," Ruby said. "I'll text you when I have news." Ruby took off down the hall toward her room.

Jane and Cora walked in the direction of their rooms.

"You know he's a good guy, right?" Jane said to her.

"I think so," Cora said. "But this has made me think, I must admit. What do we know about him?"

Jane stopped walking. "We know he's a librarian at

the school. If he had any kind of record, the school would not have hired him."

"True," Cora said. "But what about his personal life? He never talks about any women in his past or anything, except his—"

"Except his mother," Jane said. "He took care of his sick mother, Cora. He can't be all that bad."

Relief seemed to wash over Cora. "That's true. I know. But if he's such a great guy, what do the police want with him?"

"Must be a mistake," Jane said. "That's all I can think it is. Some kind of weird mistake."

"We should go to the police station," Cora said.

"I'm not sure that's a good idea," Jane replied.

"Why not? I'm his girlfriend. Shouldn't I be there?"

"Maybe," Jane said. "But let's take a rest, first. If he's still gone in an hour, we'll go and see him. How's that sound?"

But Cora didn't think she could wait. "I'll just go myself. You go and take a nap. I won't be able to sleep at all. I know myself."

"But Cashel is with him and, come to think of it, Adrian might not want you there," Jane said.

"I hadn't thought of that," Cora said. "Maybe you're right. I should stay here and take some downtime."

"Yeah, it doesn't matter if you nap. But at least take an hour to chill. I'll meet you back here, okay?"

Cora nodded. "One hour."


Cora lay on the hotel bed. She needed to lie down and rest, even if she didn't fall asleep. She tried to keep her mind off Adrian but kept going over what she knew about him.

He worked as a librarian at the school, having taken the place of the previous one, who was murdered. Thank goodness the guilty party was caught.

He was highly educated, well read, and very much a gentleman. He took care of his sick mother. The kids at the school loved him. Jane's daughter, London, loved him, too.

But he never talked about his past. She planned to rectify this during the weekend. How many relationships had he been in? Had he ever been married? She knew nothing. She always believed in the old adage that gentlemen didn't kiss and tell, but he was more tight-lipped than any man she'd ever known.

She closed her eyes and rolled over to her side. She was certain some odd circumstance had brought the police to Adrian. If not, if there was a problem, if he had something to do with the death of Marcy, best Cora know now before she became any more involved with him.

She reached over to the nightstand and picked up one of the catalogs in the stack of materials in the retreat bag, leafing through Zooey's glossy catalog. Cora hated to admit it, but Zooey was talented. What she did with macramé was nothing short of, well, art. Amazing. Wall hangings with intricate knot work. Curtains. Dream catchers. Hammocks. Lamp shades. And she crafted the most exquisite jewelry, which was her signature. She used gemstones and intricately woven macramé patterns around them. Cora was in awe. She didn't covet many things. But the necklaces Zooey made were something Cora might splurge on. She liked the vintage air of macramé meeting with Zooey's modern sensibility. The jewelry complemented Cora's retro clothing.

At least that's what she told herself.

She closed her eyes and woke up abruptly when the catalog fell on her chest.

Cora sat up on the edge of her bed and inhaled. As the air filled her lungs, she told herself it would be okay. Either Adrian had nothing to do with Marcy's death and they could move along with the retreat and their lives, or he did, and they still would move on with their lives. *Better to know.*

But why did she think he could have anything to do with murder or anything illegal at all? Why didn't she trust him? That may be what bothered her the most. He hadn't given her any cause for distrust. In fact, he'd been the perfect boyfriend.

Her cell phone buzzed. It was Jane.

"Hey, Cora. I know I said I'd meet you in a few minutes. You awake?"

"Yes."

"Something has come up with London."

"Is she okay?"

"I don't know. I think so. But I'm heading down to the day care now."

"I'll go with you. I'm not sleeping. I've barely been able to sleep."

"Okay then. Meet you at the elevator in a few minutes."

Cora stood, looked herself over in the mirror, ran her fingers through her red, unruly hair, and voilà, she was ready to go.

When she and Jane entered the hotel day care center, the Mermaid's Palace, they spotted London immediately. She held a beautiful tiara in her hands and was speaking with one of the day care workers.

"But, Ms. Shaw, we were searching for treasure and I found this. You said I could have it," London said.

"I know, sweetie, but I thought it was a toy. But this is a real treasure," Ms. Shaw said. "I need to alert the hotel and the police."

London, usually a sensible kid, started to wail.

"Oh, sweetie!" Jane said, and scooped her up in her arms. "Shhhh."

"What's going on?" Cora asked.

"I'm sorry," Ms. Shaw said to them both. "We were looking for seashells and sea glass and I told them they could keep whatever they collected."

"And?" Jane said, rubbing her daughter's back as she rocked back and forth.

"London found this tiara," she said, holding it up.

Cora's breath caught in her throat. *No! Could it be?*

"At first, I thought it was a toy. Like a part of a dress-up costume," Ms. Shaw said.

"I can see that," Jane said.

"But after I inspected it, I realized it looks like a real tiara and those stones might be diamonds," she continued.

"I think I might know who it belonged to," Cora said.

"What?" Jane said. London stopped sobbing and looked at Cora.

"Yesterday, Adrian and I witnessed this beautiful wedding and I think this is the tiara the bride wore. How many of them could there be like this, right?" Cora said. "It's exquisite."

"Well, we have to give it back if it belongs to someone else, London," Jane said, and her daughter slipped down her hip to stand on her own.

"I don't think we can," Cora said.

"What? What do you mean?" Ms. Shaw said.

"I think she's the woman, you know, on the beach last night. . . ." Cora said, not wanting to alert London.

Ms. Shaw pulled her aside. "Do you mean the woman who was killed?"

Cora nodded.

"Oh dear," Ms. Shaw said. "I need to alert the management and the police."

"I want to go home!" London yowled.

"What is wrong with you?" Jane said. "This isn't like you at all."

"I don't like it here! I miss Indigo Gap." Tears streamed down London's face.

Cora's heart fluttered as she and Jane locked eyes. Maybe they were all missing Indigo Gap. More importantly, perhaps they had all found a home—a home worthy of being missed.

# Chapter 6

Cora marveled at the scene around her. She stood in the center of a group of police officers and hotel management staff listening to the same story repeated over and over again. Why did she continually find herself in the middle of these situations?

Taking advantage of the opportunity to closely examine the tiara, Cora realized *crown* was a better word for the headpiece. Sea-green glass chunks were housed in twisted delicate wires. In between pieces of glass were seashells and what Cora had assumed were rhinestones, but all the fuss suggested diamonds. In the center of the crown, two wires shot up shaped into spirals, with glitter and stones set inside. The effect was delicate, yet bold, and Cora was in awe of the design and the skill. Even in the plastic evidence bag, it sparkled and glittered.

"Did you make this?" a police officer asked Mathilde as Cora entered the room.

"Yes!" Mathilde Mayhue said. "It's one of my

pieces." She grabbed it from the officer who was holding it.

He snatched it back. "Excuse me, but this is evidence."

"Evidence of what?" she said, almost shrill.

Cora was glad Jane had taken London back to the room to relax.

"A child found this on the beach. It's Marcy Grimm's. This might be a clue to a homicide."

"Are you talking about murder, on this of all weekends?" she said in a hushed tone. "I have a retreat to run!"

Cora walked over to her. Mathilde's face was gruesome white, yet the officer remained unconcerned.

"Oh, Cora!" Mathilde said. "How could this be? How could this have happened to me? To my retreat?"

"It will be okay," Cora found herself saying, even though she was shocked by Mathilde's reaction. After all, a young bride had just been killed. "We'll continue with the event in spite of all this."

"How?"

"One class at a time. We march forward and do what we are supposed to do. People came a long way to be here and we're going to give them what they want," Cora said.

"You're right, of course." Mathilde turned her attention back to the police officer. "I want that returned when you're finished with it."

The officer's mouth dropped open.

"Returned to me," she said. "I'll refund the money to the family, or whatever they want."

"That will be up to the family," the officer said. "In

the meantime, this is evidence. When we're finished with it, it will go back to her family, as is regulation."

Mathilde opened her mouth, as if to say something, and then changed her expression, as if she thought better of it.

"So, let me be clear about this," the officer said. "This is the piece you designed for Marcy Grimm?"

She nodded.

"She wore it at her wedding yesterday?"

"As far as I know. I didn't attend the wedding," she said, tight-lipped.

"Thank you. That will be all," he said.

"It's getting kind of late," Cora said to Mathilde. "Why don't we have a drink or something?"

She glanced at her watch. "I'm sorry, Cora. I need to help Zooey set up for tomorrow."

"Can I help?" Cora said.

"Certainly," Mathilde responded.

They walked out of the day care center, now teeming with parents, police, and hotel employees, through the vast lobby, down the Mermaid Hall to the retreat area of the resort.

Zooey was in the classroom already, her blond hair pulled into a sloppy bun, and her lithe body covered in a gauzy, nearly see-through dress.

A much younger man flitted around her. He seemed as if he stepped right off the beach—surfer blond hair and a dark tan, ripped biceps, and shoulders displayed by a white tank top. He certainly did not look like a crafty guy.

"Thanks, Tom," Zooey said to him as he finished hanging several macramé plant holders of blues and greens and a variety of knots and patterns.

She smiled at Cora. "We're going to make these in

class tomorrow. I've precut the cording. We need to place it and the tools on each chair and then I think we're done. Not much work left. Tom helped earlier."

"What a cool chair!" Cora said, noticing the hanging macramé chair in the corner.

"Thanks," she said. "It's one of my favorite things to make."

"Seems complicated," Cora remarked.

"Time consuming maybe, but not complicated," Zooey said, setting up a board with several different sample knots on it. "I listen to music, get in my zone, and go for it."

Cora studied the labeled knots. Chinese crown knot. Half-knot sinnet. Genovese waved bar. Alternating lark's head braid.

"Where do you want your books?" Mathilde asked Zooey.

"I think in the other corner there."

Mathilde scooted a table and Cora moved to help her. Tom carried over a box of books.

"I think we should leave the books in the boxes until the morning," Mathilde said. "I mean, this area is secure, but I think I'd feel better."

Zooey tucked an empty box under a table. "It will be okay," she said. "I don't think there will be time in the morning to place the books out and so on."

Cora placed the packs of cord and instructions on the classroom chairs. She wasn't going to involve herself in the decisions; this wasn't her retreat. But she wondered why Mathilde was worried about leaving Zooey's books out overnight. The area was secure and secluded.

*Not my retreat.* She repeated those words in her head. She liked being in charge of her own retreat.

But this was a pleasant feeling as well. All she was responsible for was showing up and giving her blogging class. Plus, she wanted to take some crafting classes if she could. She might even do some crafting herself.

Cora checked her phone. No messages yet, which led her to believe Adrian was still detained at the police station. Once this business with the police was resolved, Cora was sure this craft retreat was going to be fabulous. But for now, she needed to know what was going on with Adrian.

# Chapter 7

Cora had planned a room service dinner on her balcony for her crew—a relaxing breather before the madness of the retreat. But there was unmistakable tension in the air. On Cashel's return for dinner, he informed them that Adrian was still being detained at the island police station. As much as Cora poked and prodded, he kept his mouth shut.

"I'm sorry, Cora," Cashel said. "I can't tell you anything. But I'm doing my best."

"Why are they keeping him?" Jane asked. "It makes no sense."

Cashel's expression was secretive. Jane realized there must be more to the story than Cashel relayed.

"I'm his lawyer and there's this client privacy thing," he said, and bit into his burger.

"Oh, for God's sake, Cashel!" Ruby said. "I'm your mother. Cora is his girlfriend."

He finished chewing his burger and reached for a chip. "Cora and Adrian need to have a chat. This doesn't concern you at all, Mother."

"Humph," she said, and waved him off. "That's the

thanks I get for busting my ass to put you through law school."

He grinned. "Precisely."

"Do you need to be so cocky about it?" Jane said. "I mean, seriously, we are concerned about him."

"He's going to be fine. After all, I'm his attorney," he said.

Everybody quieted. London had fallen asleep in the lounge chair.

"The idea he had anything to do with a murder is preposterous," Cora said, and took a sip of her wine.

Behind Cora, the sun was setting over the beach. Crimson, dusky blue, and orange splayed out in the skies.

"I agree," Jane said.

"I'm glad you feel that way," Cashel said as he placed what was left of his burger back on his plate. "Your belief and trust in him is likely to be tested over the next few days. But I'm with you. I don't think he could hurt a fly, let alone kill someone."

Ruby dropped her fork on her plate. "Cashel! You can't say stuff like that and expect us not to want to know more."

"It will all be revealed in due time," he said, twitching his eyebrows.

Jane wanted to throttle him. She saw his mother did, too.

"Can we please change the subject?" Cora said, slurring her words a bit. Just how much wine had Cora drunk?

"Are we all set for the morning?" Cora asked.

They all nodded.

"Shall I remind you all we are guests of this retreat and we need to behave ourselves?" Cora said.

The group quieted.

"Of course," Ruby finally said.

"Mathilde is nervous," Cora went on. "This retreat has already been marred because of the murder on the beach. She asks for us to keep it light and engaging and try not to speak about it."

"We know what that's like," Jane said.

"Yep," Ruby said.

They'd not been in Indigo Gap long when the school librarian had been murdered, then her ex-husband. It was during their first retreat—and Jane had ridiculously been suspected of the murders. Several retreaters had canceled as a result.

The sound of the ocean called to Jane and she allowed it to lull her, as she preferred not to think about being a murder suspect and how it made her feel. She wondered how Adrian was managing.

"Is he okay?" she asked Cashel.

"Who?"

"Adrian!"

"Oh." He glanced nervously from woman to woman, all three of them waiting for answers. "He'll be fine."

"He's in jail," Jane continued. "I didn't spend the night in jail, but I know what it feels like to be wrongly accused."

"This is a posh island resort. It's not like he's in jail with a bunch of lowlife criminals," Cashel said. "In fact, his accommodations are nice, as far as jails go. I wouldn't worry. But he is upset, of course."

"Can I see him?" Cora asked.

"Not now," Cashel said. "They don't allow visitors past a certain time. I imagine he'll be out this time tomorrow. You can see him in the morning. But don't you have a class to teach?"

Cora nodded. "I do."

Jane might be mistaken, but she thought Cashel was amused. She knew he'd do everything he could to help Adrian, but he seemed to be enjoying the moment. She questioned his reason.

Cashel and Cora had had some chemistry between them when they first met—but Cora nipped it in the bud because Ruby worked for her. She didn't think it was appropriate to date her employee's son. But maybe Cashel harbored feelings for Cora. Was that the reason he didn't warm up to Adrian?

"Don't worry, Cora," Jane said. "Of course Adrian is innocent. And as you always like to say, if you're innocent, everything will be fine. And he's one of the nicest people I've ever met. That's why I wanted you two to meet. We have nothing to worry about."

"I beg to differ," Cashel said. "We have plenty to worry about."

"What? What do you mean? Not about Adrian?" Cora said.

"No, I wouldn't worry about him. After all, he's a big boy," Cashel said, with a bitter note in his voice. "Nah, what I'd be worried about is a murderer somewhere on this island. A killer who murdered a woman who'd just been married. Which is particularly heinous to me."

A chill traveled through Jane, even though it was a warm night. She glanced over at her daughter, sleeping peacefully in the chair.

"Also particularly personal," Cora said.

"Absolutely," he replied pointedly, lifting an eyebrow.

# Chapter 8

Cora woke up the next morning, grouchier than usual. As she drank a cup of coffee in her room, she sorted through her feelings.

Cashel's face flashed in her mind's eye. She remembered his attitude from the night before and she must have been on the edge of having too much to drink; otherwise, she'd have told him a thing or two. Why couldn't he tell them what was going on with Adrian? He was just being a brat.

And why wasn't Adrian out of jail? Why would they have kept the man without good cause?

"You picked another winner," Cora said as she checked herself in the mirror. She ran a brush through her unruly red hair and pulled it back into a ponytail. Her cheeks still held the sun-kissed pink from yesterday. No matter how much sunblock she used or how covered up she kept, she always got a little burned.

Adrian clearly had a secret. Maybe many secrets.

She fixed the twisted strap on her "granny" sundress, a stunning find for her at a vintage shop in

Pittsburgh. Green and blue paisley swirls, an elastic bodice, and a long, flowing, almost sheer skirt. She loved the gauzy cotton so popular in the 1970s.

She clipped on her long, Indian-inspired earrings.

Was she being a bit unfair to Adrian? After all, she had a few secrets of her own. She hadn't planned to tell him every little thing about her past any time soon. They hadn't been dating long and hadn't even been intimate with one another. They were taking it slow. *By the time people were in their thirties, most had a secret or two.*

But what secret of his could possibly be keeping him in jail as a murder suspect?

The alarm on her phone pinged, reminding her to meet Ruby and Jane for breakfast. She grabbed her purse and slipped on her sandals and left her room.

Ruby and Jane were waiting near the elevators. Ruby shot her a worried glance.

"Good morning. How are you?"

"I'm okay—how about you?" Cora said.

Ruby looked at Jane. "She hasn't seen it yet," Ruby said.

"Cora, listen—" Jane started to say.

"Seen what?"

"There's an article in the local rag," Ruby said.

"Article? About what?" Cora said, and reached for the elevator button.

"No," Jane said, stopping her. "Let's not go down yet."

"But we need to go," Cora said.

"Look!" Jane said, and held up the newspaper.

Jilted Ex-Lover Held in Grimm Murder Case, read the headline.

"What?" Cora said. "Who are they talking about?"

"Adrian!" Ruby said in a hushed tone as a couple walked by them.

"Adrian knew the woman who was killed," Jane said. "It doesn't prove he killed her, though."

The air *whooshed* out of Cora's body. "Of course not," she managed to say. She sucked in air. Now was not the time for a panic attack or a pill.

Jane took her elbow. "Why don't we call room service instead of going to the restaurant?"

"Fabulous idea," Ruby said. "We don't need a bunch of people gawking at us."

With London already safely at the child care center, the three of them walked to Jane's room and ordered breakfast.

"This was a good idea," Cora said. "With this news, I need some time to gather my wits."

"I figured," Ruby said.

"He's a grown man. Of course he's had other girl-friends, right?" Jane said. "I'm sure it's going to be okay, Cora."

Cora's stomach growled. "I hope they bring the food soon."

"Me too," Ruby grumbled.

"It's just that . . ."

"What?"

"We watched some of the wedding. We went for a long walk on the beach and stumbled on the scene. Which was gorgeous, by the way."

"And?"

"Well, why didn't he say something then? That he knew the bride?" Cora said. "It's just weird."

"Have some coffee," Ruby said. She had brewed a pot in the room while they waited for room service.

Jane shrugged. "Maybe he felt awkward about it. You know, his new girlfriend happening on the wedding of his old girlfriend."

"I guess," Cora said.

"Men don't think like us," Ruby said after a moment. "Communication is foreign to them."

"Room service!" came a voice and a knock at the door.

After Cora ate, she felt better, but still slightly perturbed. She needed to shake it off. She was on today. A class of fifty students had paid for her services.

"What else does the article say?" she asked.

"Not much. You know the police can't reveal all their secrets," Jane said, waving her hand.

Cora nodded. "I guess I'll read the details later. I'd like to check out my classroom and see if everything is ready."

She stood to go. "I'm hoping Adrian will be let out sometime today."

"Cashel is on his way to the courthouse," Ruby said.

"Poor guy, we're making him work on his vacation," Jane said.

"Don't worry about him," Ruby said. "Trust me, he's loving every minute of this."

"But why?" Jane asked.

"I don't know, but I don't think he's a fan of Adrian," Ruby said.

"I've wondered about that. What's going on?" Jane said.

"I don't know," Ruby said.

Cora picked up her bag and checked her cell phone to make sure it was fully charged. Then she picked up her camera bag and said, "I've got to go."

She must keep her mind off Adrian and Cashel and whatever or whomever else Jane and Ruby were talking about. This conference was too prestigious to mess up by being unfocused, whatever the distractions.

"Okay," Jane said. "We'll see you at lunch."

Cora left the room and headed down the hall to the elevator. Her goal was to keep her thoughts off the situation, so she went over the schedule in her mind. While she was leading her class, Jane and Ruby would also be teaching theirs. The macramé class was more of a workshop and would be going on all day—as was the crochet class. Cora hoped to sit in on some classes after her morning-long blogging class.

The elevator stopped and she stepped on, smiling at the few people in the car.

"Isn't it awful?" a woman said in a low voice to the man standing next to her. "She had this beautiful wedding and the next day she shows up on the beach dead."

"There's more to that story than we know," the man muttered.

*No truer words were ever spoken,* Cora mused.

# Chapter 9

Cora wondered if it was in her mind or if the students in her morning class had been particularly distracted. It took about an hour for them to settle in, but by lunch time the class was in full swing. The questions kept coming, but Cora was ready for the break—and her crew waited at the back of the room for her.

Many of the questions were about how to increase readership. Did craft challenges help? Contests? Interviews with other crafters? Was it better to focus on one craft or to have a general craft blog?

Some had more technical questions about photography. What was the best digital camera? Did she have tips and tricks for taking good photos? What crafts were easiest to photograph?

"Let's break now for lunch and come back tomorrow with your questions," Cora said.

Ruby and Jane, fresh from their own morning classes, whisked her away to a café on the far side of the resort, hoping there'd not be many crafters around to interrupt their conversation.

They sat down in a booth, decided on sandwiches to keep their lunch quick, and gave the server their order.

"Your class didn't want to let you go," Jane said.

"How did your class go?" Cora asked Jane.

"It went well," she said. "I have a much smaller group and they seemed almost advanced."

"My class went well, too," Ruby said. "It was a lot of fun."

"Well, where to this afternoon?" Cora asked.

"I'm not sure. I can't make up my mind between the macramé and the chime class," Jane said.

The server brought their sandwiches, placed them on the table. "Will there be anything else?" he asked.

"No, thank you," Ruby replied.

"I'm going to check on London before I do anything, though," Jane said.

"I think I'm going to take the chime class," Cora said. "It makes more sense for the blog. I'm going to attend the evening macramé miniclass." She wondered if Adrian would be joining her. That had been the plan, before he was carted off to jail. They would do the class, then go to dinner. But now she didn't know what to expect.

"Oh, that's a good idea," Ruby said. "The miniclasses are an excellent idea, because you don't have enough time to experience all of the classes."

"I think tonight's class is a basic intro 101 thing," Jane said. "We'll see how London is."

"What do you mean?" Cora said.

"Well, she was unhappy to go back to the day care this morning. Even though they planned to go on a little field trip. She's decided she doesn't like the lady who took the crown from her," Jane said.

Ruby cackled. "I get that!"

Cora couldn't help but laugh.

"I explained, again, that we couldn't keep something that doesn't belong to us," Jane said, and bit into her crab cake sandwich.

"It's been a weird few days," Cora said. "The wedding, Adrian, and poor London finding the tiara belonging to Marcy. Any word from Cashel yet?"

Ruby checked her phone again. "Nothing," she said.

"I wonder what's going on," Cora said. "You'd think they'd at least keep us informed."

Ruby sighed. "That son of mine is so straight it hurts."

Jane poked her in the ribs with her elbow. "What did you expect? He is a lawyer."

She waved Jane off and went about eating her sandwich.

"The tiara was astonishing," Cora said. "When I saw it on the bride's head the night of her wedding, I was in awe. But seeing it up close like that. Wow."

"Yes, Mathilde is quite gifted," Jane said.

"The wedding was stunning. Right on the beach. She was so beautiful and her dress, I don't know, reminded me of a mermaid. You know, it had that cut."

"Well, you know she was a mermaid scholar," Ruby said.

"That's what I heard," Cora said.

Jane leaned forward. "Yeah, she was a well-known mermaid folklorist."

"How interesting," Cora said. "I never realized there was such a thing as a mermaid folklorist until this weekend."

"She grew up on this island," Jane said. "Wouldn't this be a magical place to grow up?"

"I don't know," Ruby said. "Marcy moved away to study, of course, but according to the paper, she never really moved back here. I think it might be a little small for some folks. She was ambitious. Obviously."

"Yet, she came back here to marry," Cora said.

Jane rolled her eyes. "Her family owns about half the island."

"What?" Cora said. They were talking about the murder victim, but they were also talking about her boyfriend's ex-girlfriend. Her family owned about half the island? She was a mermaid folklorist? And drop-dead gorgeous. Pangs of insecurity poked at her. No wonder Adrian had not made any serious moves toward her. Next to Marcy Grimm, she was about as interesting as a piece of dry toast.

"You know they're not letting anybody leave the island without a good cause," Ruby said.

"What? Why?"

"Because of the murder. They're questioning everybody who leaves."

"Well, I suppose it makes sense, but the killer might have fled before the police even realized Marcy was dead," Jane said.

"They don't think so. Evidently, they keep a pretty close watch on the waters," Ruby said.

The island had no bridge. A ferry escorted people on and off.

"That's lovely," Cora said wearily. "No wonder Mathilde was so worried about the retreat. It's possible a killer is still on the island." Her stomach soured.

"Yes, but the killer isn't Adrian. You know that, right?" Jane said.

"I'm sure he didn't kill Marcy Grimm, but I'm

learning there's more to him than what I knew,"
Cora said.

"There always is, honey," Ruby said.

"So, the question is, if he didn't kill her, who did?"
Jane said.

"Hopefully, Adrian will be released soon, and we
can move forward and leave the police to consider
such questions," Cora said, twisting her napkin in her
sweaty palm. Why hadn't they let Adrian go?

# Chapter 10

Cora and Jane found their way to Mathilde's class. She looked every inch the put-together crafty diva. She wore silk slacks and a bright blue and yellow tunic, with large chunky beads and sea glass jewelry draped over her neck and hanging from her ears.

The effect was a bit much for Cora. She glanced over at Jane, who rolled her eyes. Yep, it was a bit much for her, as well.

Cora pulled out her cell phone and texted Adrian yet again as the class commenced. He hadn't responded to any of her texts, so far, but she tried once more. I'm worried about you. Text me when you are back at the hotel. SEND.

"Welcome to my sea chime class," Mathilde said.

A sample of sea chimes encircled the room. Simple shells hanging on wires. Shells entwined with macramé wire and sea glass. One chime appeared to be more of a wall hanging with a huge twine square with little squares of macramé inside. In each square was a colorful little seashell. Cora liked the simplicity of the design, but she wondered if it would be easy to make.

"This is one of my most fun classes," Mathilde said. "Because once you've got the basics down, you can do so much with a little twine or strings and a bunch of seashells. Then you can experiment with adding beads, sea glass, pieces of driftwood, and so on."

Cora struggled to pay attention. Something about Mathilde's delivery made her want to sleep. Or was it the big sandwich she just ate? Or the fact that she'd tossed and turned all night long, worrying about Adrian? She yawned. She might not make it through this class.

Jane caught her yawn and poked her. They were expected to attend other classes. They were being paid well for this gig and they were "on" all weekend. A relaxing retreat for everybody—but the teachers. Cora drooped and sighed.

"Coffee?" Jane whispered, and pointed to the carafe in the opposite corner of the room. "I'll get it."

"Thanks," Cora said.

"I like using this stretchy see-through cord, rather than the ropey twine," Mathilde said. "It gives the piece an airy feel and helps it to move a little more."

Cora propped her elbows on the table she and Jane were sharing. Gosh, she hadn't realized how exhausted she was. A nap might be just what she needed.

Jane sat the cup of coffee on the table and the scent perked her up. She sipped from the steamy brew and blinked. Lord, why was Mathilde's delivery so monotonous? How were her classes so popular? Cora wanted to scream. It was bloody awful.

"In the center of your tables, you have a selection of seashells, sea glass, and other pretties," Mathilde said.

Cora fiddled with their seashells.

"You've also got a little drill on your table, which you can use to make the holes. I suggest playing with your chime arrangements, laying it out on the table, before you drill," she said.

Jane's long fingers placed shells and sea glass on the table, switching one for the other, and yet again.

"Now, remember not to make your holes too big, or else your knot might slip through and you don't want huge knots," Mathilde said.

Cora ran her fingers over the smooth, oblong shells. She loved the colors—caramel and cocoa—and the spotted patterns of this particular shell.

"If you have any questions, Hank and I will be moving about the room. Grab one of us."

Hank, Mathilde's assistant, waved his hand with a flourish. He was always by her side and Cora wondered if they were involved. Neither wore a ring, so she assumed they weren't married, but they did seem quite close.

Cora lined her shells up. She was drawn to the beads and sea glass. Jane, however, selected several of the same kind of shells. Flat, half circle, all muted colors. Simple and elegant, like Jane herself.

"Just lovely," Hank said, as he glanced over Jane's shoulder.

That voice. Where had Cora heard it before? She was certain she'd never conversed with Hank. Why did his voice sound so familiar?

She continued working on her arrangement, even though his voice made her uneasy.

Shells, sea glass, beads. She was settled on the design. She drilled tiny holes into the objects.

But she couldn't shake Hank's voice. Why was it affecting her like this?

Jane was already on to knotting her string.

The two of them finished, with Jane helping Cora finish quickly, as she was lagging. Even though the coffee helped perk her up, she was still cloudy and not moving quickly enough to keep up with the class—though she did notice there were a few still working on the arrangement of their shells.

The two of them took their chimes and left the room.

"I need a nap," Cora said. "Her voice drove me bonkers."

"Okay," Jane said. "I'm going to head back over to my classroom."

Cora reached in her bag and pulled out her cell phone. There was a message from Adrian. She showed it to Jane.

I'm sorry. Must be some kind of mix up. Didn't
Cashel tell you? I've been out since this morning.
I've been waiting to hear from you.

"Cashel!" Jane said, and balled her hand into a fist.

"He was supposed to come to lunch with us and he didn't. Maybe that's why he never told me," Cora said.

"You're too kind," Jane said. "Cashel is up to no good."

"What?"

"I swear he doesn't like Adrian. I've no idea why," Jane said.

"It doesn't matter. I'm going to find Adrian," Cora said.

"Text me and let me know what's up," Jane said as she walked away.

"Will do," Cora said, as she texted him. **Where are you?**

His response came right away: **In my room. Join me?**

# Chapter 11

Adrian was standing with the door open when Cora arrived. His normally pale self was even paler and large dark circles framed his eyes beneath his glasses, which he scooted back up on his nose.

"Cora," he said, and pecked her on the cheek.

She stiffened.

"Come inside," he said. "Listen, I, ah, need to explain all this to you."

"Yes, I think you do," she said.

"Shall we talk outside on the balcony? I have some wine out there and—"

"No," she said. "Let's talk here." She sat down at the desk chair. He plopped on the bed.

"I should have told you about Marcy," he said. "I was just, so, um, floored over seeing her wedding."

But Cora persisted. "I was right next to you. We walked back together. There was plenty of time for you to tell me."

"I know," he said with a note of defeat. "It's just, well . . . I like you a lot and I didn't know how to say it to you. We saw the harpy who broke my heart get married."

Cora felt her heart hitch. "What?"

"Yeah, well, she did a number on me and I'm not going to lie to you. If I had any real tendencies to kill someone, I'd have killed her a few years ago," he said.

They sat for a moment in awkward silence, Adrian drumming his fingers on his thigh.

"So you felt uncomfortable about telling me she had been your girlfriend?" Cora finally said.

"Yeah. Of course I've been involved with other women, um, until I met you, but I'd rather not talk about any of them. You're the one who matters now."

Cora felt the knot in her stomach loosen as she breathed deeper.

"I'm so sorry I didn't tell you. If it's worth anything, I would have told you at the right time, if a right time came up. It felt awkward."

"Okay," Cora said. It wasn't as if they were married, or had even gotten serious. She wasn't going to make a big deal out of it. She was here to teach and have fun. He was here to be with her and have a little vacation, neither of which had happened so far.

"So, why did they haul you in to question you for her murder?"

He stood and walked toward the glass sliding door as a knock came at his room door.

"It's me," Cashel said, and opened the door.

Cora eyeballed him and crossed her arms.

"What are you doing here?" Cashel asked.

"What do you mean?"

"Don't you have some class to attend?"

"I do," she said. "But my boyfriend texted me and

wanted to talk, so I'm here, as if it's any of your business, Cashel."

Adrian stood behind Cora's chair and placed his hand on her shoulder. "What's up?" he said to Cashel.

"Have you told her everything?" Cashel said, red faced.

*Everything?* Cora wondered what that could mean.

"I was working on it, Cashel, before you came bounding in," he said. "What's going on?"

"The court is refusing to take away your tracking bracelet," he said. "Looks like you might be stuck here, on this island, long after we leave."

"Unless they find the real killer," Adrian said, holding out his hand to show Cora the apparatus around his wrist.

*Great, my boyfriend is on a lead.*

"I'm trying to make other arrangements so you can leave the island. I mean, your livelihood is in Indigo Gap," Cashel said.

"I'm sure you can handle it," Cora said to Cashel.

"Well, thanks for the vote of confidence, but that text message is the problem," Cashel said.

"Text message?" Cora's eyes traveled from Cashel to Adrian and back again.

"I hadn't quite gotten to that yet," Adrian said.

"Oh, sorry," Cashel said, but his tone showed that he clearly was not sorry—not in the least. Cora surmised he was enjoying this, enjoying the fact Adrian was squirming, that he had half dropped a bombshell into the situation.

"Marcy saw us," he said to Cora. "And sent me a message."

"And?" Cora said.

"She wanted to meet me. She said she'd never gotten over me and blah, blah, blah."

"So why would they suspect you for killing her because of that?"

"I replied that I never wanted to see her again."

"Oh." Cora's heart thudded in her chest.

"She wrote back pleading with him to meet her on the beach," Cashel said. "And then he sent a brusque response."

Now Cora hyperfocused on Cashel.

"Cashel, I—" Adrian started to say.

"Yeah, he wrote her back. He said, 'No way. Drop dead.'"

Cora gasped.

Adrian smacked himself in the head. "I know, right? How stupid. But how was I to know someone was going to kill her? I'm innocent. I didn't kill her. I told her to drop dead, but my God, I didn't kill her."

"How do we prove he didn't kill her?" Cora asked Cashel.

Cashel waved her off. "I'm working on it. Try not to worry about it. Don't you need to be knitting or something?"

Cora's emotions zoomed from worry and anger and back to worry, and now she was pissed. What exactly was going on with Cashel? Why was he acting like such a jerk? She stood.

"I'm not quite sure what to say, Cashel," she said. "But you know me better than that. When someone I care about is in trouble, I never stay out of it."

# Chapter 12

**Where are you?** Jane texted Cora.

She stood in the Mermaid Hall, leaning against a wall, and waited to hear back. Jane was worried about Cora. Here she was, one of the main teachers at this retreat, and her boyfriend had been carted off to jail. How was she supposed to be her best? Well, so far, she was managing. But barely.

"Hi, Jane." A young woman came up beside her. "I was in your sea creature pottery class this morning. It was so much fun."

"I'm glad you're enjoying it," Jane said.

"I'm making a turtle," the woman said, smiling. Her blue horn-rimmed glasses overwhelmed her small face. "I'm Rose, by the way."

"Hi, Rose," Jane said, and shifted her weight.

"I've never done pottery before," Rose said with exuberance. "It's so much fun."

"So do you think you might want to do more?" Jane asked.

Rose nodded. "Well, this weekend, yes. I'm not sure about once I'm home. I have good intentions, you know," she said, and smiled. "But once I'm home there doesn't seem to be enough time for anything but taking care of everybody else."

"I hear ya," Jane said. And she'd heard this a lot over the years. "But the kids will grow up and leave someday."

"Oh, I'm not talking about my kids. I'm talking about my mother and my aunt," she said. "I take care of them."

"Oh, I see," Jane said. "It's good that you're able to do that."

"I suppose so," she said, and pulled her bag closer to her.

Jane's phone buzzed, alerting her to Cora's text message.

"Excuse me," Jane said, and pulled out her phone. "I have to take this."

"Oh, no worries. I'll see you in tomorrow's class," Rose said, and walked away.

I'll be there in five minutes. On my way, Cora said in her message.

Nothing else? Jane rolled her eyes, aware Cora was dolling out information in bits and pieces. Why was she making her wait?

Jane stood among the mermaids. Several retreaters with their bags flung across their shoulders passed by her.

"I absolutely hate them," a woman said to another woman. "Mermaids creep me out."

Jane recognized her. She had been in her class this morning and was making a starfish.

"Why?" the woman who was with her asked.

"God! Think about it. She's half fish, half woman. How creepy," the woman said.

"I never thought about it like that," she replied, and they kept walking.

Strange, Jane thought, but mermaids were kind of creepy in that context, weren't they?

"There you are," Cora said.

"We're late for Ruby's candle class," Jane said. "But how's Adrian?"

Cora's mouth turned into a frown. "It's not good."

Jane's heart raced as she leaned closer. "What do you mean?"

"I mean, he was involved with her," Cora said.

"Yes, that's what the paper said," Jane replied.

"Evidently, she saw us on the beach that night and texted him," she said.

Jane leaned forward. "He didn't text back, did he?"

Cora nodded. "Of course he did, and that's why the police suspect him."

"Is that the only reason? I mean, that's flimsy," Jane said.

"It was the last text message on her phone and he told her"—she lowered her voice—"he told her to drop dead."

"What? That doesn't sound like the Adrian I know. He's always been such a gentleman. I can't imagine him even saying such a thing," Jane said.

"I know," Cora said. "But evidently they have quite a history." Cora's eyes were lit.

"How does Cashel feel about all this? I mean, does he think this is going to be a problem?"

"He's trying his best. Or so he says," Cora said.

"We need to find the classroom. Is it to the left or right? I've forgotten."

They walked together down the hall. The crowd thinned as the retreaters selected their classes and settled in their rooms.

"Adrian is wearing a tracking bracelet and can't go off the island." Cora stopped in her tracks. "Can you believe it?"

"That sounds serious," Jane said.

"It is," Cora said. "I needed to do some digging on Marcy Grimm."

"Wait, what?"

"Adrian despised her. So she probably had some other enemies, too."

"Cora—"

"It won't take much of my time to check into her background. And poor Adrian. He's a mess," Cora said.

"But why should you bother? I'm certain the police will be investigating this," Jane said.

"Probably, but what's wrong with helping move the investigation along? If we wait for them and all their procedures and so on, Adrian might not ever return home," Cora said.

"I don't like the sound of this," Jane said. "You need to stay out of it and let Cashel do his job."

Cora spun around to face Jane. "Do you know what? I've an odd feeling Cashel is okay letting Adrian stay here forever. I don't know why he doesn't like him. But it's so obvious Cashel hates him."

Jane's left eyebrow hitched. "I think Cashel likes

you and is jealous," she said as they arrived at Ruby's classroom.

"That might be the most ridiculous thing I've ever heard," Cora said, and opened the door.

"Come on in, ladies," Ruby said when she saw them enter. She glanced at her watch and back up at them. "Glad you could make it."

Cora might have been more concerned about Ruby's obvious displeasure at their late arrival if she wasn't so blown away by what Jane had just said. She doubted it was true. But if by some strange chance it was true, then Cashel was the worst person to be representing Adrian.

# Chapter 13

Only a few "social" events were scheduled at the retreat. Mathilde's retreat was different than Cora's. In truth, most of the retreats offered their own flavor. Cora preferred her own—where she and the other teachers hung out as much as possible with their students. But Mathilde's retreats were much larger and it would be nearly impossible for the teachers to give all the retreaters a slice of personal time—one of the reasons for the policy of teachers not mingling with the students outside class.

But today, a late afternoon tea was on the schedule, held in a sunny atrium.

Cora, Ruby, and Jane made their way over. A pianist played on an elevated platform. The room was gorgeous, with tropical plants and overstuffed furniture, wicker furniture, and tables of scones, cucumber sandwiches, and tiny tarts. On each of the tables were huge bowls of fruit as well.

"Since when do you put milk in your tea?" Cora asked Jane as they settled into a wicker couch together.

"I don't know," Jane said. "I am feeling very British." She lifted her pinky as she brought the tea to her lips.

Ruby had been pulled aside by a group of women. Cora had noticed them before—they seemed to love each other's company and not socialize much with the other retreaters. One of them had this amazingly loud but beautiful laugh.

"Ruby does so well at these things," Cora said.

"I loved the class. Who would have thought to make a candle in a seashell?" Jane said, and bit into a scone. "Mmmm. My God, it's delicious."

Huge, indoor tropical trees donning big, shiny, green leaves clumped together to form a stand. Another cluster of chairs sat behind the trees, where people were seated, drinking tea and getting acquainted. Cora's ear picked up a nasally voice from behind the trees. It belonged to Hank, Mathilde's assistant.

Cora strained to hear, but she couldn't make out any words. She suddenly remembered the conversation about the tiara the night before when Mathilde and someone were arguing about it. Odd that the tiara kept coming up. First, that night, next London finding it on the beach, and now. It was an extraordinary tiara. Cora saw why Mathilde might want it back.

"What are you thinking about?" Jane said.

"The tiara," Cora said, and lowered her voice. "Just eavesdropping. Or trying to. "

Jane laughed. "You know that's rude, right?"

Just then, two women walked up to them, and one sat on the chair beside Cora and the other on the chair next to Jane. They looked familiar, but Jane had met so many new people.

"Are you enjoying the retreat?" Cora asked.

"I'd be liking it even more without all the darned mermaids everywhere," the woman said.

Cora's face fell.

"Oh, I'm sorry," the woman said. "I'm Katy Carlson. I took your class this morning. It was awesome, by the way."

"You don't like mermaids, though?" Cora said.

"Hate them. Half fish, half woman? Freaks me out," she said, and bit into her cucumber sandwich.

"They pretty much are everywhere, aren't they?" Cora said.

"Yes, we're in Mermaid Hall," she replied. "But I guess if your family owns most of the island and you're a mermaid scholar, there'd be some mermaids around."

Cora leaned in.

"Yeah, you heard me right. Mermaid scholar," she said, and chortled.

"Are you talking about Marcy Grimm?" Cora asked.

"Yes, I am," she said. "The island darling who died a few days ago." The note of sarcasm in her voice was undeniable.

"Are you a local, then?"

"Yes," she said. "Well, my family is. I live in Leesburg, Virginia, now. This is my friend Jana. We're here with a group from Leesburg." She gestured to a woman who was tucking in to a bag of Swedish fish candy.

"Want one?" she asked them.

"No, thanks," Cora said, and Jane shook her head.

"Shame about what happened to her," Jane piped up.

Katy sighed. "Yes, I'd not wish that on anybody."

They sat for a few moments, with the strains of piano music filling the air.

"But, Lord, if anybody asked to be killed, it was her," Katy said, and rolled her eyes.

Cora choked on her tea, coughing.

Jane's hand went to her back and patted her. "Are you all right?"

Cora took a deep breath and nodded.

"I'm sorry," Katy said. "I shouldn't blurt things out. But it's always been a problem for me. I'm opinionated."

After Cora had settled down and took another sip of tea, she said, "Don't apologize. I'd love to know more about her."

"Cora—" Jane said.

"Oh, there's not much to say," Katy said. "Only that she grew up here, her family owning much of the island, and was always a brat. Got away with everything. Think of the proverbial snotty rich kid. That was Marcy. She moved away and made quite a name for herself as a mermaid folklorist. Published several books. They're in the hotel gift shop. My mother worked as a maid for her family for years. Let's say, what goes on behind closed doors . . ." The woman wiggled her eyebrows.

"Oh my," Jane said.

"Oh my, indeed," Katy replied. "She didn't have many friends here. She'd just been married and it was only family attending. No real bridal party. Nothing."

Cora had noted the very small wedding.

Cora and Jane exchanged expressions of curiosity. Why would sweet, gentlemanly Adrian be attracted to someone like Marcy? Cora's curiosity sparked. She might find out more about Marcy tonight. She and

Adrian planned on attending a macramé workshop together, then having a quiet dinner.

She rarely asked men she dated about their past love lives. It wasn't good practice. But in this case, it might help take the bracelet off her new boyfriend's arm.

# Chapter 14

The mystery of Marcy Grimm was now even murkier. Noted mermaid folklorist with five books in the gift shop. Five. And Cora could not even write one—even though she'd been approached over and over again.

Jane picked one up and read over the back cover copy. "This one is about the Sea Glass Island Mermaid. Evidently, there's a legend about her."

Cora refrained from rolling her eyes. A touristy lure if she'd ever seen one. But some of the other books appeared quite academic. Except for the mermaid art book, which was a large coffee-table book full of mermaid art from all over the world—some of it ancient.

"Oh, there's the Waterhouse mermaid I love so much!" Jane said.

"That's the print you have hanging in your bathroom," Cora said.

"I love the Pre-Raphaelites. Waterhouse is my favorite," Jane said.

"It's kind of fancy for you," Cora said.

"I like *some* fancy things," Jane said. "Just not all fancy things." She grinned. "I don't like fancy doilies."

"But you do like my doily skirt, right?" Cora said, flipping through one of Marcy's books.

"We are selling out of those books. I think that might be the last one of the art book," the saleslady said.

"Really?" Cora said.

"The author of the book recently passed away," the woman said. "So all of the sudden people want her books."

"Well, this is a beautiful book," Cora said, and placed it back on the shelf.

The saleslady nodded. She was dressed in a beach-appropriate, colorful, floral print dress.

"Did you know Marcy?" Cora asked.

"I guess you could say I did," she said, smiling at a passerby. "We had a book launch party here for her once."

"I've heard she wasn't a nice person," Cora said. Jane poked her in the ribs.

"Well, she was always pleasant to me," she replied. "But I know people who've had run-ins with her." She lifted an eyebrow. "But the whole family is like that. Wealth does that to you sometimes. So they say. I don't know many wealthy people so I couldn't say."

"Such a shame about what happened to her," Jane said in a hushed voice.

"Yes, a tragedy, after she married the love of her life," the woman said with a sigh. "It's the stuff of romance novels."

"What do you mean?" Jane said.

"They dated in high school, on the sly. He was from a poor family and her family didn't want them dating. Eventually they broke up. But years later, they found each other again. Romantic, don't you think?" She smiled.

A customer came up to her. "Do you have this shirt in pink?"

"No, I'm sorry. We only have what's on the floor," she replied.

"I suppose that's romantic," Jane said once the customer wandered off.

"He must be devastated," Cora said.

The woman nodded her head slowly. "I heard he's been sedated."

Cora's hand went to her chest. "How awful. Is he in the hospital, or is he at home?"

"Oh, I'm sure he's with his mother," she said. "Now, there's a character for you."

Cora picked up another book. "What do you mean?"

"She's a psychic, or voodoo queen, or something," she replied. "Lives near the swamp. I never go over there. It scares the bejesus out of me. Are you going to buy a book?"

Cora thought a moment. What would Adrian say if he saw her with one of Marcy's books?

"I'll take this," Jane said, reaching for the mermaid art book.

"And I'll take this one. I might be back for the others," Cora said, grabbing *The Mermaid of Sea Glass Island* book. It was the cheapest one. She would buy the other books as e-books. Her curiosity about Marcy needed to stay private, for now.

"Voodoo queen," Jane said, as she purchased her book. "I've never met a voodoo queen."

"At least not that you're aware of," Cora joked.

"She's a perfectly lovely woman," the saleswoman

said as she slipped Jane's book into a bag. "You don't want to cross her." She winked.

"No, I suppose not," Jane said.

Cora assumed she was joking, but she still felt a cold shiver. Psychics. Mermaids. Murder on the beach.

She handed the saleslady her book.

"Now, this is an interesting book," she said.

"I thought so," Cora replied.

"I had an uncle who swore he saw her," the woman said as she swiped Cora's card.

"Saw who?" Cora said.

"The mermaid, dear," she said, looking at her above the top of her glasses.

Cora laughed.

"I'm serious," the saleslady said, as she place Cora's book into a bag. "Of course, it was a long time ago, before the storm took away a large chunk of our island. My uncle was not a man to invent stories. He said he saw her plain as day, swimming. Said he's never seen such a beautiful creature and she glowed like an angel or fairy." A wistful note came through in her voice.

Cora refrained from rolling her eyes. She was aware of things in this world that couldn't be explained and she didn't want to be the kind of person who was closed off to angels, for example. But mermaids? Mermaids were another matter.

# Chapter 15

Cora and Adrian sat in the small classroom with a few others. Jane was right; most people were drained by this point. These miniclasses were designed for the few who weren't. Several more days of teaching craft blogging loomed ahead of Cora. She was almost tapped out. But that was for personal reasons. She couldn't allow the situation with Adrian to seep in to her professional life.

"Should be starting soon, hey?" he said.

He wore a pair of khaki slacks and a short-sleeve, floral shirt. The green in the flowers on the shirt brought out his jade-green eyes even more.

"I hope so," Cora said, as Zooey walked in the room. Blond, tall, and flashy, she was everything Cora was not.

Adrian sat back, glanced at Cora, and raised an eyebrow. She knew he'd rather be somewhere else; a macramé class was not what he came here for. He came to be with her—and he'd gotten way more than he bargained for, with the ex-girlfriend's marriage, then death, in quick succession.

"I'm so glad you could make it," Zooey said. "This

evening is a miniclass and I'm going to give you a little background on macramé." She paused. "Macramé is my life. I think, eat, and dream macramé."

The room silenced. Oh boy, Cora thought. And she dared not glance at Adrian. She didn't want to see his reaction to such pretension.

"But you are not expected to feel that way. Not tonight anyway," Zooey said, and smiled.

*Maybe she is trying to be funny.*

Zooey walked across the room and preened over the supplies. She glanced at her assistant. "Can we pass these out now?" She held up strands of colored cord.

He stepped in and passed out the provisions. A few bowls on a table nearby contained charms, sea glass, and seashells. Cora assumed they would be selecting their materials from those bowls.

"When most people think of macramé, they imagine the 1970s version," Zooey said. "Right?"

There were murmurs of agreement in the small classroom. "Well, it was popular in the 1970s but has made quite a comeback."

"I remember the owls," one woman said, and laughed. "Everywhere, those owl wall hangings?"

"Yes," Zooey said. "And some of them now are worth a fortune to the right collectors."

"What?" Adrian mouthed to Cora, who shrugged. She had no idea. She displayed a few macramé items purchased from a vintage shop in her attic apartment back in Indigo Gap. But a few of the crafters she had met through the years sent her wall hangings and rugs, now scattered through Kildare House.

"But macramé's history goes back to the Babylonians and Assyrians," Zooey continued. "The word itself comes from the thirteenth-century Arabic weavers' word *migramah,* meaning 'fringe.' Macramé is a form of textile making using knotting rather than weaving or knitting. Its primary knots are the square knot and forms of 'hitching'—full hitch and double half hitches."

"I read it was popular in the Victorian era," a woman said.

"Yes, quite," Zooey replied. "It's had moments of popularity over the decades."

All the students now had their cords. Cora loved the way it felt in her hands.

"You can do so much with it, which is one of the reasons I love it. Wall hangings, articles of clothing, bedspreads, tablecloths, draperies, plant hangers, and other furnishings, to necklaces, anklets, and bracelets," Zooey said. "And tonight, we want to keep it simple before you all run off to dinner."

At the mention of dinner, Cora was suddenly aware she should have eaten something this afternoon instead of shopping. But she couldn't resist learning more about Marcy Grimm. She wanted to know all about her. Not only was she Adrian's ex-girlfriend, but he was suspected of her murder. The more she could find out about her, the more she felt she might be able to help Adrian.

"Okay," Zooey said. "Let's get started. Some of you have ribbons, some have yarn, and some have cords. If you'd rather have something else than what you were given, feel free to switch."

After everybody made their switches, Zooey told them to choose a charm or a stone or tiny shell from a bowl. "Or several, whatever you want," she said.

She showed them how to make the knots for the

bracelets, and Adrian's long fingers moved with a dexterity that Cora admired.

After the class, Cora wore two bracelets, both made of sea glass and mermaid charms, one she crafted and one Adrian made for her. And off they went to the Drunken Mermaid, a bar-restaurant, which was not in the resort.

"Thank goodness, we're going off site tonight," Cora said, reaching for Adrian's arm.

"Do you feel like you're in a fishbowl?" he said, grinning.

"Sometimes," she said. "Though I suppose it's to be expected. But it will be wonderful to relax and just be with you."

"Thank you, Cora."

"For what?"

"For not making a big deal of this ex-girlfriend business," he said.

They had decided to walk to the restaurant instead of taking a cab, and Cora was glad of it. She wanted the opportunity to speak without the gossipmongers surrounding them.

"I'm still not sure what you mean," she said.

"I mean by the fact I didn't tell you about Marcy," he said.

"Well, Adrian, I'm not thrilled about it, but we've just started seeing each other. I don't know how much of your private life before me I need to be aware of," she said.

"You're amazing," he said, and leaned over to kiss her.

She allowed herself to enjoy the kiss. The ocean sounded in the background. The scent of the ocean breezes wafted. The kiss. The ocean. The knot of tension inside her unraveled and loosened.

"Besides," she said, "I have a past, too." She moved away from him and pulled him along the path.

"Um . . . in what way?"

She waved him off and kept walking.

# Chapter 16

Cora nearly swooned when she entered the Drunken Mermaid. The scent of garlic, onions, and rosemary wafted toward them.

"Table for two. Adrian Brisbane," Adrian said, as he walked up to the host.

The eyes of the eaters followed Cora and Adrian as they were seated. Was it because they were a couple of tourists at a restaurant frequented by locals? Or was it that Adrian was so tall and gorgeous? Cora wondered.

"It smells fabulous in here," Adrian said.

"I know, right?" Cora said. The delicious aromas alerted every one of her senses.

"That's him. I know it is," came a voice across the dining room.

Cora strained to see what was going on. She didn't see anything but a group of people sitting at a large table in the corner. The restaurant was dimly lit.

Their server came up to the table with the menu and wine list.

Cora glanced over the menu. Italian seafood. Shrimp scampi—yes, that was what she wanted.

"Goddamnit!" The male voice came across the room again. "Let me go. I want a word with the bastard!"

Now the other eaters were agape as several servers ran to the area, and a manager as well.

"What's going on?" Cora said, looking around the place.

"I have no idea," Adrian said, and sipped his water. "But I'm hungry and would like to order." He grinned, revealing his deep dimple.

"Me too," Cora said.

But as soon as the words came out of her mouth, a strange, wild-eyed man ran to their table. And the next thing Cora knew, other men were trying to hold him back. Cora's heart raced. What could he possibly want with them?

Adrian turned his head and started to rise from his chair. "What—" he began to say, but the man tore away from the servers trying to hold him back and he lunged at Adrian, who fell to the floor as his chair tumbled.

The man pummeled Adrian, his fist coming down on his face.

Several onlookers gasped and screamed.

Cora stood and edged her way in between the men who were trying to grab Adrian's attacker and yanked the guy by his hair.

"Ayyy!" he yowled.

She straddled him and wrapped her arm around his neck and squeezed.

"Call the police, you idiots. Don't just stand there!" she cried.

"They're on their way," a server said.

"Let me up!" the man said.

"Not on your life," she said. "Are you okay, Adrian?"

"I think so," he said. "I'm a little squished. But I'm okay." He was still underneath the crazed man whom Cora was straddling.

"What the hell, lady?" the man said to her. "Why are you helping a murderer?"

"What?"

"He killed my Marcy!" the man said.

"It's okay, miss, we've got the situation under control," a newly arrived uniformed officer said as he pulled her from the man, with a not-quite stifled grin.

"Adrian didn't kill anybody," Cora managed to say, though her chest felt as if it were on fire and there was a lack of oxygen in the room.

"You're crazy to be involved with him!" the man said.

"Can we please calm down?" the officer asked.

"Yes, please," the manager said. "Let's take this into my office, now."

Another officer helped Cora pull Adrian to his feet. His nose was bloody and his left eye was swelling already.

"Your eye! How awful!" Cora said, and pulled a napkin from the table, wiping his face.

"Attractive, right?" Adrian winced.

"Let's go into the office, please," the officer said. Cora and Adrian followed.

He looked sheepishly at Cora. "Thanks for rescuing me."

She tried to smile but couldn't. Her mind was trying to catch up with what her body had done. Trying to make sense of what had happened. That man thought Adrian had killed Marcy. That man must be . . . must be . . . Her head was swimming and she dizzied. He must be Marcy Grimm's husband.

Adrenaline coursed through her. Did he believe Adrian killed his wife?

Why?

What was going on here?

The group of them entered the small office.

"I think we need a medic," the officer said.

"We told you it was not a good idea to go off the resort," the other officer admonished Adrian.

"He's done nothing wrong," Cora said. "Why should his movements be curtailed while we're here? I don't understand."

Her eyes skimmed the room as the men took her in. She was certain she was a mess, but she didn't care.

"Are you okay?" the manager said to the man who attacked Adrian.

Cora studied him. The man was certainly *not* okay. His wild-eyed bearing and dark hair contrasted against his sickly pallor. Yet, he was strong and had knocked Adrian right down. She guessed he was about her age. His eyes were circled and swollen. A brief pang of sorrow and regret moved through Cora. Grief did strange and awful things to people.

The door opened. An imposing woman entered the room. "What a scene," she said. "Son"—she turned and looked at him—"we're going home. Adrian, I think you should go back to the resort and stay there. Marcy Grimm was a popular person on this island and we all want her death avenged."

She took in Cora. "And I don't know who you are, lady, but great moves."

Cora extended her hand. *You always catch more flies*

*with honey than vinegar*, she heard her grandmother's voice say in her head. "Why, thank you. I'm Cora Chevalier, one of the teachers at the craft retreat. And I'm Adrian's girlfriend."

The woman cupped both of her hands. "Nice to meet you. I'm Rue Dupres. I'm sorry for my son's behavior, but he's grieving."

"What exactly happened here?" the officer said. "I need statements from everybody."

"Come now, officer. We all know what happened. Let's call it a day, shall we?" Rue said.

"Adrian? Would you like to press charges?" the officer asked.

"Yes, I think I would," he said, and he turned to Cora. "Can you please call my lawyer?"

"Why would you do that?" Rue said.

"I was attacked. I want it on record," Adrian said. "I'm a person of interest in a murder case. And I think it's better safe than sorry. I'm sorry. I realize he's grieving. But I didn't kill her and I won't be treated as if I did."

Cora dialed Cashel's phone number on her cell phone.

It was going to be a long night.

When Cashel walked into the room, he was all business. Gone was the goofy, moody man annoying everybody. Cora sat next to Adrian, who held an ice pack to his swollen eye.

They were at the local police station—the restaurant manager having politely asked them to leave. Cora and Adrian were in a separate room from Josh and his mother, Rue.

"What have you gotten yourself into?" Cashel said, and flung his briefcase on a table.

They recounted the story.

Cashel sat down. "I advise you not to press charges. The man is bereft. He thinks you killed his wife. It might be considered a goodwill gesture for you to drop it."

"Or an admission of guilt," Adrian said.

"No, I don't think so," Cashel said, glancing at Cora, back to Adrian. "But suit yourself."

Adrian turned to Cora. "What do you think?"

"I can see both points of view," Cora said after a moment. "Cashel, you should have seen Josh. He was like a madman. I can see why Adrian is concerned. But a big part of me agrees with Cashel. It does you no good to press charges. Let's stay at the resort, mind our own business, and then go home."

"Except that I can't go home," Adrian said, lifting up his arm.

Cora's empty stomach went sick. "I know, but I'm sure by Monday they will let you go."

"Not until they recognize he didn't commit the crime," Cashel said.

"Can't you do something about that?" Cora asked.

"It was part of our bargain. He wanted out. The only way they'd let him out was with that bracelet."

The room quieted. Cora's mind was reeling. She needed food. She needed out of this place. And she needed Adrian to be free.

"Well then," she said. "We'll have to find the real killer."

"What? What are you talking about?" Adrian said.

"We're going to need to prove your innocence and

the best way to do it is to find the person who killed Marcy," Cora said.

"I was afraid you might get some crazy ideas," Cashel said. "You need to stop with your meddling before it gets out of control."

"Yeah, Cora, it might backfire. You're not a cop. I don't want you to get hurt," Adrian said.

"You both are aware I can take care of myself," she said.

"Don't you have some quilt to make?" Cashel said, with a note of sarcasm.

"I don't quilt, Cashel," she said back to him. "Though it is a goal of mine."

"You know what I mean," he said. "You're here to teach classes, not mess around in police business."

She decided to keep her thoughts to herself. What Cashel didn't know wouldn't hurt him. Adrian was another matter. She needed to find out more about Marcy. If she had learned anything in the past, it was most murder victims knew their killers. Usually, if it was a woman, husband, boyfriends, and lovers were at the top of the suspect list. Which meant Josh was also under suspicion—maybe that's why he'd had such a violent reaction to Adrian. Maybe he killed her and desperately wanted the police to think otherwise.

"Cora!" Cashel said, awakening her from her daydream.

"Yes?"

"I want your word that you won't mess about in this case. You could screw things up for Adrian," he said.

She reached over and placed her hand on Adrian's. "I wouldn't want that," she said.

"Your word," Cashel said.

Cora answered him with silence.

"Can we please leave?" Adrian said. "I hate this place. And I'm starving. Cora and I were going to have a romantic dinner and boom, I was attacked."

"Mom and Jane have that taken care of for you. Just check in with the concierge and room service will be brought up to you immediately," Cashel said. "They figured you hadn't eaten."

A wave of gratitude swept over Cora.

"You don't have to make up your mind immediately about pressing charges. You have some time. I suggest you give it some thought," Cashel said.

"Okay, that's what I'll do. I want it on record. You know what happened. The man has a dangerous temper," Adrian said.

"Exactly my thoughts," Cora replied.

Cashel stood. "What?" He eyeballed Cora sideways.

"Never mind," she said. Josh was at the top of her list for suspects. After seeing the way he attacked Adrian, she thought him certainly capable of murder. But why would he kill Marcy on their wedding night?

# Chapter 17

"He must have killed her," Cora said to Adrian, after they finished their relatively quiet dinner in Cora's room. They were both exhausted, stressed, and famished. The food went down quickly.

"What? Who?" he said, yawning. The swelling around his eye had lessened, but he still looked pitiful.

"Her husband. Marcy's husband. Don't you think?"

Adrian leaned in and tilted his head slightly, the way he always did when he was thinking. "Why would he kill his wife on their wedding night?"

"You saw his temper," Cora said, and sat her wineglass down on the table.

"Yeah," he said. "I couldn't imagine her with someone like him."

"What do you mean?"

"I mean, she was always so strong. I can't imagine she'd put up with any kind of abuse. She was smart and had her act together, most of the time," he said.

"You know, Adrian, you could say the same thing about most of my clients at the women's shelter," she said. "It's a fallacy that all women who are abused are uneducated."

His right eyebrow went up. "You'd think if they were educated they'd realize they wouldn't have to put up with mistreatment."

"It's complicated," she said.

It quieted as Adrian gazed out the window. The moon was shining brightly over the ocean and sand, giving the beach a glow.

"I loved her," he said, after a moment. "I never would have killed her."

Cora felt a sting. She couldn't say why. Was she jealous over a dead woman? Or was he still in love with a dead woman? He was a sensitive guy. He didn't give his heart away quickly. He hadn't even made any advances with Cora. Which was refreshing. But now she wondered: was he ready for a relationship?

"How long ago was that?" Cora asked, after pouring herself another glass of wine.

"We broke up around three years ago," he said. "We were together all through college and grad school. We met in a research methods class. She was vivacious and brilliant. We broke up a few times, over silly stuff, really. You know how it is in college. So stressful. But we were very close. It was intense."

"Why did you break up? I mean the final break?" she asked, after another sip. Why not? Why not ask the burning question on her mind?

"She'd gotten a fellowship in Greece," he said, and drank deeply from his wineglass. "I had planned to visit, but never could manage to get enough money together. She met someone and that was the end of it. We were planning to get engaged the following summer, but she met someone and was blunt about . . . things."

"Was it Josh?"

"No, not from my understanding. It was a local guy from Athens," he said. "I didn't keep up with her and her life. If I had any idea she was back and here on this island, well, I'd never have come with you."

"These things happen," Cora said.

He looked at her sideways. "Yeah, I guess." He reached across the table and held her hand. "Thank you for being so understanding."

"Adrian, I—" Cora was at a loss for words. Did she have a choice but to be understanding? It was a weird circumstance. The two of them had just started dating and they decided to take things slowly. Now, she was glimpsing why Adrian wanted to ease in to their relationship.

"For a long time, I had no interest," he said, slurring his words at the edges. "Not until I met you."

Her heart fluttered in her chest and he lifted her hand to his lips and kissed it.

The kiss spread through her arms and warmed her.

"It's getting late," she said. "I need sleep. I have an early class tomorrow."

"Yeah," he said, standing up. "I'll pull the table out into the hallway."

She opened the door and he scooted the room service out.

She leaned into him and kissed him good night. She kept it short and sweet. No complications. Not tonight.

Later, in bed, she mulled over everything she'd learned today. Her boyfriend had been heartbroken. Hadn't they all?

Marcy Grimm's new husband had quite a temper. Cora planned to investigate him on the Internet the next morning after she wrote her blog post about the retreat. Josh's mother, Rue, seemed to have it together. To have a son like him must be hard for her.

Marcy Grimm had been not only a beautiful woman but also intriguing and smart. But she also seemed to have a mean streak. To break up with Adrian, whom she had planned to marry, over what? A fling in Greece? Oh well. Cora tried not to judge, especially when it came to matters of the heart. Marcy and Adrian simply were not meant for one another.

Cora's neck and back ached, and she fought to fall asleep. So far, this retreat was not a retreat at all.

# Chapter 18

Jane had also tossed and turned all night. She was concerned about Cora. Concerned about Adrian. When they'd gotten the word about what had happened, she and Ruby wanted to run to the restaurant or police station to meet them, but Cashel stopped them. He was right, of course. They didn't need a bunch of people clogging up the works. And, by that time of night, she would've had to take London with her—not a good idea.

But it gave her the idea to call Zora, who was taking care of the Kildare House and Luna, Cora's cat. She asked if Zora could also watch London. She really wanted to get her daughter off this island. Jane said she'd meet her halfway between Indigo Gap and Sea Glass Island. But Zora insisted that her sister would be happy to pick up London and bring her home. Evidently, Zora's younger sister lived near the island. By the time Jane had gotten off the phone with Zora, Ruby had already ordered a meal for Cora and Adrian. And Jane couldn't help but wonder how it went after they'd gone back to Cora's room. It turned out Adrian had quite a past. Who knew?

He was reserved, smart, and cute. When Jane first met him, he'd given off "Cora vibes," and she figured Cora and Adrian would suit one another. And they did. But something niggled at Jane as she downed a cup of coffee before taking London to the day care center for a few hours before Zora's sister Lulu came to fetch her. Cora and Adrian had been dating a few months now, and had yet to become intimate. Unless Cora had not told her about it. And she certainly would.

The last time Jane asked about it, well, Cora said they were not in any hurry. Jane understood—but, geez, months?

But now the plot thickened. Adrian had this past relationship with Marcy and evidently it did not end well. He was a sensitive sort. But most men Jane knew were not so sensitive as to not at least try to have sex with their new girlfriend. Men were like that. They separated sex and feelings much more easily than most women. Though God knows she's had some one-night stands—which she felt herself blushing over.

"I'm ready, Mommy," London said, as she came out of the bathroom.

"Good," Jane said. "Me too."

London slid her backpack across her shoulder. "It might rain today. I hope not. I wanted to build a sand castle before Miss Lulu comes to get me. "

Jane checked her cell phone. Ruby and Cora were already at the breakfast buffet.

"I'm a bit late. We need to hurry." Jane was thrilled that London couldn't wait for Lulu to take her home.

She adored Zora—which didn't hurt, but she also adored Indigo Gap.

The two of them scampered into the elevator and off to the day care, then said their good-byes for a few hours. Jane made her way to find her colleagues.

"What's with you two?" Jane said as she slid into the booth they shared at the hotel restaurant, her plate piled high with eggs and potatoes, and fruit from the buffet.

"I'm not feeling well," a disheveled Cora said.

How unlike her on a teaching day. She wore a bright yellow minidress, 1970s vintage, which usually suited her. But her normally peachy skin held a gray cast this morning.

"Well, it's no wonder with everything that's been going on," Ruby said.

"It's not your—" Jane said.

"No, it's not a panic thing. It's a stomach thing. Ruby gave me some medicine. I hope it works," Cora said.

Ruby nodded. "It will."

"I thought Adrian would be here," Jane said.

"He begged off. He wanted to sleep in. It was quite a night," Cora said. Two pieces of dry toast sat in front of her. She lifted one to her mouth.

"I bet," Jane said.

"Listen," Ruby said, lowering her voice, "I did some checking last night on Josh."

"What?" Jane said. "What kind of checking?"

"I searched on the Internet," Ruby said.

Cora's mouth dropped. Jane leaned forward.

"Don't look so surprised," Ruby snapped. "I may be old, but I understand how to use the computer. Or a tablet, as the case may be."

"What did you find out?" Jane asked, while Cora crunched her dry toast.

Ruby leaned in closer. "Not much," she said. "Except he did have a record. Barroom brawls. That kind of thing."

"And?" Jane said.

"There was an article about some sort of gala here on the island a few years ago," Ruby said. "It was a charity event for the storm damage from some hurricane or other. This was back when Adrian was dating Marcy, evidently."

Jane's stomach soured. Was this going where she thought it was going?

"I don't know about this, but Adrian knew Josh. Looks like they were friends," Ruby said.

"What? That can't be," Cora said. "He never said anything about that."

"So they knew each other," Jane said. "What does that mean? Did he specifically tell you he didn't know the guy?"

"No, he didn't say anything at all about him. We talked about Marcy last night, but not Josh," Cora said.

"Well, then, what's the problem?" Jane said.

Cora placed her toast down on the plate. "The problem is Adrian is holding back. He's aware of more than he's telling me. Getting anything out of him is like pulling teeth."

"Most men are like that," Ruby said.

"Yes, but most men weren't in love with a woman who's just been killed," Cora said.

"What are you implying?" Jane said.

Cora's coloring was edging back. "I know Adrian

didn't kill her. I know that," she said in a hushed voice. "But I think he knows more than he's letting on."

"I'm certain he doesn't want to worry you. Cashel probably knows the whole story. I mean, how much do you need to know? You're here to teach. Cashel will take care of all this, right?" Jane said.

Ruby harrumphed. "One would hope."

# Chapter 19

Was a half-truth the same as an outright lie?

As Cora prepared for her class, Adrian stayed ever present in her mind. Her sick stomach, at least, seemed to calm down.

She'd never thought to ask him if he was acquainted with Josh. But he didn't volunteer the information. Neither of the men did, as a matter of fact, not in the restaurant and not any time later. Odd. Cora shivered.

Why would Adrian not mention last night that he knew Josh?

She turned on her laptop.

Several early crafters entered the room, laughing. It was Katy and her crew.

"Good morning, Katy," Cora said, and waved. She remembered the group from yesterday morning. They were a scrapbooking group who had established a blog that was succeeding and growing, but they wanted to learn how to grow it even further from this point, technically and financially.

They sat in the front of the room, each of them clutching a Starbucks cup, and the scent of the coffee filled the room.

"Meet my friends," Katy said. "You met Jana, yesterday, and this is Renee Rodgers, who is our webmaster, Sabrina Isaac, Linda Emonds, and that's Lisa Iekel, who helps with the photos on the site."

"Nice to meet you all," Cora said. "I checked out your Web site and it's gorgeous."

"Thanks," Renee said.

"We need to post more frequently," Linda said.

"Yes, I'd agree that you do. It's best to post on the same day, as well, like every Wednesday, so your readers expect a post from you," Cora said, while flipping through her handouts for the morning.

"What cute bracelets," Sabrina said.

Cora's bracelets slid around on her wrist as she flipped through the pages. "Oh, thanks," she said. "We made these at the macramé miniclass last night." Once again, she thought of Adrian. His long fingers knotting the bracelet. And the way he slipped it over her arm. He might just be the perfect boyfriend. Perhaps too perfect. Was he hiding something? Okay, she was not going to allow those thoughts to enter her brain. Not now.

"I wish I had the energy to attend last night, but I was exhausted by that point," Sabrina said.

"It's a retreat. You're supposed to find it refreshing, not exhausting. Calm down. Relax. We don't need to do it all in one long weekend," Katy joked.

"That's true," Cora said. "Remember, we're focusing on allowing ourselves some time to explore. Let's not do it at a breakneck pace."

"These computer classes hurt my brain. I recognize I should learn the more technical side, but geez," Jana said.

Had Cora been too technical yesterday? She hoped not. Her classes were as untechnical as they could be, given they were about blogging.

During today's class, Cora planned a primer about the business part of blogging, or rather how to earn money by blogging. Which she was a wiz at, surprisingly enough. Her blog earned her more money every year than her full-time salary while working as a counselor in the women's shelter in Pittsburgh. Her place of employment had become her second home since she had camped out in the back room almost every day. It wasn't worth it to go home each night just to get three or four hours of sleep and head back to the office.

She was so grateful her blogging and crafting allowed her to start a new career—one that could help women in a different way. Sometimes it was about finding a craft to help you overcome depression, well documented by knitters and crocheters, and sometimes it was about spending time alone, etching out time for oneself. But for this group of women, the scrapbookers from Leesburg, this class would give them a wide range of knowledge and skills to apply to their own blogging business. Who knows where it would lead them?

Cora's heart lifted as she gazed out on the crowd forming in the room. Staying present was not going to be as hard as she thought. She allowed herself to feel the incredible, positive energy in the room.

\* \* \*

After her class, Cora stopped by Chloe's café and ordered a sandwich to go and hightailed it to her room to update Cora Crafts a Life, her blog. She liked to keep her readers up to date—she wanted them to feel as if they were attending the retreat alongside her.

She uploaded a few photos of her class today. She also uploaded some photos from the macramé class last night. She glanced at the clock and took another bite of her egg salad sandwich. Gosh, she was hungry. That's what came of being sick first thing in the morning, she supposed.

With a little time on her hands, Cora decided to research Marcy Grimm.

She keyed in her name. A list came up. First, her obituary and then some online articles from the local paper.

Cora skimmed it—she knew all this information already—except the cause of death. An allergic reaction to a jellyfish sting? Why would she be in the water that time of night if she were that allergic to jellyfish? And on her wedding night? As Cora read further, she learned that Marcy hadn't actually been stung. Instead, it was implied that whoever killed her was aware of her allergy and must have injected her.

*Or something.* Mmmm. How could Cora find out? She doubted the islanders would give her any information. She wondered if her friend back home in Indigo Gap could. She dialed Detective Brodsky.

"Cora?" he said into the phone.

"Yes, it's me," she said. "Have you heard about what's going on here?"

"No, but you're going to tell me, right?" he said with a chuckle.

She filled him in and explained Adrian was a suspect and told him about what had happened last night.

"And you're calling me for what reason?"

"I was wondering if you had access to her death information. She was allergic to jellyfish. How did the venom get inside her body?"

"Look, Cora, I realize Adrian is your new beau and all that, but are you sure you want to be messing around with this?"

"Yes, I'm sure. I'd like to learn how she was murdered by a jellyfish allergy," she said. "It had to be an injection, right?"

"One would assume," Brodsky said, and sighed.

"The thing is, Adrian is not going to be able to come home until we prove his innocence," she said.

"That's what his lawyer is for," he said.

"Well, his lawyer is Cashel and I'm not sure he's helping at all," Cora said.

"Cashel O'Malley is a fine attorney," Brodsky said. "Adrian is in good hands."

"I don't think Cashel likes him," Cora said.

Brodsky laughed. "Oh? Never mind. That doesn't matter."

She heard some noise in the background. "I can check a few things out for you."

"Thanks, Brodsky," she said. "And while you're at it, can you check out Josh Dupres?"

"Give you an inch and you want a mile."

"I owe you," Cora said.

"I like the sound of that," he said, and hung up the phone.

Just then her phone alerted her to a new text

message. It was from Jane: **Where are you?** They
planned to meet for the crochet class.

**I'll be there soon,** Cora texted back.

She Googled Josh Dupres, and a long list of entries
came up. Most interesting was an article about his
mother, Rue, who had assisted in a recent murder investigation on a neighboring island. The article said
her psychic abilities helped the police solve a murder
case. Another murder so close by? A few months
ago? Odd.

Cora sent Brodsky the link to the article.

She read further. Rue was a well-known psychic on
the island, a daughter of a voodoo shop owner from
New Orleans and an antiques dealer from Charleston. She'd helped to solve at least three murders in
South Carolina and a few in other states.

Cora keyed in her name.

A photo of her appeared on the screen, standing
in front of her house, which was in the swamp neighborhood of the island. If she was so talented as a
psychic, what was she doing living there?

Cora remembered the words of their tour guide.
"Some of these folks have more money than God, but
choose to live here."

Rue had presence. And behind her in the photo?
The beautiful, sparkling chimes that Cora had noticed during the tour! She zoomed in for a better
view. The wind chimes were made of sea glass and
macramé. Interesting.

Her phone buzzed another alert. Once again, it
was from Jane and simply said: **Cora!**

**OK,** Cora texted her back.

She grabbed her purse and headed out the door of
her room.

On her way to crochet class, Cora mulled over what she knew, which still wasn't much. But connecting with Brodsky—and his being in such a helpful mood—gave her hope she might be able to move the case along so Adrian would be able to go home with them on Monday. She walked briskly through the hallway until she saw Jane standing beside the mermaid statue, hands on her hips.

"Where've you been? We're late. You know I hate going to classes late."

"I was updating the blog," Cora said.

"It doesn't take you that long to update your blog," Jane said.

"I dug around online and had a conversation with Brodsky," Cora said.

"Oh no," Jane said.

"We've got to clear Adrian, don't we?" Cora said.

"Adrian is going to be fine," Jane said. "He's innocent. We believe in the justice system, right?"

"Yes," Cora said, as they reached the classroom where the crochet class was being held. "But we're also aware of how slow it can be. Adrian needs to leave this island and go home."

# Chapter 20

As Cora and Jane settled in, the class had just started. Ryan Anderson, the teacher, oozed the presence of superstar. Cora would bet her life that half the women in the room already crocheted. But a handsome, personable guy who could also crochet? Women swarmed around him at all the craft events. It was almost as bad as Jude Sawyer, the "rock star" broom maker guest teacher during Cora's first retreat at Kildare House.

Cora eyed the room and recognized some of the crafters. Katy and her group were clustered around their own table. Mathilde, her assistant, and Zooey were gathered around another table with a few others Cora didn't recognize.

"So yesterday," Ryan said, "we made these beautiful coasters."

He held up an example, a coaster shaped like a flattened seashell. How clever, thought Cora.

"Some of you were surprised by how versatile crochet is," he said. "It's more than Grandma's afghans and shawls."

A little twitter from the crowd.

"Though there's nothing wrong with that. We love afghans and shawls," he said. "Today, we're going to make something more traditional, but still basic. We're going to make hats."

His assistant passed out booklets and baskets of yarn.

"While you are situating yourselves, I'd like to tell you a little about crochet," he said.

Cora reached into her basket and felt the yarn. There was something so soothing about the feel of quality yarn. She could almost feel her heart rate slow and her cloud of worry dissipate. Almost.

Ryan went on. "The word *crochet* comes from the French *croche*, meaning 'hook,' but it was most likely developed from a Chinese form of needlework called 'tambouring.' This technique was similar to modern crochet, except it was worked on a fabric background with fine thread and a fine needle with a hook on one end."

"How did it move to Europe?" someone asked.

"Well, nobody knows for sure, but the theory is once tambouring reached Europe in the 1700s, someone discovered the thread stitches would hang together without the fabric background, and voilà, crochet was born," he said.

"Now, while I'm filling you in about the fascinating history of crochet, I want you to choose your color scheme from the basket of yarn we're passing out. If you don't like the colors in your basket, feel free to trade," he said, smiling his million-dollar smile.

"I like him," Jane mouthed to Cora.

"So," Ryan went on, "this discovery happened in

time to help Ireland during the famine. Can you believe it? Crochet to the rescue!"

Laughter from the crowd.

"It was the 1800s, and the potato blight sent many poor Irish families who depended on the crop for income into poverty. Mademoiselle Riego de la Blanchardiere decided something must be done about the situation. The peasants desperately needed a new trade, something that offered easily accessible materials that could be worked on in less than ideal conditions, and would appeal to the nobles as a treasured commodity. Crochet provided all these requirements, and soon the unique style of Irish crochet lace became coveted worldwide. But most importantly, it gave the people a way to feed their families."

"I had no idea!" Mathilde said loudly.

"Okay, so maybe it hadn't occurred to Mademoiselle Riego de la Blanchardiere that Irish lace would be the savior of the country, but she's the person generally credited with inventing the style. She also wrote the first book of crochet patterns, which was published in 1846," he said, chuckling.

Cora and Jane traded baskets. Jane hated pink and her basket was full of shades of pink. Cora didn't mind it. Pink wasn't her favorite color, but she didn't despise pink like Jane did. Jane refused to allow anyone to buy pink things for London when she was born.

"Today, of course, crochet is known in many forms. Our pioneering grandmothers, poor from the Great Depression and later World War Two, would save every scrap of yarn and turn them into what are now known as granny squares," Ryan said. "Of the laces, there is broomstick lace, which was originally worked on the end of a broomstick; and hairpin lace, which is worked over two pins. Tunisian or Afghan crochet almost seeks to combine crocheting and knitting techniques. And even Japan has its own form of crochet known as *amigurumi*, which is the art of crocheting small stuffed toys.

"And it doesn't end there. Now creative crafters are incorporating beads, wire, plastic bags, and countless other notions into their work. Every day it seems someone thinks up something new to do with crochet. The possibilities are endless. And many of those possibilities are right here in this room," he said, beaming.

Jane's attention was focused on choosing a crochet hook, digging around in the basket.

"I want to tell you about these hats," Ryan said. "They are from a pattern by my dear friend, Edie. I'm sure many of you have heard of her."

Murmurs of acknowledgment rumbled from the crowd.

Cora glanced at the pattern booklet and saw Edie smiling and dressed in colorful garb on the cover. Maybe she'd have Edie to Kildare House sometime in the future.

"Let's jump in, shall we?" he said. "Oh, I see some of you are off to the races."

Cora's fingers found a rhythm as she followed the pattern. It was written so well that she didn't have a hard time following. She was not great with knitting and crocheting, but today, it was like her fingers took over. As she focused on creating the hat, her mind emptied of thoughts about Adrian, Marcy Grimm, and Josh Dupres. Practicing what she preached.

There was something about the feel of the yarn, the rhythm of her fingers, that was so soothing.

She hung on to the feeling throughout the rest of the class and even as it finished. She felt renewed.

But when Cora exited the room, she noted her phone alerted her to messages.

One was from Adrian: Went for a walk, came back exhausted. Catch you for dinner?

Another one was from Detective Brodsky: Call me when you can.

Jane peeked over her shoulder at the phone. "Well, he didn't waste any time, did he?"

"He must have found something," Cora said.

The two of them escaped to a quiet corner and sat down on overstuffed wicker chairs. Floor-to-ceiling windows provided an excellent view of the beach. A sudden longing to go outside and spread her toes in the sand came over Cora, but instead she dialed Brodsky.

"What do you have for me?" she said once he'd answered.

"Well, here's the scoop," he said. Cora could almost see the twinkle in his eyes. "When they found her, they thought it was an allergic reaction to a jellyfish sting. Right?"

"Yes," she said. "That's what I read."

"But her family insisted she would not be out for a midnight swim—for that very reason," he said. "She never went in the water because she was deathly afraid of getting stung."

"Makes sense," Cora said. Jane watched her intently as several women passed by.

"So that's why they did a tox report and so on. But

at the autopsy, the ME found several needle pricks," he said.

"Needle pricks?"

"Yes, someone who knew about her allergy injected her with jellyfish venom," he said.

Cora chilled. "How many people would know that? I mean, it's not something that would come up in everyday conversation."

"That's where your boy Adrian comes in," he said. "He would have known, right?"

"Yes," she said. "And he'd texted her, evidently."

"No wonder he's a person of interest," Brodsky said. "You've got your hands full."

"Unless . . ." Cora said.

"What?"

"Well, he wasn't the only person who was aware of it."

"Are you talking about her new husband?"

"Of course," she said.

"Don't you think if he were going to kill her, he'd wait awhile? I mean, killing her on their wedding night? I don't know, Cora. It sounds far-fetched, even for you," he said, and laughed.

But a chill moved through her. Did it matter to a man who'd kill his woman whether it was their wedding night or not?

"Well, what would your theory be, Brodsky?" she asked him.

"I'd say spurned lover."

Cora's heart sank. That would be Adrian.

"Okay, how about neither spurned lover nor husband?"

"Drugs? Money?" he said. "Look, I know you want

to help Adrian. But I think he's in good hands. Cashel's a capable attorney."

"So you say," she said. Where was Cashel, anyway? Why hadn't he been around?

Brodsky laughed, again. "You're too much. How is the retreat, otherwise?"

"The retreat is fine," Cora said.

Ruby spotted her and Jane and walked over toward them.

"How's it going with you?" Cora asked.

"It's quiet here," he said. "I've got some queries out on your psychic, as well, even though you didn't ask. I couldn't resist. I'll call you later."

"Okay, thanks so much for calling," she said.

"What did Brodsky have to say?" Jane asked.

"That was Brodsky?" Ruby said, and rolled her eyes. "What did he want?"

"I asked him to do some checking around for me."

"About the case?" Ruby said.

She nodded. "I realize Cashel is doing his best, but I wondered what Brodsky could tell us. I'm worried Adrian won't be able to come home with us on Monday."

"I'm worried about that, too," Ruby said, which surprised Cora. She was such a champion of her son's legal prowess. Did she know something Cora didn't know? "Cashel said the authorities around here move much slower than he'd like. It's almost as if we stepped back in time when we came to Sea Glass Island."

"Well, that's a good thing when you go on vacation or on a retreat," Jane said.

"Yes, but not a good thing when there's a murder,"

Cora said. "And when someone you know is accused of it."

"Well, what did he say?" Jane said.

"Oh, not much. I mean he told me someone gave her a shot of jellyfish venom. That's how it was done. But he's still working on the Rue question," Cora replied.

"Rue?" Ruby asked.

"Yes, she's Josh's mother," Cora explained. "I met her last night. She was at the restaurant with her son."

"I still think it's odd that they were out," Jane said. "I mean when someone close to you dies, you don't go out to eat. People bring in food."

"Not so much anymore," Ruby said. "It's unfortunate, but true. They probably wanted to grab a bite and didn't want to cook."

"Possibly," Jane said.

"So back to Rue," Ruby said. "Why are you having her checked out?"

"Evidently, she's a psychic," Cora said with more than a note of sarcasm. "She's helped the authorities out on a previous murder case on a neighboring island."

Ruby's face brightened. "Now, that's the most interesting thing I've heard in a long time. Does Cashel know about her?"

"I haven't seen him. Have you?" Cora said.

"The last I saw him was this morning and he was muttering something about being on an island and having to work," Ruby said.

"I'll text him and see where he is," Cora said.

"If Rue is such a good psychic, she should know Adrian is innocent," Jane said.

"And if the local police rely on her—" Ruby said.

"Now, hold on a moment," Cora said, as she texted Cashel and hit SEND. "I don't hold with that nonsense. So much of the time, it's smoke and mirrors. Very few real psychics exist in this world."

"Well, now," Ruby said. "True enough. But it's possible she's for real."

"Even if she's not," Jane said, "we should go and see her."

"She'll want money," Cora said.

"Of course she will. And we'll give it to her. It's about exchange for energy and talent," Ruby said.

"I don't know about this," Cora said. "It makes me nervous."

"She has a track record," Jane said.

"Yes, but Brodsky is checking in to all that," Cora said.

"Well, I'm going to see her, maybe after I drop off London. I've gotten special permission for her to leave the island and Zora's sister is coming to get her," Jane said.

"Good idea," Cora said.

"If you'd like to come, you're welcome to. Someone has got to do something. Poor Adrian," Jane said.

Pangs of guilt shot through Cora. Of course, poor Adrian. But if she was honest with herself, she was a little miffed at him. She still had no idea how well he knew Josh, and why he'd neglected to mention it.

"I'm not sure visiting a psychic will help him," Cora said.

"It can't hurt," Ruby said, with a finality in her voice that Cora knew only too well.

Cora's phone beeped, alerting her to a text.

"Cashel?" Jane asked.

"No, Mathilde, asking me to fetch you two and come to her office," Cora said.

"What do you think that's about?" Jane asked. "I've got to go soon."

"I have no idea, but let's go and find out," Cora said.

# Chapter 21

They hurried to Mathilde's office. It was more than a bit of a mess, which made Jane nervous. Piles of books and magazines were scattered about the room, along with craft materials. Shells. Yarn. A variety of paintbrushes and knitting needles.

"Shove some of that off the chair and take a seat," Mathilde said as she looked up from the computer. "I saw your lovely blog post."

Cora had been updating her blog all along, despite everything going on. Jane was impressed with the way she managed it.

"How's it going with you all?" Mathilde turned away from the computer and toward them.

"Fine," Jane said. The other two muttered in agreement.

"Well now, that's not what I heard," she said.

"What do you mean? My classes are rocking," Ruby said.

"Oh no," Mathilde said, waving her bangled arm. She wore beautiful abalone bracelets. "Your classes are all going well. I have scouts out, you know, plus I have retreaters filling out forms all along. No. That's not what I'm talking about." She eyed Cora.

Jane wondered what the heck was going on.

"I'm talking about your boyfriend," she said to Cora.

Cora's face reddened. "I'm sorry?"

"I heard he had some trouble last night," she said.

"He was attacked," Cora said.

Mathilde sat quietly and regarded her. "That's what I hear. I also heard you came to his rescue."

"Of course," Cora said, almost stammering.

Jane's hand brushed against Cora's—a gesture meant to calm. She hoped. The last thing they needed was a panicked Cora.

"Cora is trained in martial arts. Her last job saw to it. What's the point of all this, Mathilde?" Jane said.

"We don't like our retreat teachers bringing any undue attention. It's bad for our reputation," she said. "You understand."

Ruby harrumphed.

"It wasn't as if I sought it out," Cora said. "A local attacked us."

"I'm aware, but I'm going to have to ask you to stay at the resort and not go to any of the local establishments," she said. "The locals have decided Adrian is a killer and they want revenge."

"That's absurd!" Ruby said, as if she'd been holding it in too long.

But Jane understood what she said had some truth. That's why Adrian had been attacked, of course.

Mathilde ignored Ruby. "I can't force you to stay on site," she said. "But it's in your best interest, as well as the retreat's, that you do."

"Adrian didn't kill anybody," Cora said, after a moment. "And he's not going to behave as if he did. I know him better than that."

"Where is he now?" Mathilde asked pointedly.

"The last I heard from him he was taking a nap after walking on the beach," Cora said.

"He didn't tell you, then," Mathilde said.

"Tell her what?" Jane said. "What's going on?"

"A group of locals on the beach . . ."

"What happened?" Cora stood.

Jane reached for her.

"Nothing much," Mathilde said. "Calm down, please. A group of them sort of chased him away. They didn't hurt him. But they were throwing things at him."

"What? What kind of a place is this?" Ruby said, as Cora took off out the door.

"Cora!" Jane said, on her heels, Ruby behind her. The three of them headed to Adrian's room.

"He never tells me anything," Cora said as she jabbed the elevator button.

"What did you expect? Him to tell you he was attacked on the beach?" Ruby said as they entered the elevator. "He's a man. He didn't want you to know."

Cora's jaw tightened.

"He probably didn't want to tell you because he realized you'd do exactly what you're doing now. He recognizes you're here on business," Jane said, concentrating on keeping her voice calm and even. But she was frightened.

"I understand," Cora said, as the elevator moved. "But every time I turn around I find out something else that, well, he should've told me. It's like he's keeping secrets. Telling half-truths."

"I agree that he's not seemed himself since he's been here," Jane said, as they exited the elevator. "But consider what he's been through. Saw his ex-girl getting married while standing next to his new one, for starters."

"Then she shows up dead the next day," Ruby said.

"And he's being accused of killing her," Jane said. "He must be an emotional basket case. Give the guy a break."

Cora traipsed down the hall, heading for his room, with Ruby and Jane close behind. She stopped in front of his room. "Maybe you're right," she said. "I like him, and I know he didn't kill anybody. But I'm also aware that if he and are going to have a relationship, he's going to have to communicate. I can't keep second-guessing him."

Well, then. She was right, of course. But it was reassuring to hear her say it. Jane wanted it to work out between them. She predicted they were perfect for one another, but she could be wrong.

Cora knocked on the door and they heard him coming to the door to open it. He looked groggy.

"Were you sleeping?" Cora said. "Sorry. Are you okay?"

"Yeah, yeah," he said. "Come in."

The three women entered his room. His clothes were folded neatly on top of his bag. A T-shirt was flung across his chair. He picked it up and placed it over the other clothes.

"It's a bit of a mess. I'm sorry," he said.

"What's that?" Cora said, pointing to a black bag with hypodermic needles sitting beside it.

"That's my medicine," he said.

"Medicine?" Cora paled.

"I'm diabetic. Didn't I tell you?" he said.

"No, Adrian, you didn't tell me," Cora said with a stiff jaw. She glanced at Jane.

It was almost as if Jane could read her mind. No wonder the cops suspected Adrian. Not only did he text the victim right before she died, but he also traveled with needles. Someone who knew and despised the victim—and owned the very equipment that had killed her.

# Chapter 22

"Sit down," Jane said to Cora as she led her to one of the chairs in Adrian's room.

She read Cora so well. Cora concentrated on getting more air into her lungs. Her heart raced. Maybe she was making too big of a deal about this.

"Diabetes is a pretty big deal," Ruby said, and snorted. "I'd think you'd tell the woman you're dating."

"We just started dating," Adrian said. "And I'm so used to it, I don't know, it never occurred to me. I mean, I guess I thought you knew. I've been having some trouble regulating. We're trying different things now in order to regulate me. I'm sorry, Cora."

She found her words. "It's not just that," she said. "I keep finding things out. Things you neglect to tell me. What the heck, Adrian?"

"What are you talking about?" he said.

Ruby sort of looked away, but Jane stood beside Cora. She wasn't going anywhere.

"We just came from Mathilde's office. She said you had some trouble on the beach today," Cora said.

"Oh, that," he said. "Yeah. I didn't want to worry you. I'd have told you about it at dinner."

"That's a big deal, don't you think?" Cora said. "I mean, you told me you were tired and would see me at dinner. You made no mention of an angry mob."

"That's an exaggeration," he said, and laughed a little. "It was a group of high school students or something. They caused a scene but not much more. If it was that big of a deal, I would have said something on the text. But," he said, "I wasn't that concerned about it."

He was so chill it was disturbing. How could he not be a nervous wreck? He was a murder suspect. Couldn't even go for a walk on the beach and was hounded by people who thought he killed his ex-girlfriend.

"Sounds like Mathilde has a flair for the dramatic," Ruby said from her corner.

"I'd say," Jane said. "Now we're not allowed off the resort."

"What? That's ridiculous," Adrian said. His voice raised, eyebrows gathered into a *V*.

Cora crossed her arms. "There's plenty to the resort. We don't need to make a big deal of this. It's safer for us to stay put."

"Safer? What the heck?" Ruby said. "I can see Adrian staying on the resort. He's had trouble."

His hands went to his hips. Ruby tilted her head in exaggeration and gestured with her arms.

"But us?" Ruby said.

"Mathilde doesn't want any bad publicity surrounding the retreat," Cora said. "She's doing what she thinks is best for the retreat. We are guests here. Remember. Let us comport ourselves."

Ruby rolled her eyes. "I don't know about you sometimes. But I've got to go. My class starts in about thirty minutes. I have some prep to do. Has anybody heard from Cashel?"

Cora checked her phone. "I texted him a while back and haven't heard from him."

"He's around," Adrian said. "I think he said he was going to the courthouse to research some documents."

"What kind of documents?" Jane asked.

"I think he said something about property and a new development and so on," Adrian said.

"Why would he be researching that?" Cora asked.

Adrian shrugged. "It has something to do with the case. You don't need to worry about it. You're working here, right?"

That stung just a wee bit.

"I was curious," Cora said. "But you're right. I'm working. I have other things to do."

She stood.

"Cashel left clear instructions for me," Adrian said.

"Really?" Cora said. "What about?"

"About you," he said, with a slow smile spreading across his face. "He said you have the best intentions and this incredible need to please."

Why did that sound sort of sexy coming from his mouth? Well, sexy or not, she was miffed. And she planned to stay that way until she found a reason not to. Men!

"Cashel had no right to tell you that," she said.

"I don't know what's wrong with that boy," Ruby said. "He's not quite been himself."

"Well, I can understand. He thought he was going on vacation and it turns out he's working," Adrian said. "I'd be a little upset, too. I told him I'd help with the research, but he insisted I rest."

Cora warmed. Cashel was doing him right, after all. Cashel was a man full of surprises. What kind of property records was he researching? Maybe she should do some checking to help out? This was ringing a bell. Didn't she read about a new resort? Or had someone mentioned it to her?

Jane snorted. "Good to know he's got some sense," she said.

"What's that supposed to mean?" Ruby said.

"Sorry, Ruby. I know he's your son, but I wonder about him," Jane said.

Ruby waved her off. "Yeah, me too."

"Wait. What? He's my lawyer," Adrian said.

"Oh, no worries," Cora said. "Cashel is a fine lawyer. It's the rest of him we all wonder about."

# Chapter 23

"Are you coming to my class?" Ruby asked as she headed for the door.

"I planned to go to Mathilde's mosaic class," Cora said, her heart still racing, as she wiped her sweaty palms on a tissue. She wished for her own bed now. Her bed at home, quilt covered and with her purring cat Luna curled into a ball on her chest. "But I don't want to look at her now."

"C'mon," Jane said. "Ruby can show us how to make a bowl out of seashells any time. I say we go to Mathilde's class and show face."

"What are you going to do?" Cora said, eyeing Adrian.

"I'm whipped. I'm hoping to hear back from Cashel any minute." He leaned over and kissed Cora on her check. Cora lingered in the scent of him— spicy, musky man.

But he increasingly was becoming a man of mystery. Cora didn't need mystery or drama in her life. This was why she had set off on a new life, wasn't it? Her anxiety had gotten so bad she was almost paralyzed with it. But then again, the situation was the problem, not Adrian. She stood on her tiptoes and kissed him back on his cheek.

"We'll resolve this situation," she said.

He blinked. "Thank you. You know I'd never hurt anybody, right?" he said in a lowered voice.

She nodded. Ruby and Jane walked off. Jane held the door open.

"Let's go," Jane said.

Cora followed them.

"I'm not sure I can sit in a class for an hour," Cora said.

"You realize you have no choice, right?" Jane said. "It's part of the package."

"Yes, but I need to do something," she said.

"What?" Ruby said.

"I need to sit and think about this murder," Cora said.

"Why?" Ruby said. "Cashel's got it under control. I'm sure."

Cora checked her phone again. Still no message. Maybe Ruby was right. He was so busy that he'd not checked his phone.

"You have to wonder what the motive was to kill someone like that. It had to be planned for a while. An injection of jellyfish venom?" Jane said as she pushed the elevator button.

"Well, she was rich," Ruby said. "The rich are more vulnerable in some ways. Because everybody wants what they have."

Cora's heart nearly stopped. "That's it. Money is one of the biggest reasons people commit crimes, right?"

"So, after this class, let's examine Marcy's finances," Jane said after she exited the elevator.

"They should all be public record," Cora said.

"Well, I've been hearing about this new proposed resort," Ruby said. "I wonder if her family had anything to do with that."

"It's a small island," Jane said. "I'm betting the Grimm family has something to do with everything on the island."

"Hey, Cora!" Katy and crew came up to them. "I enjoyed your class this morning."

"Thanks," Cora said. "Where's your gang heading to?"

"We're going to Ruby's class. We want to make one of those beautiful shell bowls. How about you?"

"We're going to the mosaic class," Jane said. "Look, here we are."

People gathered in the classroom. Ruby said her good-byes and headed into her class.

"I heard about your trouble last night," Katy said with a lowered voice.

Cora felt air escape from her. Why was she so surprised? It was a small island.

"Word travels fast, doesn't it?" Jane said, and smiled politely.

"I want you to understand if you need anything from any of us, all you have to do is say the word," Katy said.

Cora warmed. "Thanks," she said. She felt her face heat. She was certain it was bright red, the curse of being so fair. It was hard to hide her embarrassment. How many of the crafters here knew about what happened last night?

"Well, we'll see you later," Jane said as she dragged Cora into the mosaic room.

"Oy," Cora muttered. "Does everybody know?"

"Take a deep breath," Jane said. "Let's concentrate. Hold your head high. We're going to make some kick-ass mosaics."

Cora drew in oxygen. She needed it. She glanced over at the bins of sea glass and seashells. Sparkling. Colorful. She dug her finger into some aquamarine-colored glass and relished the feel of the smooth, cool bits and pieces of glass.

"Now," she heard Mathilde saying. "You can either make your own thing or use a template. We've got flowers, a starfish, and a mermaid."

Cora had nothing against mermaids, but she'd had her fill of them this weekend. Between Mermaid Hall, the *The Mermaid of Sea Glass Island,* and her boyfriend's ex-girlfriend, the mermaid scholar, if she'd had any appetite for mermaids, it had been satiated—and then some.

# Chapter 24

Cora received a text from Detective Brodsky as she was finishing up her starfish mosaic: Your psychic checks out. I can't find anything on her.

She's really psychic? Cora typed back. Cora believed such things existed, but that they were few and far between.

I don't know about *that*. But she has no record, he texted back.

Interesting, she responded. She wondered how difficult it would be to pay her a visit. The she remembered she was not supposed to leave the resort, was she? She was teetering on running out of the place—she was feeling hemmed in. She'd probably be fine sitting here, if Mathilde hadn't asked them to stay. Cora understood. But it didn't make fighting her impulse any easier. She wanted out.

"A mermaid?" Cora said to Jane, glancing at her mosaic.

"What's wrong with mermaids?"

"It's a little mermaid-intensive for me."

"I'm a big fan. Ariel is my favorite Disney princess."

"Oh, that's right," Cora said, smoothing over some grout. "Belle is my favorite princess. She's way smarter than Ariel."

"Not true," Jane said, with a gleam in her eyes.

"Them's fightin' words, girl," Cora said.

"Really?" a woman behind them said. "You two talking crap about Disney princesses?"

Cora's face heated.

"Everybody knows Cinderella is the best," the woman said, and the group laughed.

"Who are you texting?" Jane said, after it calmed down.

"Brodsky. Our psychic checks out," Cora replied.

"Psychic?" Jane said a little too loudly.

"Remember, Josh's mother is the island psychic and she's helped with other murder cases."

"That's bizarre. Other murder cases on this island?"

"No. On neighboring islands."

"It's a little too coincidental for me," Jane said, completing her mermaid mosaic and holding the finished tray up.

"Lovely," Cora said. "Your own Ariel."

Jane grinned. "You know it, baby."

"What do you mean about coincidence?" Cora asked her as they gathered their things to leave the classroom.

"Well, first, that it's Josh's mother. Second, murder? On a neighboring island? That's two murders in unlikely places."

"Actually, I think there may have been more, but that's something I'm going to check into," Cora said. "But I'd like to talk to Cashel and see what he's researching. I don't need to reinvent the wheel."

"Oh, he's researching something about property," Jane said. "I ran into him this morning when I was dropping London off at day care. He mentioned something about a property dispute."

Cora realized that had been mentioned several times. She made a mental note to check further into it. She realized some people considered their land important and would do a great deal to save it—but to kill? And who exactly was involved in the land dispute?

"I don't know about you, but I feel like a quick walk along the shore before I take London to meet Lulu," Jane said, with an impish grin. "She's packed and ready to go."

"But—"

"Yeah, I'm aware, but we can still walk on the resort's beach, right?" She raised an eyebrow. "I can't have someone telling me where I can and can't go."

Cora thought of the wind chimes hanging in Josh's mother's doorway. "I'd like to talk to a psychic."

"Oh no, you are not going that far alone," Jane said. "That's on the other side of the island in the damn swamp area. Besides, what are you going to say to her? Her daughter-in-law was killed. I don't think you should go anywhere by yourself. You better leave that alone, Cora."

Perhaps Jane was right. Maybe she should leave that alone. But in the meantime, she wanted to go back to her room to do a little surfing on the net to see what she could find out about the property dispute on the island.

"Okay," Cora said. "I won't go. I'm going to my room to write a blog post and rest, if I can."

"Who are you kidding?" Jane said. 'You're going to do some research."

Cora bit her lip.

"Well, have fun," Jane said. "I should get London, anyway. Then I'm going to take that macramé mini-class."

"Okay," Cora said. "I'll see you later."

"I want a full report," Jane said, as Cora walked away.

"Sure thing," Cora said, and found the elevator.

When she exited the elevator, she heard raised voices. It took her a moment to figure out where they were coming from—around the corner. She planted herself.

"Are you happy now?" a female voice said. "I'll never get my hands on the gorgeous tiara now. Her family has it."

"The police gave it to them. There was nothing I could do. You need to get over it, Mathilde," the voice said.

*Oh, it's Hank, Mathilde's assistant.*

What were they doing here, on the third floor, standing in the hallway arguing? And so quickly? Mathilde must have slipped out before anybody else. *Odd.*

"That tiara is priceless," Mathilde said with a hiss. "You screwed this up."

"You don't understand. What I did was best. Some-day you'll understand," he said.

"Don't speak to me as if I'm a child," she said, her voice shrill.

The voices grew closer. Cora took off down the hall in the other direction. She remembered a similar conversation between those two on the eve of Marcy Grimm's murder, and her chest reacted with a crushing sensation. She needed to retreat to her room—and fast.

# Chapter 25

Cora was a kickass researcher—if she did say so herself. Her fingers took control of the keyboard and her screen lit up. She focused on the task in front of her so that the panic sensation would diminish. What was going on with Mathilde and her assistant and the tiara? The second conversation she overheard heightened her curiosity. Extremely unpleasant. But, as the images popped up on the screen of the newly planned Sea Glass Resort, she feasted her eyes on the travesty of it. The resort she was sitting in took up a big chunk of the island. This proposed resort would take up about half of the remainder.

It was on the other side of the island—near the swamp and marsh area. Hmmm. She remembered reading something about Disney filling in swamp in order to build in Florida. And that looked like what was happening here. Images of the row houses and the somewhat dilapidated homes played in her mind. What would become of those folks?

Were the developers offering to buy?

She clicked on the image of the article. She scanned

it and recognized several of the names: Rue, Josh, and the Grimm family were mentioned several times. Interesting. And no wonder Cashel was researching this situation. It seemed the perfect motive for murder. Well, no perfect reason existed in reality—but given what she knew about people, money was always at the top of the list for reasons for murder—that or love, or drugs. Her little town of Indigo Gap had even been infiltrated by the drug problem.

Her heart fluttered as she thought about Indigo Gap. Wow, she hadn't expected to miss it so much. She'd always thought of Pittsburgh as home. It was where she grew up, where she went to school, and where she had built her life as a social worker. But, ultimately, it was the place she was compelled to leave. She understood the city too well, knew the secrets of its residents, and it became like a weight on her chest. She thought she had her anxiety under control, and for the most part she did. But she didn't like confrontation—even other people's confrontations.

She sighed.

According to the article she was reading, the Grimm family was trying to stop the new resort. They had more money and influence than anybody on Sea Glass Island, apparently. But other residents wanted the resort. It would mean jobs to those who couldn't land jobs at the already built resort. Unemployment was high on the island. Several people commuted to other islands for work, or to Charleston.

The Grimms were allied with the preservationists and the conservationists, trying desperately to save what was left of the landscape, the plants, animals, and the swamp. Interesting family.

Most wealthy sorts would be on the other side, the side of the developers. Of course the developers were backed by even more money. Adair Development was a huge corporation. Cora hoped they'd lose. Sea Glass Island was so charming—she hated to see it developed even further.

But how did this have anything to do with the killing of Marcy Grimm?

Would a developer send someone to kill a woman who belonged to an opposing wealthy family? Cora doubted it. That was the stuff of fiction—wasn't it?

And why Marcy and not her parents? Or her new husband, for that matter? Everything she owned was now his.

Once again, the fleeting thought came to her that love was often the reason for murder. A twisted kind of love. But this story offered everything: love, murder, and money. Which thread to follow?

Her phone buzzed. It was Jane. Was her macramé class over already?

"Yes," Cora said, picking up the phone.

"Something terrible has happened. Thank God I just got London safely off this island."

"What?" Cora felt a bolt of panic travel along her spine.

"It's Zooey . . ." Jane's voice quivered.

"What's going on?"

"She never showed up for class and . . ."

"And what?"

"They found her body. She's dead," Jane said.

"What?"

"Now, calm down," Jane said. "Take some deep breaths, my friend. You've not heard the worst part."

"Worse? Worse?" *What could be worse?*

"She, her body, was, um, cinched in a huge macramé bag," Jane said.

Cora didn't think she heard right. "Come again."

"She was found in a macramé bag," Jane said.

Cora sat, stunned.

"So Mathilde is having a meeting in another part of the resort and wants all the teachers to attend. Can you meet me at the Golden Seashell?"

"Yes," Cora said. "I'll be there."

She shut off her laptop and caught a glimpse of herself in the mirror. She was normally pale—but now she was as white as a sheet. Gosh, she needed to put on a happy face for the retreaters—how was she going to do that? Poor Zooey. How gruesome. How perfectly awful.

She smoothed her vintage baby doll dress and reached for her crochet bag. Lipstick should help. Her heart thudded. How could such a terrible thing happen? Two murders on such a tiny, beautiful island. She drew in air and headed out the door. Memories of what she had heard when she entered the hallway tugged at her, along with all the stuff she'd read about the resort. Surely, Zooey had nothing to do with any of that. Could Zooey and Marcy have anything in common?

Cora pressed the elevator button. At least her boyfriend had an alibi; he was still in his room fast asleep. Well, the last she'd checked on him, he was safely tucked in.

Where are you? she texted him.

In my room, he replied. Just got out of the shower.

She stepped on the elevator and took advantage of

being alone. She called him and filled him in on the story.

"And you're going down there? I don't like it," he said.

"It's in another part of the building. Why don't you join us?"

He was silent. "Okay. I've not heard from Cashel. I suppose he'll call when he has something to tell me."

One would hope.

"See you in a few?"

"I'll be right down," he said. "And, Cora?"

"Yeah?"

"Please be careful," he said.

"I will."

# Chapter 26

Jane stood in the room with the other craft retreaters, trying to calm her nerves. She wasn't the sort to have anxiety problems, like Cora. But the situation scared her. Someone had killed Zooey. *Today.* Could be someone in this room. Who knew? People were getting offed left and right. Women. First Marcy Grimm, now Zooey, the macramé artist. Tom, Zooey's assistant, was rushed off in an ambulance. For a few moments, Jane herself thought she'd have to ask for medication, as well. How bloody awful.

She was surrounded by strangers. Okay. Some of them were her students. But still, they were strangers. Poor Katy and her crew—they had walked in on the body. Linda was okay. She was a nurse. But the rest of them? In shock, every one of them. They were whisked off to a quiet room.

Finally, in a sea of strange faces came one she recognized, one she yearned for at times like these: Cora. Cora, even with all her own issues, was the person to have near you in crisis. She knew what to say. She knew what to do.

"Hey," Cora said, and reached for her, giving her a warm hug. "Are you okay?"

"A little shaken," Jane said. "I didn't see . . . Zooey. But a group of women did. She was in the room when they walked in."

"Why don't we sit down," Cora said, and led her to a group of chairs.

Jane sat down and watched Cora walk to the bar, where they were handing out glasses of wine like it was candy. The room was hushed.

"I'm not sure this is the best idea. Maybe Mathilde should have sent them off to their rooms," Cora said.

"She was probably in shock herself," Jane said. "Can you imagine?"

Cora probably could. But Jane understood Cora didn't want to think about what would happen if one of her retreat teachers or guests was killed. Other things cropped up, though. Identity theft. A male teacher who couldn't keep it in his pants. And Cora's own best friend accused of murdering the town librarian—that would be her. That was enough. They both wanted smooth sailing from here on out.

Cora sat down in the chair next to Jane. "I was reading about the Adair Development thing online and examined some of the drawings and proposed resort."

"Isn't that kind of what Cashel is doing?" Jane asked, and took another drink from her wine. A warming sensation traveled through her body.

"Who knows what the man is doing? I've not heard from him. I wanted to read up on the situation. The Grimm family has been trying to put a stop to the proposed resort," Cora said.

"Well, that's interesting," Jane said. "That took you . . . what fifteen minutes? . . . to find out, and Cashel's been gone all day?"

"Forget about Cashel," Cora said. "He's not even going to tell us anything he finds out."

*Forget about Cashel.* She should. He annoyed Jane more and more. She was certain he liked Cora. At one point, she thought Cora liked him. But Cora was crazy about Adrian.

"So what did Zooey have to do with anything?" Jane said in a hushed tone. "I mean, she's not from here, is she? Why would she care about this island like that?"

"I may be barking up the wrong tree, but people get crazy when it comes to big money, property, and saving their land, and so on. I'm betting these murders are linked and that it has something to do with all the proposed development," Cora said.

"But Zooey had nothing to do with any of that," Jane said.

"Not that we know. But what do we know about her?" Cora said, and sipped from her wineglass. "Even her last name is secret."

"Well, that's easy enough to find out. There will be obituaries, articles in the paper, that kind of thing. We'll know all about her soon enough. She was quite popular," Jane said. "A very successful macramé artist."

Her words hung in the air.

Poor woman.

Cora nodded. "She was gifted. But I tell you, something was off about her."

"What do you mean?"

"First of all, I don't like the one-name thing. What's that about? Second, I didn't like the way she shook my hand. Or didn't shake it. I mean, her hand was limp. It was off-putting," Cora said.

"I noticed that, too," Jane said.

Adrian was making his way toward them. He wore a green shirt that matched his eyes. Cora lit up as she waved to him.

"He's into you," Jane said.

"Of course," Cora replied.

"But how into him are you?"

"What do you mean?" Cora said, her face falling.

"I mean you don't trust the guy. It's obvious," Jane said. She drained her wineglass.

"That's not quite true," Cora said, but her face was getting pink.

"Yes, it is," Jane said.

Cora appeared to be mulling over what Jane said. "Well," she said, "I don't trust people easily. You understand. Especially men. I'm just getting to know him."

"He's not given you any reason not to trust him, Cora," Jane said.

"His half-truths bother me," Cora said.

"Get over it," Jane said. "Not everybody opens up as easily as you do. Besides, he's a guy. He's more quiet and reticent than most. But I thought you liked that."

"I do, but this weekend has been strange. He's been acting oddly, you know? But I think we're on the right track," Cora said.

"I think it would help if you slept with him," Jane said, with a wink.

Cora's face turned bright red and she laughed. "As if that would solve everything."

"What's going on?" Adrian asked as he reached them.

"Girl talk," Jane said.

Adrian grinned and nodded, then looked off in the direction of the podium, where Mathilde stood in front of a microphone.

"I want to apologize," Mathilde said. She divulged all the information she'd learned about the murder. "There's no point in pussyfooting around. Security on the island is on red alert. Nobody is leaving and nobody is allowed to enter the island. For the time being, I'd appreciate it if you'd all stay close by. All indications are the person who killed Zooey was after her—and her alone. Your lives are probably not in any danger. But the police want you to stay as alert as possible—and as safe."

Mathilde's face reddened and splotchy patches surfaced. Cora felt for her. But she read between the lines and didn't like the use of the word *probably*. Probably not in any danger. Probably.

*So if the murder was personal . . . just what was Zooey involved in? And did Zooey know Marcy?* thought Cora.

"Do you know if Zooey was acquainted with Marcy?" she asked Adrian.

"What?" Adrian said.

"Zooey, the woman who was killed. Was she familiar with Marcy?"

"Why are you asking?" Jane said.

"I'm wondering if the murders had anything to do with one another," Cora said. "It's odd, you know—two within the past few days, isn't it?"

Adrian paled. "Uh."

"What?"

"I think they did know each other," he said. "I wanted to ask Zooey and I never got around to it."

"What? What do you mean?" Cora said, the weight of her plate suddenly becoming too much. She sat it down on the edge of the nearest table.

"Well, the thing is," Adrian said, "Zooey looked familiar to me, though her name didn't ring a bell. But the other night I remembered that she reminded me of someone and wondered if it was her. I never got around to asking her."

"Who was the person?" Jane said.

"Someone who used to work for Marcy. I think her name was Susan," he said. "I feel like I should have recognized her right away and felt bad that I didn't. But I'm pretty sure it was her."

What? Zooey was a Susan? Cora felt her mouth drop open.

"What did she do for Marcy?" Jane asked.

*Yes, Jane, ask questions.* Cora stood with her mouth open trying to take this news in. Zooey, who had just been killed, had a secret identity. As she mulled that over, it sort of fit. But it was shocking to hear it.

"She was a research assistant," he said. "Marcy, though a good writer, and a decent researcher, didn't have time to do most of her own research. Her publishing schedule was so tight."

"And so Zooey, the great macramé artist, was a researcher?" Jane said, smirking.

"Yeah, she was a struggling artist not so long ago," Adrian said. "I mean, if it's her."

"What was her last name?" Cora asked. Her brain had finally caught up.

"I'm not sure I ever knew it," he said.

"Of course," Jane said, and rolled her eyes. "She will forever remain with no last name."

"Of course," Cora muttered. Her head was spinning—Zooey was Susan, who a few years ago had worked for Marcy Grimm. Now they were both dead. A stone cold dread came over her. Of course, their killings were connected. She surmised the only other person on the island who was familiar with this past was Adrian. Was he next on the killer's list? She drew in air. *Get a grip, Cora*, she told herself. Adrian was here, next to her, and wasn't going anywhere.

But Zooey or Susan or whoever the heck she was, was killed right here in this resort. So it didn't matter that they stayed in. Cora wanted out of here. Out of the resort, off the island, and to Kildare House, Indigo Gap, and Luna, her cat. She wanted to be home.

Pangs of panic moved through her. First, her chest felt the pressure.

"I need to head back to my room," she said.

"I'll come with you," Jane said.

"Me too," Adrian said. "Are you okay?"

Suddenly, the room spun. Cora was not okay.

Adrian took one elbow, Jane the other, and they managed to escort her out of the room, past the re-treaters, past the other teachers, past the group of police officers in the hallway, on to the elevator.

"Let's relax, shall we?" Jane said as they entered the elevator.

"This is crazy," Cora managed to say.

"What has got you so upset?" Adrian said.

"It doesn't have to be any specific thing," Jane

said. "It's just how she reacts to stress. Her body just takes over."

Cold; Cora was so cold. They exited the elevator and made it to her room. She opened the door and fell into her bed.

Jane reached into Cora's bag, found her pills, and handed her one, the way she had done so many times before.

Cora took it, with no argument.

"It will be a few minutes," Jane said.

After some time, with Adrian and Jane sitting on either side of her on her bed, Cora's mind stopped racing.

"I think it's too strong of a coincidence. I think Marcy and Zooey were killed by the same person," Cora said.

"That makes sense," Adrian said. "But why? I mean, what were those two into?"

"The other thing I was thinking about, Adrian," Cora said, "is that you are one of the few people, if not the only one, who knew that Zooey was Susan, right?"

He nodded. "Probably. Though I'm not sure it's a secret or anything."

"But it is," Jane added. "Zooey was very well known in the crafting world. And I've never read anything about a name change or anything, even about her past."

"You're missing my point," Cora said. "Adrian might be in danger."

"What? Me?"

"Why not you? You knew them both. Knew of their past connection."

"Yeah, but nothing sordid or seedy about the connection existed," Adrian said. "I could see if they were hiding something that I might know about. But, nah, that's the stuff of fiction."

"Yes, I agree," Jane said. "Cora's imagination takes over sometimes. The only secret past is Zooey's and it was a name change. Who wouldn't rather be a Zooey than a Susan? She carefully constructed it all."

Cora mulled that over a minute. "Well, maybe you're both right. Maybe I need to let this all go, get through this weekend, and go home."

"If they let us," Jane said.

"If, indeed," Adrian said, holding up his arm, with his tracking bracelet still clasped on his wrist.

# Chapter 27

Adrian and Jane left Cora's room, insisting she rest. But she was too keyed up. Relaxed from her pill, yes, but not sleepy. So she picked up a book. It was Marcy's *The Mermaid of Sea Glass Island*. It was a beautiful book, with gorgeous illustrations and type throughout.

It told the story of a mermaid captured by a fisherman, who became enamored by her and kissed her, after he untangled her from the net. Even though a mermaid's kiss is usually deadly, she spared him because she had fallen in love with him—and because he saved her life. It was this mermaid who blessed the island with the sea glass and shells it became so famous for.

What a lovely story, Cora thought. In the back of the book it explained that the geography of the island and the tides and currents of the sea was the geological reason for the sea glass on this island. But Cora closed her eyes and decided she'd rather think about mermaids than riptides.

But she did love the shiny sea glass and the way it sparkled in mobiles, mosaics, and tiaras. Using the glass in crafts and jewelry was a gorgeous way to up-cycle, which was a practice that Cora believed in wholeheartedly.

As she drifted off, a pounding came at her door and she was brutally snapped back awake.

"Cora! Cora, let me in, please," the voice said. A male voice. She kind of recognized it.

She struggled to emerge from the bed. She felt as if she were swimming—her legs and arms were heavy with slumber.

She made her way to the door and peered through the peephole.

"Cashel!" she said, and opened the door.

He fell into the room and onto the floor.

"What are you doing? Where have you been?" she asked as she helped him to his feet. He didn't look himself at all.

He stood, wobbling on his feet.

"Are you drunk?" Cora said. The straight-laced Cashel drunk in the middle of the day?

"I swear, I only had one drink," he said, but he smelled of alcohol.

"What? You can hardly walk," Cora said, and led him to her bed. "You better lie down."

"No, wait. I had *two* drinks. Yes," he said.

"Cashel! You can't be this drunk on two drinks!"

"Shhhh!" he said. "I know. Listen. I'm being followed. Nice cabbie brought me here. But, I'm being . . . followed."

"What?" she said, leaving him to sit on the bed alone as she walked back over to the door, opened it,

and looked both ways down the long corridor.
"Nobody is out here. Honestly, Cashel!"

She turned back around and walked over to her
bed. "Cashel?"

He was out.

So strange. Cashel drinking in the middle of the
day? Two drinks made him this drunk? He must be
lying. But why would he lie to Cora? More importantly, why had he come to her room, instead of his
own? And where had he been all this time?

Her phone beeped, alerting her to a text message.

Late afternoon classes will resume. Thank you,
Mathilde Mayhue.

*Great,* Cora thought. *And I have a drunk man in
my bed.* Not just any man. Ruby's son. And Adrian's
lawyer.

Momentarily torn between wanting to take care
of Cashel and needing to meet Jane and Ruby, she
stood for a moment. After watching Cashel slumber,
she determined that he wasn't going anywhere. She
better get going.

The walk over to where her friends were had never
seemed so long.

"Ruby, I need to talk to you," Cora said, as she entered the hallway and saw Ruby and Jane standing
with a few other women. It was Katy and a few of
her crew.

"What is it? We need to go," Ruby said.

Cora pulled her aside. "It's Cashel," she said.

Ruby leaned in.

"He's drunk and in my bed," she said.

"What?"

"He's drunk and in my bed," Cora repeated.

"Cashel? My Cashel drunk on a Saturday afternoon?" Her eyes widened as she clutched her chest.

Cora held back a laugh. "He came to my room, pounding on the door, and I let him in. The next thing I know, he's passed out on my bed."

"Did he say anything? Like about why he'd been drinking? That's not like him," she said. "He's always been straight as an arrow."

"He said someone had been following him."

Ruby lurched back. "Maybe he was getting too close."

"Too close to what?"

"Too close to figuring out who actually killed Marcy Grimm," she said. "And someone followed him."

"For what purpose? To harm him? To scare him?" Cora mulled it all over. If the developers were behind these murders, they were nobody to mess with. They'd killed two women. They'd not flinch at killing another person.

Ruby nodded. "Probably both. If they were on to him."

Cora dug in her crocheted back and fetched her room key card. "I doubt that. He'd only been researching for a few hours. How would they realize it so quickly? Here's an extra key to my room."

"Why would I need that?"

"I thought you might want to check on your son," Cora said.

"Nope," Ruby said, and smacked her lips together. "He's a grown man. He'll be okay in your bed."

Cora felt her face heat. "Would you like to escort him out of my room and tend to him?"

Ruby shook her head. "When he wakes up, he'll leave on his own accord. I can't pick him up and carry him like I did when he was a boy."

Cora imagined Ruby twenty years younger carrying her son around on her hip. She liked the image. But for now, she wanted him out of her room.

"He'll be gone by the time you're back," Ruby said. "He'll wake up and figure out where he is and high-tail it to his own room. Mark my word."

Cora sighed. Ruby was probably right. She'd go to the afternoon classes, concentrate on the craft in front of her, return to her room to prepare for dinner, and he'd be gone. As far as she was concerned, they'd never have to speak of it again.

"What's going on?" Jane said, sidling up to them.

Cora filled her in.

Jane's face reddened as she burst into laughter, which made Cora start to laugh, and the next thing she knew they were all laughing.

"I can't imagine him drunk!" Jane said.

"Elevator's here," Katy called.

"Oh, okay," Ruby said, and they all filed into the elevator.

Cora wished she had gotten some sleep. Ten minutes would have helped. She loved her ten-minute naps with Luna. She'd counted on having an interesting weekend, but not quite this interesting, and she hadn't counted on missing Indigo Gap so much. They'd only been living in the quaint, historic town about eight months. Funny, she was missing it and not her home before that, in Pittsburgh. Oh, she loved the city and would always hold it special in her heart. But too much pain was attached to the place. The women she could not help. The ones she lost. The years she lost. No—she took a deep breath—she would not dwell on it.

Indigo Gap, however, was a fresh place, a place of comfort, mostly. Oh, there'd been a few . . . unfortunate glitches. She'd not allow herself to dwell on those, either. She was certain the murders and kidnappings were flukes. Stuff like that didn't happen in places like Indigo Gap. And they didn't usually happen on secluded islands, either.

What was going on here? Did the killing of Marcy and Zooey have a connection? If so, what was it? Did it have anything to do with the big development deal? It seemed as if it were the only thing happening on the island of any newsworthiness.

"It was the oddest thing I ever saw—and I'm a nurse," Linda said. "The way Zooey's body was folded and fit into that macramé bag. At first it was the odd knots that attracted me. I've never seen macramé knots like that. Then the body . . ."

"How awful," Ruby said.

"I had no idea what was inside," Linda went on. "I thought it was someone's bag left behind. But the closer I got to it . . . I saw her hair and then her cold, unblinking eyes."

"Okay," Cora said. "I think that's enough. I don't want to hear any more."

The elevators hushed and came to a halt. The women filed out.

"Good for you," Jane said. "I was beginning to feel a little sick."

"Nobody needs to be aware of the gruesome details. I'm sorry," Cora whispered.

"Gruesome is the right word," Jane said. "Now, which class are we off to?"

# Chapter 28

Cora's heart wasn't in it. None of the classes interested her. She wanted to walk on the sand, smell the salty air, and listen to the waves.

"I'm tired of being inside," she muttered to Jane. Ruby was off to the seashell wreath-making class.

"You know, I was thinking the same thing. Let's go outside. We're allowed on the resort beach, right?"

Cora nodded. "I think so. Security will stop us if we're not."

Jane sighed as they walked in the other direction down the long hallway to the lobby. "It's just, well, we are at the beach. I'd hoped for more downtime."

"Nobody could've predicted the way things have turned out," Cora said.

"That's for sure, and it's not over yet," she said.

When they walked outside, the fresh sea air filled Cora. "I love the scent of the beach," she said.

"Ah, yes, I know what you mean," Jane said.

"Look, there's two empty chairs," Cora said.

The resort's cushioned lounge chairs sat in strategic places along its quiet section of the beach. Cora supposed most of the visitors this weekend were the retreaters and they were mostly inside.

"I read the legend of the Sea Glass Island Mermaid," Cora said, after situating herself in the chair. "It was interesting."

"I've been examining my book, too," Jane said.

A server arrived with a flourish. "May I bring you ladies drinks?"

"Oh yes, that would be lovely. I'll have a piña colada," Jane said.

"Oh, that's sounds good. I'll have one, too," Cora said. The sun was warming her skin and she allowed herself to relax—a bit. She slipped her sweater off.

She despised the air-conditioning. It could be one hundred degrees outside and she'd be freezing indoors. Seemed unnatural.

Jane slipped her sunglasses on, as did Cora.

"You won't be able to be out here long," Jane said. "You're getting pink."

"Sucks," Cora said.

"Yes, but when you're old and gray you will be glad," Jane said. "The rest of us will be wrinkled prunes and you will still have your peaches and cream skin."

"So they tell me," Cora said, looking over her shoulder for the server. She was thirsty and the piña colada sounded refreshing.

"So Cashel is upstairs in your room, drunk?"

"Yep," Cora said.

"I wonder if we should check on him."

"He's passed out cold," Cora said.

"We need to sober him up," Jane said, as their drinks came.

Gorgeous, fluffy white drinks with pink umbrellas

and jewel-toned fresh fruit. Now, they were living the life. Sitting on the beach, watching the waves ebb and flow, listening to its rushing rhythm.

Cora leaned back into her chair after sipping from her large glass. "Mmmmm," she said. "Good."

"Yep." Jane nodded with her lips still on the straw.

"Why do we need to sober up Cashel?" Cora asked.

"We need to find out what he knows," Jane said.

"Yes, but if he's still drunk it won't do us any good," Cora said. "The whole Adair Development thing is interesting. The Grimm family is against the development. And there were some others, some sort of conservationists, wanting to save what wild lands are left."

"You know what was beautiful?" Jane said. "The swamp area. I never thought swamps and marshes could be pretty. I'd like to see that area saved, too."

"It was nothing like I had imagined. The swamps and the marshes. Lovely in their own right," Cora said. She remembered the kudzu, the live oaks, and the unusual grasses—and she remembered what she thought must have been Rue's place, with the gorgeous, glittering chimes. "You know, I met Josh's mother, Rue. I liked her. She seemed formidable."

Jane quieted as she sipped more from her drink. "Maybe she didn't like her new daughter-in-law."

"Possibly," Cora said.

"That's more than possible. I've never known a mother who thought her son's wife was good enough," Jane said.

"Okay," Cora said. "But would she have hated her enough to kill her? And why would she have killed Zooey?"

"That, my friend, is a good question. I suppose

money was involved," Jane said. "Or some kind of seedy affair."

Cora's ears pricked at the words *seedy affair*. She thought of her Adrian being sucked in to this situation. Surely he hadn't been involved with any of it. Yet, the police insisted he wear the tracking bracelet.

"Don't look now," Jane said in a hushed voice. "Here comes Hank. Speaking of seedy affairs." She wiggled her eyebrows comically in reference to his rumored involvement with his boss, Mathilde.

Hank? What was he doing here? Cora wondered.

"Hello, ladies," he said. "May I join you?" He dragged a chair over and sat it on the other side of Cora.

"Sure," Cora said. "I thought you'd be busy helping Mathilde in her class," she said.

"I've been fired and I don't feel like drinking alone," he said, turning. "May I get a drink, please?" The server came close to him and he asked for a scotch on the rocks. A strong drink to be sipping on in the sun, Cora noted. "No pleasing that woman. I've had it. I stood up for myself and she fired me."

Jane's mouth dropped open.

"I'm so sorry, Hank," Cora managed to say. "It's been a trying weekend for everybody. I'm sure she's stressed. Having all these murders happening when you're trying to have a retreat . . ."

"Well, that's what we argued about, frankly," he said. "I thought we should cancel the classes. She refused. The woman has more money than God and she refused to cancel for fear of losing money. It's so, I don't know, crass. Zooey's body isn't even cold yet, I'm sure. And here we are making seashell wreaths."

Well, there it was. He'd verbalized what Cora had been feeling under her skin this whole time.

Hank took his drink from the server. "Thank you," he said.

Cora noted the slight trembling in his hand as he held his drink.

"I shouldn't be talking with you two," he said after he sipped from his drink and leaned back into his chair. "You're in the crafting community and I don't want any rumors flying around about my departure. So, please."

"No worries," Cora said. "Mum is the word."

She sipped from her long straw, enjoying the smooth heat of the liquor as it traveled, remembering Hank and Mathilde arguing in the hallway of the resort—and standing outside the first night she and Adrian were walking back after seeing the wedding. What was the argument about? That's right—the tiara. She sunk more into the relaxation of the moment and wondered if it mattered.

# Chapter 29

The rushing sound of the ocean lulled Jane into an almost-sleep state. She was not one for naps, like Cora, who insisted her power naps were part of the source of her amazing creativity. And amazing it was. Jane loved the gorgeous coasters Cora fashioned out of old CDs, just last week.

Cora and Hank were in a conversation of sorts, about sea glass, shells, and something about a tiara. Jane was half listening. Thoughts of her morning pottery class rolled through her mind. She'd need to check on some of the pieces that had been fired that morning.

"A tiara worth that much money?" Cora's voice raised. Jane snapped awake.

"How much?" Jane said, sitting up.

"Well," Hank said. "It was worth about half a million. But now, since Zooey has died, it will be worth more."

"Zooey designed it?" Jane said.

"Yes, that's what we were talking about," Cora said. "Weren't you listening?"

"No. I think I was almost asleep," Jane said.

"In any case, Mathilde and Zooey designed it together," Cora said. "It was part macramé and part wire."

"Plus the sea glass was exquisite," Hank chimed in.

"Not to mention the diamonds," Cora said.

"Real diamonds?" Jane said.

"Absolutely," Hank said, as if it were an everyday thing. Real diamonds in a tiara to be worn only once in a woman's life. "Nothing was too good for Marcy Grimm."

"Oh," Jane said.

"So you knew her?" Cora said.

Sadness came over his face. "Yes, yes, I knew her. God rest her soul."

The three of them sat quietly for a few seconds.

"Well, it turns out my boyfriend knew her as well," Cora said.

*My boyfriend* sounded odd coming out of Cora's mouth. It had been more than a few years since Cora had a boyfriend. Jane liked the sound of it.

"Speaking of boyfriend," Cora said, glancing at Adrian as he walked toward them.

"Here's your hat," he said, and handed it to her, eyeballing Hank.

"Thanks," she said. "I needed this." She placed it on her head.

Adrian kissed her cheek and placed his hand on her shoulder, as if to claim his woman. Jane smiled. Adrian wasn't like that, but maybe he was jealous. If only he recognized how long it had been since

Cora was interested in a man, let alone was able to trust anybody, especially a man, Adrian might have a little more confidence.

Hank stood. "Please take my seat. I'm off. Suddenly I'm starving."

"Thanks," Adrian said. "I'm Adrian, by the way," he said, and extended his hand.

"Oh, sorry. I thought you two had met," Cora said.

"I don't think so," Adrian said as they shook hands.

"Well, lovely to meet you," Hank said, oozing charm. "I must be off. I'll catch you later."

A weird clenching feeling grabbed at Jane's guts. Something about Hank niggled at her. Why? He seemed charming. Except that he and Mathilde argued and he was only too happy to tell them about it. She didn't like that. These were private matters. It was unfair to Mathilde that her employee went around talking about her like that. Well, ex-employee.

"Isn't he Mathilde's assistant?" Adrian said, wiggling his eyebrows. He plunked himself down in the chair.

"Yes, he was until recently," Cora said. "Though I doubt there was any of THAT going on."

"Why?" Adrian said.

"He's gay," she said.

"He is?" Jane said.

"I'm sure of it. My gaydar was beeping," Cora said.

"I didn't get that idea at all," Adrian said. "Oh well," he said. "I guess he's not having a torrid affair with his boss."

"Now, that's a bit disappointing," Jane said with a laugh.

"But he did seem devoted to her," Cora said. "He'd been with her for years."

"But he's no longer with her," Jane said. "I found it tasteless, for him to tell us all that."

"What's going on?" Adrian asked.

Cora filled him in.

"It's interesting because I'd heard them arguing twice this weekend," Cora said. "Both times it was about that bloody tiara."

"The tiara that London found?" Adrian said.

"Yes," Jane said. "It's worth half a million apparently."

"That doesn't surprise me," Adrian said. "Nothing was too good for Marcy Grimm."

Jane's and Cora's heads twisted toward him.

"What?"

"That's what Hank just said," Cora said. The breeze was picking up and Cora's red hair was blowing around, even with the hat on.

"She must have been one spoiled rich girl," Jane said.

The sky was starting to darken.

"Yes, she kind of was," Adrian said. "But she had high standards for everything, even her work. She was meticulous about it. But on another note, where the hell is my lawyer? I'd like to know what's going on."

A grin spread across Jane's face. She couldn't help it. This was going to be delicious.

"He's drunk and in my room sleeping it off," Cora said.

"What?" Adrian sat up in his chair.

"Yeah," Cora said. "He came pounding on my door, drunk, fell into my bed, and there he remains."

"Why would he be drinking when he should be working?" Adrian said. "What kind of a lawyer is he?"

"He's a capable lawyer," Cora said. "I don't understand what happened."

"I think we should go and check on him," Jane said.

"Damned straight," Adrian said.

# Chapter 30

A police officer walked up to Adrian when they reached the lobby of the hotel.

"Adrian Brisbane?"

"Yes," Adrian said. Cora reached out and grabbed his hand.

"A word, please," he said, and led them into a long hallway.

What was going on? Was Adrian going to be questioned about Zooey's murder? Was he suspected for that, too? Oh, this was getting ridiculous! And his lawyer was sleeping it off in Cora's room!

The officer opened the door and turned to the group. "Only Mr. Brisbane, please."

Adrian's brows knitted as he glanced at Cora and Jane.

"We'll wait right here," Cora said.

He nodded and went into the room.

"Actually, I should go and fetch Cashel. You wait here," Jane said.

"Good idea," Cora replied. "Here's my key."

"How drunk is he?" Jane said as she grabbed the key.

"He passed out on my bed," Cora said. "What does that tell you?"

"If you can rouse him, throw him in the shower," Cora added.

"With his clothes on?"

"I doubt he'd have time to change . . . it wouldn't work," Cora said. "How else can we sober him up quickly?"

"Coffee? Does that work?" Jane asked.

"Yes, but you have to wake him up first," Cora said.

"Okay, Well, it's been a little while, maybe he's slept it off," Jane said, with a note of hope in her voice.

"Good luck," Cora said.

"Thanks," Jane said as she turned to go.

Cora leaned on the wall outside the room where Adrian was being questioned. Of course, since he was suspected for the first murder, they'd question him about the murder of Zooey. It was procedure, right? But he'd been in his room most of the time because he was so exhausted from all that had been happening, especially from getting roughed up on the beach. They couldn't even try to pin Zooey's murder on him, could they?

The door opened.

"Ms. Chevalier?" a voice came from inside. "You may enter."

"Oh," she said, and stepped across the threshold.

"Adrian says you can vouch for his locale between the hours of one and three this afternoon," the officer said.

"He was in his room," she said.

"How do you know?"

"Well," she said, and found herself blushing, even

though she had nothing to blush about. "I saw him and then we texted a few times," she said, and pulled out her phone.

"Not necessary," the officer said. "We have his phone. We needed some corroboration."

"Do I need my lawyer?" Adrian asked.

"No, you are free to go. For now," the officer said. "Just please don't go off resort grounds."

Cora's stomach tightened. He was still being watched. Still wearing his bracelet. At some point his rights as a person to move about freely would have to be considered.

"Can he take that thing off?" Cora asked, pointing to the bracelet.

Adrian held up his arm.

"No, not yet," the officer said. "Sorry."

"You know his every move," Cora said. "Then why did you question him for Zooey's murder?"

Adrian bit his lip.

"We don't owe you any explanation," the officer said. "But the murder did take place in the same resort as your boyfriend here is staying. He's the number one suspect for a high profile murder case on Sea Glass Island. You're dammed straight we needed to question him."

The room silenced.

Cora's chest tightened, again. *Calm down*, she told herself. It was procedure. And they were letting him go. Now all they had to do was clear him for Marcy's murder. She inhaled air, felt the oxygen circulate in her body.

He reached for her hand. "It's okay," he said. "I have faith this will work out."

She smiled at him. "Me too."

"Now, if you don't mind taking all this sweetness out of the room, I have other things to do," the officer said.

"Oh, okay," Cora said. He didn't have to tell them twice. They exited the room right as Cora received a text message from Jane.

He's not here, it said. Cashel is not here. I've gone to his room. There's no answer at the door.

Adrian's phone received a message next.

"It's from Cashel. Finally!" Adrian said. "He's at the hospital. He said he thinks he was drugged and is getting blood tests."

"Drugged?" Cora's heart lurched. His search must be leading him in the right direction. Someone was watching him. That same person could be watching them now.

He's at the hospital. Just got word, she texted Jane back.

"We need to check on him," Cora said.

"I can't go," Adrian said. "I don't think you should go either." He glanced around and lowered his voice. "It might be dangerous."

"Poor Cashel," Cora said, remembering Mathilde asked that they stay on the resort grounds. "You're right. I told Mathilde we wouldn't leave."

Where's Ruby? With him? Jane texted.

I don't know, Cora replied.

I'll find out and meet you at the mermaid fountain, came Jane's response.

"Let's head over to meet Jane," Cora said, slipping her arm through Adrian's.

"I'm going to need a drink—soon," he said. "Something sweet."

"Okay, once we hook up with Jane, we'll bring you some juice," Cora said.

"Sounds good," he said. "With a splash or two of vodka would be better."

Cora saw the strain in his eyes. Such a sweet guy being hounded for murder. Two murders, that is.

As they walked toward the mermaid fountain, Cora noted knitters and crocheters scattered about the area. They were working out their stress via their craftwork, which was exactly what they were meant to be doing here. Relaxing. But this weekend had gone terribly, terribly wrong.

# Chapter 31

Cora saw Ruby marching out of her classroom to where the rest of them stood at the mermaid fountain, with Mathilde close behind.

"I'm going to have to ask you to stay. I'm sorry. It's best for all us if you stay," Mathilde said.

Ruby spun around, as if she might take a swing at Mathilde. Cora's muscles tightened. Was there going to be a fight?

"Just try to stop me, lady," Ruby said. "That's my son lying in the hospital room." Ruby's face was red, eyes bulging.

Cora touched her shoulder. Ruby's panic was almost palpable.

"Cashel is in the hospital. I'm going to see him. Are you coming with me?" Ruby said.

"Absolutely," Cora said, then sneezed.

"Me too," Jane said. "Bless you."

"Um, well, I can't," Adrian said, holding up his arm, revealing his bracelet. "But I'm going to do some research from here."

"Research?" Mathilde said. "For what?"

"Never mind. It's a personal project," Adrian said, leaning down and kissing Cora on the cheek. "Stay in touch," he said.

"There she is!" a voice rang out. It was Katy and her group. "Hi, Cora," she said. "We have a question for you about WordPress. Do you have a minute?"

Mathilde crossed her arms, as if to say *what are you going to do now?*

"Yes, I can take a quick question," Cora said. "But I'm on my way out. How complicated is it?"

"Well, it's about monetization. How do you find your sponsors?" Katy asked.

"Actually, I have a handout I'll be giving you tomorrow with all that information in it," Cora said.

"Good, let's go," Ruby said, and pulled Cora by the arm.

"Well, that's good to know," said Linda, Katy's friend. "We'll see you then."

Cora, Jane, and Ruby headed out to find a cab.

The three women rode in silence all the way to the other side of the island.


The hospital turned out to be not much of a hospital; it was more like a medical outpost or emergency center. But Cashel was well tended. Cora was surprised to find him in much better condition than he had been the last time she had seen him. They had bags of fluid hooked up to him and a blue hospital gown covered him. When he glanced up at Cora, his eyes looked bluer than ever. Her stomach knotted. She had been more worried about him than she realized. He was becoming a good friend.

"Cashel," Ruby said, and kissed him. "What the hell happened?"

"I wish I knew," he said. His chin tilted toward Cora. "I had one drink."

Cora's heartbeat quickened. "You were drunk," she said.

"I wasn't drunk," he said with a note of defensiveness in his voice.

"When you came into my room, you could barely walk and you smelled of booze," she said.

"One drink," he said again. "I think I was drugged."

"But why would someone do that?" Ruby said.

A nurse walked into the room and checked his vitals.

The rest of them stood hushed as she took his blood pressure.

When she left, Ruby asked the question again. "Why would someone drug you?"

"I've been asking myself that same question," he said.

"Cashel, do you think this had something to do with whatever you were doing at the courthouse?" Jane asked.

He nodded. "My research suggests that this beautiful island has a lot to hide."

"But how would someone know that quickly that you were on to them?" Cora said.

"I was there for a few hours, in their archives, on the Internet, and so on. Someone at the courthouse knew I was there and made the connection that I'm Adrian's lawyer," he said. "It's simple."

"Where did you go for your drink?" Ruby asked.

"I went to the same place Cora and Adrian were last night, the Drunken Mermaid," he said. "I had a spot of lunch and a beer. One beer."

"You looked absolutely drunk," Cora said. "I had no idea you'd been drugged. I'd have never left you if I'd known."

"I know that," Cashel said. "But I knew . . . I knew something was wrong."

"I'm going to kick someone's ass," Ruby muttered.

"Cashel, do you think someone was trying to hurt you?" Jane asked.

"I don't know. Maybe," he said. "Maybe someone was trying to kill me." His eyes swept to his mother. "But they didn't succeed, did they? We'll find out soon from the blood tests what exactly they gave me."

"Why would anyone want to kill you?" Cora said. "What is going on here?"

"Let's talk about that later, shall we?" he said with a lowered voice.

"How are you feeling now?" Ruby said, her hand to his face.

"I'm fine, Mom," he said. "I feel a little weak. But nothing a bloody steak can't rectify."

"When will they let you leave?" Cora said.

"In about an hour or so, I imagine, with strict orders to rest up," he said. "Which I plan to do. I'm going to do the rest of my research from the resort."

Cora saw the lines of worry gather at the edges of his blue eyes. Someone might have tried to kill him. Because he was Adrian's lawyer. Someone wanted Adrian to take the hit for this murder case. Why?

Why Adrian?

Cora had assumed it was a matter of convenience.

He happened to be on the island. He happened to have been Marcy's ex-lover. He happened to have texted her before her death. But was there more evidence that she knew nothing about?

"Cashel, what does this have to do with Adrian?" she asked.

"Someone wants to make sure he takes the rap for the murder of Marcy Grimm," Cashel said with a low voice. "And I can tell you now he had nothing to do with it."

"Then why him?"

"You don't know?" Cashel said with a smirk.

"Know what?"

"Your boyfriend stands to inherit a lot of money," he said. "Money that many islanders feel should stay on this island with Marcy's family."

Cora's jaw clenched. Adrian! Why didn't he tell her?

Because he's Adrian!

Ruby *tsked*.

Jane grunted. "Typical of him, isn't it?"

"I sure am getting to know Adrian," Cora said. But other thoughts were occurring to her. She took comfort in knowing his whereabouts were being traced by the local law enforcement. If he was inheriting a large sum of money, he might be in even more danger than she had imagined.

# Chapter 32

Ruby decided to stay at the hospital with Cashel, while Jane and Cora felt they should head back to the retreat. As they waited for their cab, Jane fought off the urge to take off running through the sand. It was so beautiful, with the sun lowering against the horizon, and the waters were calmer and reflecting the coloring sky.

"I don't want to go back," Cora said.

"Funny, I was kind of thinking the same thing," Jane said. It was like that with them a lot. Sometimes she thought they were like an old married couple.

"Something is rotten in Denmark," Cora said.

"And on Sea Glass Island, as it turns out," Jane said.

"Such a famous retreat," Cora muttered.

"It's about to be even more famous," Jane said.

A cab pulled up. Both women slid inside.

"Where to?" the cabbie said.

Jane noted that Cora was raising an eyebrow at her. "The Drunken Mermaid, please," Cora said.

"Mathilde is not going to be happy with us," Jane said, grinning.

"Neither is Adrian," Cora said. "I texted him and told him about Cashel. He doesn't need to be aware of my whereabouts at all times."

"Why do you think he didn't tell you about his inheritance?" Jane asked.

"I have no idea. He's so reticent," Cora said, her fingers balling up a piece of her pink granny skirt.

"But then again, I have to wonder if Cashel is being forthright," Jane said.

"Why wouldn't he be?" Cora said.

"I don't know. It's just a feeling," Jane said. "He might like you and maybe isn't being as helpful as he could be."

"That's ridiculous. We're friends," Cora said. "His mother works for me. We've discussed this."

The cab pulled up to the Drunken Mermaid.

"Isn't this where you and Adrian got into the fight?" Jane asked.

"Yes, and it's also where Cashel was drugged or poisoned or whatever. First order of business. We need to check this place out more thoroughly," Cora said, and handed the cabbie his money. "Keep the change," she said.

"Is this a good restaurant?" Jane asked the cabbie.

"I don't know," he said. "I've never been."

"Really?" Cora said.

"Are you a native?" Jane asked.

"Yes, ma'am," he said. "I don't like what goes on in this place."

"What do you mean?" Jane asked.

He frowned. "Drugs mostly, any kind, you name it. But you didn't hear that from me."

Jane's heart lurched. "Why are we going here again?"

The man laughed. "You'll be fine. Just don't stay after, say, ten P.M."

"Thank you," Cora said.

"We'll be back before six. I need to check in on my daughter," Jane said. "Wasn't this place recommended by Mathilde?" Jane asked.

"I don't remember," Cora said. "Maybe."

"Well, we sort of found out what we came here to find out," Jane said as they stood outside the Drunken Mermaid.

"There's more to this place than meets the eye," Cora said. "Now we're aware. But what we don't know is why someone here would drug Cashel."

"How would we find that out?"

"I'm not sure," Cora said. "But let's go inside, get a drink, and snoop around. Maybe we'll figure it out."

They walked in the place and Cora stopped.

"Are you okay?" Jane said.

"It's just that this is where Adrian got hit and I kind of, um, lost it. It's weird for me," she said.

"Well, let's go in, have a drink, and leave," Jane said. "We don't need to stay long. I've no idea what we're searching for, do you?"

"Something out of place or someone suspicious," Cora said.

They walked in the Drunken Mermaid and were seated right away. It was the same hostess who had seated her when she and Adrian came. She held a gleam in her eye when she saw Cora. Cora knew she recognized her. Her red hair identified her—most of the time.

"I'll have a glass of merlot," Jane said to the server.

"That sounds good," Cora said.

"Two merlots coming right up," said the server. She wasn't the woman who had served them last time.

"Have you heard back from Adrian?" Jane asked.

"Yeah, he's researching in his room," Cora said. "I wonder what Cashel found."

"He certainly wasn't telling us anything."

The server brought their drinks.

Cora picked up a menu. "This is different from the dinner menu," she said to the waitress.

She nodded. "Yes, we've three different menus. If you turn it over, there's the story of the restaurant. It's kind of interesting actually."

"Have you worked here long?" Jane asked.

"No, only a few months," she said. "Grateful for the job. You two here for the retreat?" She placed her hands on her hips.

"Yes," Cora said. "How did you know?"

"Most of the strangers who come in on weekends are from the retreat. I'd love to go someday, but it's outrageously expensive."

Jane felt a pang of embarrassment. It was true—this retreat was one of the more expensive ones, and she couldn't see the cause for the expense.

"If you like to craft, you should come to our retreat," Cora said, and handed her a card. "In fact, if you can get away, please come and be my guest."

The woman's face fell. "What? You mean . . ."

Cora grinned. "Yes. Certainly. Check us out. We have a retreat coming up all about felt and fiber. We're planning a Christmas retreat, also, with a focus on embroidery and needlework. Just go online and pick out which one you'd like to come to. My treat."

"I don't know what to say," the waitress said. "Nobody's ever done anything like that for me."

"Well, it's about time," Cora said.

Cora loved this kind of thing, mused Jane.

"Thank you," the waitress said, and slipped Cora's card into her pocket.

"Izzy!" a man called.

"I'll check on you in a bit," she told them.

"Sure thing," Jane said, and took a sip of wine. After Izzy left Jane asked if she was the server when Cora and Adrian were here.

"No," Cora said. "But the hostess was here that night. I'm sure she recognized me."

"It was so nice of you to invite Izzy to our retreat," Jane said. "Did you come into some money or something? We need to make a living, lady."

Cora sighed. "Yes, I know. But we also need to make some friends." She winked. "And besides, one freebie every now and then is not going to hurt."

"I guess not," Jane said, begrudgingly.

Cora's eyes scanned over the back of the menu. "Izzy was right; this place has an interesting history. Look at who the owner is."

She handed Jane the menu.

"Mathilde Mayhue?" Jane said.

"Sshhh," Cora said. "Good God. Do you want to get us drugged, too?"

Jane blinked. And she blinked again. She felt the blood drain out of her face.

"What's wrong?" Cora said. "I was kidding. Kind of."

"You'll never believe who just walked in the door."

"Who?" Cora said with her voice lowered.

"Hank," Jane said. "Mathilde's ex-assistant."

# Chapter 33

Cora and Jane sat in their booth in the corner and hoped he hadn't seen them. It was dark, barely lit, so they might remain in the shadows.

"We need to leave," Cora said.

"But we've not finished our drinks," Jane said.

"Keen sense of the obvious," Cora said. "As soon as Izzy comes back, let's settle up."

"Okay, well, I better drink up," Jane said, and took a long drink of her wine.

Cora took a drink of hers.

"What do you think of him?" Jane said.

"I hadn't thought much about him, frankly," Cora said. "He was Mathilde's assistant. But they'd been arguing, you realize."

"Well, yeah," Jane said. "That's why he's no longer her assistant."

"No, I mean before that," she said. "I'd overheard them a couple of times."

"What were they fighting about?" Jane said.

"The first time was the first night we were here and

Adrian and I were coming back from the beach. They were fighting about the tiara," Cora said.

"What about it?" Jane said.

"He'd given it to Marcy as a gift, hoping the publicity would elevate their business, bring more people in, and Mathilde was furious. I got the distinct impression she did not like Marcy—nor her husband," Cora said. The word *husband* nearly tripped her up. Husband of one day. A wave of sadness moved though her.

Jane sat back in her seat. "Mmmm. It is an extraordinary piece, but I'm not sure it's worth arguing like that over."

"I hear you," Cora said. "But they were arguing about it again yesterday in the hallway around the corner from the elevators."

"Well," Jane said, "it sounds like those two had issues. It's a good thing they are moving on from one another."

Izzy sashayed up to the table. "Can I bring you another drink, ladies?"

"No," Cora said. "We need to leave. Hadn't noticed the time. Do you have the bill?"

"Sure," Izzy said, and tore it off her pad with a whoosh.

Cora sat it and a twenty-dollar bill on the table. "Keep the change, Izzy. Maybe we'll see you again, soon."

Izzy smiled. "I hope so. And thanks." She picked up the money and the paper. "Enjoy the retreat and the island, ladies."

"Thanks," Cora said, before slipping out the side door.

"Hopefully, he didn't see us," Jane said.

"Yeah, he was too busy talking with the bartender," Cora said. "I don't think he noticed anything or anybody else."

Cora's phone buzzed, alerting her to a text message.

Our schedule has changed. We're having a craft-in this evening at 7. You are required to be there. Thank you, Mathilde.

Jane's phone went off at the same time. "I guess we need to head back." She sighed. "This retreat has been a bit of a disappointment. Wouldn't you say?"

"I'd say," Cora said. "There doesn't seem to be any cabs around."

"I'll text our cabbie. He gave me his number," Jane said.

"Mathilde owns the Drunken Mermaid. Which is where Adrian was attacked. And where we think Cashel was drugged," Cora said, sort of to herself. Jane was texting the cabbie.

"Could she have something to do with Marcy's and Zooey's murders?"

"Mathilde Mayhue is no killer," Jane said.

"No, I can't imagine," Cora said. "But then again, you never know about people, do you? I mean, look at what we've seen happen over the last few months."

"Yes, that's true," Jane said. "But Mathilde is well off. She seems happy and successful. Why would she kill either one of those women and jeopardize her reputation? There's no real motive."

"Here comes our cabbie," Jane said, waving to him.

"Well, I guess we're heading back to the resort," Cora said. "I'm not sure how I feel about that."

"Well, feelings have nothing to do with it, unfortunately," Jane said. "We are obligated."

Cora nodded.

"That wasn't long," the cabbie said.

"No," Jane replied.

The cabbie drove them along the road and Cora took in the beach sights. The dunes. The sand. The ocean in the distance. She wanted to be at home. And she had been looking forward to this event so much! Disappointment was one thing, but murder was another. As she mulled things over in her mind, she realized they were all in the midst of a deep and twisted story. Adrian's secrets. Cashel's drugging. Two murders. A special tiara. A disgruntled employee. And land disputes. It was like something out of a B movie. Any minute, she expected another twist to the story. Or a monster to emerge from the sea. Deus ex machina.

She laughed to herself.

"Are you tickling yourself?" Jane asked.

"Yes, just thinking about this crazy trip and trying to make sense of it all," Cora said.

"But there's nothing funny about what's been going on," Jane said solemnly.

"No," Cora agreed. "But with all the strangeness . . . I was thinking I'd not be half surprised to start hearing about monsters coming out of the ocean."

"Now, that is funny," Jane said. "But you know what would be even funnier? If we heard about a mermaid sighting."

They shared a chuckle. But the cabbie cleared his

throat. "You may laugh, friends, but I have seen her with my own two eyes."

"Who?" Cora said.

"The Sea Glass Island Mermaid, of course," he said.

Cora's eyebrow went up. "I've read about her."

"There are things . . . things we don't understand in this world," he said.

"Where did you see her?" Jane asked.

"Where everybody sees her. It's always the same place, out beyond the swamps," he said.

Cora and Jane looked at one another. "Shall we?" Jane asked.

# Chapter 34

"Here we are," said the cabbie, whose name was Roy, as he pulled up to a remote section of the beach.

Wilder, rockier, and with far less people. A couple walked along the edge of the surf. A man sat on a rock and gazed out over the waters. He turned to acknowledge the car and turned back to his view.

"Follow me," Roy said, as he got out of the car.

"It's gorgeous here," Jane said.

"I agree," Cora replied, wishing they'd brought Adrian with them. He'd love this.

Sea grass bunched in tufts along one part of the shore.

Roy stood and took in the scene before moving them along to a roughed-out path. They moved over small rocks and trees, tree stumps, and patches of dirt and sand.

Cora wondered where they could be headed. It seemed as if they were more in the woods than on the beach, yet she heard the ocean sounds.

They continued moving.

"Is this the part of the island you're from?" Cora asked.

"Yes," he said. "I used to play here as a kid. My wife is from the swamps, so I spend a lot of time over there these days."

They clumped along the path. A crack of a stick breaking. Soft thuds of footfall.

"Here we are," he said, leading them down a small hill to an opening in the wooded area.

Cora viewed the patch of rocky woods surrounding a pristine cove. The deeper blue of the water calmed her. Serenity washed over her.

Jane looked back at her with wide eyes. "I wish London were here," she said.

"My favorite spot on the island," Roy said.

He must have been about fifty, Cora surmised, catching his flecks of gray in the golden sun as it shone on him. A few wrinkles gathered at his eyes and around his mouth.

"I can see why," Cora said.

"If the new resort happens, this will all be gone," he said.

"So you are against the resort?"

He nodded. "I'm aware it's probably inevitable. But I would rather it didn't happen in my lifetime."

A few moments of awkward pause as they all stood gazing at the tranquil blue sea.

"So, where's the mermaid?" Jane said, grinning.

"See that rock out there?" He pointed to a jagged rock about two hundred feet out into the sea. It jutted out and almost resembled the head of a whale. "That's where she was this morning. That's where all the sightings of her are."

"That's true!" Cora exclaimed. "I read the book."

Jane shot her a questioning glare.

"So this is the cove in the book," Cora said.

"Are you talking about Marcy Grimm's book?" he asked.

She nodded. "I read it last night. Beautiful book."

"Yep," he said. "Now, that young woman knew what she was talking about. Well educated. But now . . . you know, she was killed."

"Yes," Jane said. "So we hear. On her wedding night. Odd, isn't it?"

He pursed his lips, as if he were holding something back.

"So you've seen her here?" Cora said, wondering what the man could have seen at this spot that made him think it was a mermaid. Could it have been a woman taking a break from a swim?

"Several times," he said. "Always early on foggy mornings. I only catch glimpses of her. This morning . . . I saw her arm through the fog as she reached up to do something with her hair. I caught her face then. Not exactly what I'd call pretty."

A chill came over Cora.

"More . . . sort . . . of . . . compelling and fierce looking," he said.

"Could it have been a swimmer out there? Or a sea creature?" Jane asked.

"No, ma'am," he said. "I understand how crazy it sounds. I do. But I know what I saw."

Cora sized him up. He didn't give any of the telltale signs of lying. He believed what he told them.

"We need to head back," Jane said. "Unfortunately."

"I could stay here all day," Cora said.

"But I need to Skype with London. I promised," Jane said.

"Thank you for bringing us here," Cora said, as they headed back.

"Oh, you're welcome. I never brought a tourist out here before," he said. "You seem open."

"Thanks," Cora said.

"Some might call it naive," Jane muttered, and he laughed.

"I do hope the new resort does not destroy all this," Cora said, as they pulled away from the beach.

"We're fighting it the best we can," Roy said. "But there's only so much we can do against all that power and money. Even the Grimm family is working hard against it and they have more money than God."

*There's that expression again*, Cora thought. More money than God. It was the same one their tour guide had used when they traveled through the swamp area.

"Can we drive through the swamp neighborhood?" Cora asked.

"Sure, but why?" Roy asked. "Most people don't like it over there."

"I want to take a glimpse at some gorgeous chimes I saw," she said.

"Oh, that'd be Rue's chimes," he said.

"Rue? Josh's mother?"

"Yes," he said, looking in the mirrors. "The psychic."

Jane and Cora quieted. Cora twisted a tiny piece of her skirt.

"Yes, let's drive by there," Jane said.

Cora watched as the landscape gradually turned from wild beach to marshy, swampy beach. Houses turned from a few scattered large homes to clusters of small, colorful places. The chimes she came to see were still there. No wonder they caught her attention before. The sheer amount of them was catchy. At least ten chimes or mobiles were strung or hanging on the porch and in Rue's front window. The house was painted sea-blue; the porch sagged here and there, but the chimes . . . The chimes blew in the little breeze, and as they passed Rue's place, Cora still found herself charmed with them.

"Psychic, hey?" Jane said. "I don't know about that, but she certainly has lovely chimes."

"Spirit chimes," he said.

"What?" Jane said.

"Keeps out the bad spirits," he said. "It's old wisdom from some of the local women."

"Who makes them?" Cora said.

"She makes them. Rue makes them," he said. "Though my mom used to make them. A lot of the women around here grew up making them. But Rue makes and sells hers. They are amazing, aren't they?"

"Just gorgeous," Jane said.

"I wonder if she'd talk with me about them for my blog," Cora said.

"I'm sure she would," he said.

Cora's mood lightened even more. She intended to hang on to it as long as possible. She glimpsed the resort and sighed. Back to Mathilde Mayhue and the craft retreat. Back to Adrian and his troubles. Back to the place where Zooey, or Susan, or whoever she was, was killed, several hours ago.

# Chapter 35

It was amazing what a few moments back into the hubbub could do for you.

Each little tendon and muscle in the back of Cora's neck seized and twitched as she approached the "craft-in" room. She had dropped by her room to pick up her crochet project. She'd not gotten the hat finished, like most of the other crafters had. Within a few hours, many of the crafters in the crochet class had finished beautiful, colorful hats—and Cora was inching along at a snail's pace.

She loved crochet. Loved the idea of crochet. Loved the feel of yarn on her fingers. She understood its benefits—the same with knitting. From everything she'd read (and seen) about the health benefits of crochet and knitting, well, she wanted them. The Zen-like qualities of finding the rhythm, clearing your mind of everything but your stitching, and the actual textural benefits of the yarn against skin. Yes. She wanted that. But her fingers were not as dexterous as she needed them to be. She hadn't enjoyed it because she was too busy trying to figure it all out.

"It doesn't have to be perfect," Jane said as Cora ripped out another row.

"No, but it does have to be somewhat recognizable as crochet," Cora said with a laugh.

They were sitting on a couch, listening to relaxing music, along with the others at the craft retreat.

*Now, this is a retreat,* Cora thought, not running from class to class and stressing yourself out over learning new techniques, new crafts. And it took a murder for Mathilde to give them this space and time.

*Murder.* The word held firm in Cora's mind, even as she moved on to the next olive-green row of crochet stitches. She'd left Pittsburgh because of the stress of working in a women's shelter. She could not handle it. Her anxiety had become debilitating. And since she left and made Indigo Gap her home, she'd had the bad luck to be involved in murder cases. Well, she hoped this was the last of it.

She must help Adrian out. But what next?

The music calmed her. Women sat in groups and focused on their crafts. Low conversations were going on.

She and Adrian had been at the Drunken Mermaid when they ran into Josh and his mother, Rue, the day after his wife's body was found on the beach. Odd, but not completely out of line. People had to eat. Grieving sapped the energy from you and cooking was often set aside.

But Cashel swore he'd been drugged there. Swore he only had one drink. Yet, he appeared snockered. Drugs will do that, as well, Cora reminded herself. But why would someone drug him, unless Cashel found incriminating information at the courthouse?

The fact that it happened at the Drunken Mermaid could not be a coincidence. The fact that they spotted Hank there and that Mathilde owned the place could not be a coincidence, either, could it?

But what did Mathilde have to do with any of it? What would her reason be to kill Marcy and Zooey, and try to drug Cashel? She was an extremely successful crafter. Highly respected. And she had created and ran one of the most popular craft retreats in the world. Why would she be bothered with murder?

Cora sunk her crochet hook into the stitch.

"What are you thinking about?" Jane asked, as she lifted up her hat, almost finished.

"Mathilde," Cora said. "I'm thinking all the evidence sort of suggests Mathilde had something to do with . . . everything." Cora lowered her voice, not wanting others to hear her.

"But why would she take such a risk? More than that . . . is she capable of such hideous acts?" Jane asked.

"Yet, she owns the Drunken Mermaid. There's something about that place. Too much going on there," Cora said.

"Well, even our Roy suggested there's a lot going on there," Jane said.

"I don't care to go back there ever again," Cora said.

"But . . . ?"

"I wonder if we could help Adrian by going back and checking things out at night," Cora said.

"I don't think so," Jane said. "Imagine what somebody did to Cashel. What would they do to you or me?"

"Somebody is hiding something," Cora said. "Whatever it is, it's big enough for murder."

Jane's face paled. "I think you've hit the nail on the head. That's enough reason to stay away from the place."

"But—"

"I know you want to help," she said. "I know that."

"Adrian is in trouble," Cora said. 'I'd think you'd want to help, as well."

"I do, but getting ourselves killed is not going to help anybody," Jane said.

Cora grimaced. A chill ran through her. The impulse to help had gotten her into trouble before. She was certain she didn't want any more danger in her life. Was there a smarter way to manage?

"What do you suggest?" Cora said. "I mean, I feel utterly helpless."

Jane appeared to be mulling things over as she ran her fingers over her hat.

"I think we should talk with Adrian and see what he's found out. But while we're here, we need to work the crowd," Jane said.

"Most of these people are crafters. They came from other places. What would they know?" Cora said.

"It's not so much what they know," Jane said. "Let's listen in on how they are feeling. And what they've observed. Some of these women walked in on Zooey's body. Some of them might have observed reactions of some of the key players. C'mon, Cora. We can do this."

Cora scanned the room. She spotted Katy and her crew. She zoomed in on Linda. Wasn't she the nurse? The one who had gotten close to Zooey's body?

She sat her crochet down and girded her loins.

# Chapter 36

How's it going at the craft-in? Adrian asked in a text message, as the conversation with Linda was turning to her finding Zooey's body.

Okay, more later, Cora texted back.

She turned back to Linda. "Was there anything odd about the body?"

"What do you mean? Other than being found in a huge macramé bag?" Linda said.

"Yes," Cora said. "Other than that."

"Rigor mortis hadn't set in," Linda said. "I touched her. As I said, I thought it was some kind of macramé arm. She was . . . still warm, actually."

"So it hadn't been long," Jane said.

"No," Linda said. "Makes you wonder, doesn't it?"

"What do you mean?" Katy said. Katy was sitting behind a small craft table, working on a miniscrapbook. *Some people knit when they are stressed, others scrapbook*, mused Cora.

"I mean, the killer must have been right under our noses," Linda said.

"Stop with the drama," Jana said. "You're scaring me. We're supposed to be relaxing here."

Cora caught herself. That was true. She needed to back off.

"I have one more question," she said. "Was there anybody in the room, or outside the door? Anybody suspicious looking?"

"Why are you so interested?" snapped Katy.

"Her boyfriend is a suspect," Jane said, placing her hand on Katy's shoulder. "She's trying to clear his name."

"I can't think of anybody suspicious lurking around. In fact, the room was empty. I wondered where they were. It was nearing time for the class and the room was empty. Even her assistant was nowhere to be found," Linda said.

The women soaked that in.

"Would you like a Swedish fish?" Jana said, holding out the bag to Cora.

"No thanks," Cora said, and then almost to herself, "I wonder where her assistant was. I haven't seen him since."

"Oh, he's quite torn up," Katy said. "Back in his room medicated, I should think."

Mathilde made her way to the group.

"Hello, ladies," she said. "How's it going?"

"Okay," Jane replied.

"As well as can be expected," Katy said.

"Are we relaxing? I mean, I don't know. I thought this would help, " Mathilde said.

"Oh yes," Linda said. "Bourbon might do me better, though."

"I'd be happy to bring you a drink," Jane said, standing up.

"Oh, honey, thanks. That would be so sweet of you. Frankly, I'm having a hard time getting this out of my head. You'd think I'd be used to seeing dead bodies. Well, I am, but this was way different," Linda said, and her lip twitched.

"Oh dear," Cora said, and placed her hand on Linda's. She'd been so focused on helping Adrian. Had she been insensitive to Linda and her friends? "I never should have brought any of this up. I apologize."

"You brought it up?" Mathilde said.

"Yes," Cora replied. "Just trying to make sense of it all, I suppose."

"Besides that," Jana said, "her boyfriend is a suspect."

"Is he?" Mathilde said. "I haven't had much time to pay attention to anything other than this." There was a note of bitterness in her voice.

"Is there something else we can do to help you, Mathilde?" Cora asked.

"Try not to talk about the incident," she said.

"That's not going to help a thing," Katy said, turning a page of her scrapbook. "Trying to sweep stuff under the carpet never got anybody anywhere. People need to communicate their feelings. We can't go around repressing them."

Mathilde's carefully painted faced fell. Cora thought she saw her cheek twitch.

Good Lord, the woman was stressed. Of course she was. How would Cora feel if this happened at one of her retreats? As it was, murder had happened right down the street from her retreat, and again, not too far away—all too close for comfort. But thank goodness there had never been one at Kildare House, where the retreats were held.

Mathilde sat down next to Katy. "You know, you're right." She looked as if she were deflating. "I'm not sure how much further I can go with this. I want to go home, hug my kids, and curl up in a ball on my couch."

Cora must have looked surprised.

"You didn't realize I have kids?"

"No. I mean. I've never read anything about your kids," Cora said.

Jane came back into the circle and handed Linda a drink.

"I keep my kids out of my public story," Mathilde said.

Suddenly Cora's respect for Mathilde went up more than a few notches.

"I have three. They are at home with my mother," Mathilde said, smiling. "I hate leaving them, but it doesn't happen often anymore and it's not like I'm far. I used to travel quite a bit, but now it's only once a year and during this retreat."

"You've built something here," Jane said.

"Thanks, and I'm hoping this weekend doesn't destroy it," she said.

"I doubt that. You've got great years behind you," Cora said with reassurance.

"Yes, but this weekend . . . murder . . . fighting with Hank." Mathilde paused. "I had to fire him."

"Yes, we heard," Cora said.

"We saw him later at the Drunken Mermaid," Jane said.

Cora gauged Mathilde's reaction.

"I don't care where he goes, as long as it's away from me and this place," Mathilde said. "I'll deal with his being at the Drunken Mermaid later."

There was something about her tone. Menacing? Bitter? The hair on the back of Cora's neck prickled.

"Someone said that you own the place," Jane said.

"Partially," Mathilde replied. "But Hank is my partner. My lawyer will deal with him. I simply want nothing to do with him anymore. I want out."

"It's too bad," Cora said. "You've been partners for years."

"Yes, but he's changed. I don't understand what happened to him. The last straw was the retreat. He wanted me to close down. And that was my first inclination. But all these women have paid big bucks. Some of them have saved for quite some time. I need to respect that and give them what they came for, don't you agree?" Mathilde said.

"I suppose I do," Cora said. "There's been some trouble around my retreat, but nothing like this. I'm not sure what I'd do."

"You've got to do what you think best, of course," Jane said.

This conversation was leading in directions that Cora hadn't anticipated, but Adrian's texts kept coming in. "Excuse me, ladies. I'm going to check on my boyfriend and Cashel."

"Cashel?" Mathilde said.

"Yes, remember Ruby's son had some trouble with his stomach or something and had to go to the hospital? No big deal. But I'd like to touch base and see how he's doing," Cora said.

"Oh, that's right," Mathilde said.

"I'll come with," Jane said. "I need to try London, again. I couldn't get through the first time."

After they left the craft-in, Jane and Cora walked together down the long Mermaid Hall.

"She's stressed," Jane said.

"Of course, and the others are, too," Cora said. "Possibly Hank was right. Maybe it would have been best to call it off and have everybody go home."

"But maybe Mathilde is right, too," Jane said.

Cora's bag slid down her arm and she heaved it back to her shoulder. "There's no perfect way to deal with something like this. But I'd like to think if it happened at one of our retreats we'd pull together, not crumble like Hank and Mathilde."

"Me too. I had the feeling it had been coming awhile. Didn't you?" Jane said.

"It seemed like it," Cora said. "Why don't you check in with London and meet us at Adrian's room. He says he has news."

"Okay, we'll see you there," Jane said.

The elevator doors opened and there stood Tom, Zooey's assistant, appearing cool as a cucumber with sunglasses on his face. Cora smiled. He ignored her and walked off the elevator.

# Chapter 37

Adrian's fingers glided over the keyboard as he brought several documents up on his laptop screen.

"You see," he said. "Adair Development is completely on the up-and-up as far as I can tell. In fact, I was able to hack in to their files about this project, and it's not been made public yet, but they are giving up their plans to build here."

Cora was impressed. "My boyfriend, the hacker."

His eyes met hers again and this time bore no shame, more like lust. Pure, animalistic lust. Tingles traveled through Cora's center. *My goodness.*

He reached for her.

"Wait," she said. "We have more work to do here and you and I have to chat about another secret you've been keeping."

"Secret?" he said, wrapping his arms around her waist, looking up at her. He cleared his throat.

"Your inheritance," she said. "You didn't tell me about it."

He laughed. "Oh, that." He dropped his hands

and stood from his chair, perched in front of the computer.

"It would be nice if you'd communicate with me," she said. "I don't want to have to pry everything out of you."

He pulled her close to him, wrapped his arms around her, and he felt muscled beneath those thin clothes. T-shirt. Shorts. And long, lean muscles.

Oh, she wanted to sink into him.

"It's nothing," he said.

"What?"

"Well, not nothing, but I don't believe it. I don't believe for one minute she'd leave me a thing. It's an old will. I'm sure a new one will turn up. She married Josh. I'm sure he's going to inherit her money," he said.

Cora was startled. If it wasn't about money, why else would someone be trying to frame Adrian for this murder?

"Why else would . . ." The sentence remained incomplete because Adrian's lips were in the way. A kiss. And another and her thoughts turned to mush.

"I'm not worried about it now," he said. "What I'm worried about is this dress."

"What? What about my dress?" she said.

"It's vintage and I have no idea how to unhook the buttons. I've been thinking about it," he said, hitching an eyebrow. "From the minute you walked in here."

"Adrian, I—" *Now? Here? At this time?* When Cashel was down from being drugged and Adrian was suspected for murder? *Now?*

"So," he said, and pulled himself away from her.

"I'm thinking I'm going to watch you take that dress off."

Heat rushed through Cora. *Could she? Would she?*

A pounding at the door interrupted her thoughts. "Cora! Adrian!"

It was Jane. Cora had quite forgotten about Jane.

She cleared her throat. "Coming," she said.

Adrian walked out on the balcony. "Give me a minute, would you?"

She nodded and opened the door.

Jane frowned.

"What's wrong?" Cora asked.

"It's Cashel," Jane said. "He's back and he wants to see us all in his room. I saw him in the hallway. He looked terrible."

"They let him out of the hospital still sick?" Cora asked.

Jane nodded. "Evidently, there was nothing they could do about it. He insisted."

"What's going on?" Adrian came up behind Cora.

"Cashel wants to see us all in his room," Cora said.

"Okay, let me collect my laptop. I've been wondering when he'd be back. We've got some talking to do," he said, and went about gathering his things.

"I'm not sure I need to be there," Jane said. "I still haven't been able to contact London. The Wi-Fi is terrible. Lulu's cell phone keeps going straight into voice mail. I even called Zora. She's fine and she says Luna is doing great, by the way."

Cora eyed Jane. She had made the right decision in getting her daughter off this island. She knew it made Jane nervous sending her daughter off with Lulu, a woman she only knew through her sister. But both Jane and Cora thought highly of Zora.

"It'll be okay," Cora said to Jane, hoping she was right. It was unlike Cashel to call a whole group together. He must have his reasons.

Pangs of worry shot through her. Poor Cashel. So sick. And he had been trying to help. Even though he often annoyed and angered her, she considered him her friend and would not want anything bad to happen to him. Besides, he was Ruby's son and Adrian's lawyer—he needed to stay healthy.

# Chapter 38

Jane and Cora made their way to Cashel's room, where the others were already waiting, seated on the balcony. The sky was darkening and waves pounded on the sand. The rushing noises of the waves would have calmed Cora, but she was so keyed up from all the worry and excitement.

"So, what happened to you?" Jane said, eyeing Cashel.

Cashel was sitting in a lounger, legs propped up, sunglasses on. His coloring was still off.

"I was drugged," he said. "We've gotten the tox reports."

A hush fell over the group.

Adrian's arm slipped around Cora's shoulder. Her head went into her hands and she glanced at Cashel. "What do you think this means?"

"Someone wanted me out of the way for several hours," he said.

"Gave him a tiny bit of the date rape drug, Rohypnol. Wasn't like they wanted to kill him," Ruby said.

Cora thought about the way he had acted as if he'd been drunk and she supposed it made sense.

"So they wanted you down long enough for . . . for what?" Adrian said.

"I've been trying to figure that out."

"The only thing that's happened is, well, Zooey was killed," Jane said.

"Maybe someone wanted to you to look suspicious, you know, a lawyer on drugs," Cora said.

"But why? What would be the point?" Jane said. "He has no connection to any of these people, except that he's Adrian's lawyer."

They all glanced Adrian's way.

"Well," Adrian said, then cleared his throat. "I've an alibi for that. We tried to call you, but couldn't reach you. They questioned me and Cora and understand I had nothing to do with that one, at least."

"Good," Cashel said, nodding. "Because here's the thing. Those two murders are most assuredly connected."

"How do you know?" Cora said. She had considered this. But the women were killed in different ways. She was unable to find a solid connection between them—except for Adrian, who thought he recognized Zooey as Marcy's old, long-time research assistant, Susan.

"Zooey was Susan Twiliger," Cashel said to Adrian. "Ring a bell?"

"Yes, I thought so. Her hair is different and something else. I could not quite put my finger on it," he said.

"Nose job," Cashel replied.

"My, my, you have been digging around," Jane said.

"So Susan used to work for Marcy," Cashel went on. "First it's too coincidental that they were both murdered within days of one another. I wasn't aware of her murder until thirty minutes ago, though. But her name did come up in the research anyway."

A vision of Zooey's beautiful face came to her mind. Cora didn't care for her—it turned out she was not your ordinary fake, but a REAL fake. She had a carefully constructed new self that had become a famous crafter.

"Susan and Marcy were cousins," Cashel said. "Marcy's family was and is quite wealthy. Marcy's family lived on the other side of the island. Marcy's mother was a sister of Susan's mother."

"What part of the island does Susan's family live on?" Cora asked.

"They live in what people call the swamp area, though it's not a true swamp. It's just a marsh," Cashel said.

Cora's spine tingled. The beautiful wind chimes flashed in her mind.

"Josh's family is from over there, too," she said.

Cashel nodded. "Josh is Zooey's cousin."

"So Marcy and Josh were related?" Cora said.

"By marriage. Not blood related at all," Cashel responded.

"So, what does this have to do with anything? My case? Why you were drugged?" Adrian said with a note of impatience.

"I researched Adair Development," Cashel went on. "They are planning to back off the resort plans."

"Yeah, I found that out today," Adrian said.

"Did you happen to notice who is on the board for them?" Cashel asked.

"No," Adrian said.

"Mathilde Mayhue," Cashel said.

Once again, the group was silenced.

"So Mathilde Mayhue is on the board for Adair, and she owns the Drunken Mermaid?" Cora said.

"Odd, isn't it?" Ruby said. "How many professional crafters do you know who could afford all that?"

"Not the majority, but she is outrageously successful," Cora said. "She created this retreat years ago and helped to make this island what it is—quite a success."

"Or a travesty," Adrian said. "Depending on how you view it. Marcy hated the retreat, the resort. She said the island was better off without it. Of course, her family didn't need to worry about making a living, like some of the other residents who were gung-ho about the resort. It meant jobs for them."

Cora remembered the conversation she'd overheard between Hank and Mathilde about the tiara. Mathilde did not like Marcy. That was obvious. But Hank seemed to have a high opinion of her.

"What else did you find out?" Cora asked.

He hesitated, letting out air. "That's pretty much it. But it was enough to get me out of the way, obviously."

"Just finding out about Adair Development and that Mathilde is a board member? Ridiculous!" Jane said.

"I would agree," Cashel said. "Which leads me to believe there's more going on here than meets the eye. But my focus is not on solving all the local issues—and there seem to be a great deal. My focus is on absolving Adrian from a ludicrous murder rap."

"Do you have enough information to do that?"
Jane said.

"I don't know. But that's not quite the question.
They have to prove him guilty. If they can't prove
it, they can't hold him here. So, Adrian, if there's
anything else you could think of that you need to tell
me, now is the time," Cashel said.

Adrian shook his head.

"Don't you think that if we find the killer it will
help Adrian?" Cora said.

"Of course it would," Cashel said. "But none of us
are cops. And some of us have work to do here. Like
you. Shouldn't you be, I don't know, knitting something?"

Ruby reached over and smacked his head, playfully.

Cora ignored him, as she often did.

"Cashel, when you were in the Drunken Mermaid,
did you see anybody you knew?" she asked.

He thought a moment. "I recognized a couple of
people. Mathilde's assistant . . . What's his name?"

"Hank," said Jane. She looked at Cora, for they
had noted him there as well, not more than a few
hours ago.

"And Josh's mother? She was there with a group of
women," Cashel said.

"Rue the psychic?" Cora asked.

"Yeah, psychic," Cashel said, and laughed.

But Cora's stomach was knotting. Were Rue and
Hank acquainted? It seemed an odd connection. But
then again, Cora didn't know much about Hank,
other than he was Mathilde's assistant, they had been
quarreling for days, and finally, he quit or was fired.

"That Hank character? I don't like him," Ruby said.
"He's a bit too pretty for me. I never liked a pretty man.

Besides, his nose was always in Mathilde's ass. No life of his own, I suppose."

"You know he no longer works for her, right?" Jane said.

"I think we should talk with Hank," Cora said.

"Cora—" Cashel said.

"Can't hurt to talk with him," Jane replied.

"I think we need to talk with Rue, too. I've been wanting to interview her for my blog," Cora said.

Cashel shook his head. "Can't you control your woman?" he said to Adrian.

"I don't think I'd even want to try," Adrian said, grinning.

"Seriously," Ruby said with sternness. "If these folks are drugging Cashel for knowing too much, which is nothing at all, imagine what they might do to one of you for not minding your own business. We need to untangle Adrian from this mess and get on home. Let's not complicate things, shall we?"

Cora grimaced. Ruby was right—but of course, that wasn't going to stop her. She'd just have to be extra careful.

# Chapter 39

Rue's e-mail address was not hard to find. Cora sent the note off with a brief explanation. Cora was no trained journalist, but one thing she'd found about people was that they did like to talk about themselves. She'd met few crafters who didn't relish the opportunity to talk about themselves and their craft.

"I'll talk with Hank," Jane said. "I saw him heading into the bar earlier; maybe he's still there."

Cora's eyebrow lifted. "He's a handsome guy."

"That he is," Jane said. "But, of course, it doesn't matter. He's gay, right? And I'm a woman on a mission."

"Be careful," Cora said. Her phone beeped, signaling a new e-mail. "It's Rue."

"Already?" Jane asked.

Cora read the e-mail aloud:

"Good to hear from you. As luck would have it, my husband is at the resort now and he will bring you to our home for the interview. Does now suit? He's standing next to the mermaid fountain. Tall redhead. You simply can't miss him."

"Oh, I don't think you should go alone," Jane said. "Hank will have to wait."

"I'm sure I'll be fine. We don't know when you'll get a chance at Hank again," Cora said.

"No way," Jane said.

Cora recognized the tone of her voice and decided not to argue with her.

"Whatever," Cora said. "If you want to come, it's fine with me."

I'll be right there, Cora texted back. I'm bringing Jane Starr with me. I hope that's okay.

Cora and Jane grabbed their things and headed out to the lobby where the mermaid fountain was.

They made their way to the tall, redhead of a man standing there.

"Mr. Dupres," Cora said.

He nodded and extended his hand. As they shook hands he said, "No. Call me John. Nice to meet you, Cora."

"Jane," she said, and extended her hand.

"I don't mean to rush," Cora said. "But we need to skedaddle before someone sees us. We're supposed to be staying at the resort."

"Why's that?" he said as he led them out the door to the car.

"Because of the murders," Cora said. "For our safety."

His head tilted. "You'll be safe with me," he said. "No worries."

"I imagine," Cora said, and slipped into the car. Jane took the backseat.

They rode a few minutes in the quiet.

"I was about to leave," he said. "Then Rue texted me and said you wanted to interview her."

"Yes, I write a craft blog and I've been by your place a couple of times now and saw the gorgeous chimes. I wanted to talk with her about them," Cora said.

"The spirit chimes are special," he said, beaming. "I'm proud of her. I like the fact that she's taken folk art and made it into, well, what I'd call real art."

Cora warmed. This man was proud of his wife. How heartwarming.

"Have you been married long?" Cora said.

"No," he replied. "Just about a year."

"Oh," Cora said. So this man was not Josh's father. That's why he wasn't Mr. Dupres.

"She was married once before," he said. "Had a couple of kids with that man and then he disappeared."

"Disappeared?" Jane said.

"Yeah, took off. Nobody knows what happened to him," he said. "Finally got him declared dead after, I don't know, years of him being gone, so she could move on."

"That's sad," Cora said. She was aware that there were more missing people in the world than one could imagine. Sometimes they'd been killed and simply never found. Sometimes, something snapped in them and they were confused and wandering. Other times, it was deliberate. A popular scenario was running away to be with a new love. Cora wondered which scenario could have been Rue's husband's.

"Rue's excited about this," he said as he pulled up the driveway.

The house sat in a long row of other houses. Some were sort of ramshackle. But others were painted in bright colors. Rue's place was painted sea-blue and the trim was in cobalt-blue. The chimes hung on the front porch and in the bay window facing the driveway.

Spirit chimes. Cora loved the idea of them. Loved the name. Some crafts had such interesting histories. The chimes tinkled in the slight breeze and the sunlight caught in the sea glass and beads. She viewed them closer as she followed John onto the porch. Small feathers, tiny pieces of driftwood were also on some of the chimes. She hadn't seen it before. And . . . were those . . . bones? Bones of small animals? Birds? What?

Shards of fear and disgust moved through her. Were they killing animals to make crafts? She'd have to find out, wouldn't she? She absolutely could not profile a person on her blog who was killing animals.

Rue opened the door. "Cora!" she said. "Pleased to see you again." Her smile was broad across her face and welcoming. A confident charm oozed from her.

Her skin was a light mocha and was radiant. Her eyes were dark and almond shaped. She was a large woman who moved with grace and assurance. She wore blue jeans and a light blue peasant shirt. Beads hung around her neck and earrings that matched dropped from her ears.

"Please come in," she said.

"Thank you," Cora replied. "This is my colleague, Jane Starr," Cora said after they were situated.

"Pleased to make your acquaintance," Rue said. "Can I bring you iced tea or something?"

"No, please," Cora said. "We want to hear about your chimes and take some photos. How does that sound?"

Rue's eyebrows lifted. "Honestly? It sounds like heaven."

# Chapter 40

"First, let me say how sorry I am for your loss," Cora said.

"Thank you," Rue said. "She was a wonderful woman who would have made an excellent daughter-in-law."

"How is your son?" Jane asked.

"He's not handling things well at all. But what can you expect? It's an awful thing," she said. She frowned and folded her hands on her lap.

"Let's change the subject," Cora said. "Let's talk about the spirit chimes."

Rue brightened. "Well, I grew up making them," she said. "I'm one of the few Sea Glass Island natives who are actually from here. There's fewer and fewer of us remaining."

"Any idea how it began? Who started it?"

She shook her head. "No. Sea folk are superstitious," she said. "Hence the tales you sometimes hear. Fishermen and their wives founded this island. Generations of fishing, until the tides shifted, I suppose. But in any case, the spirit chimes are supposed to keep the bad spirits away and invite good spirits to stay around. It's that simple."

"I wouldn't want any spirits around," Jane said.

Rue leaned in to her. "Oh, my dear, they are every-where. And you . . . you have such goodness around you."

Cora shivered slightly and cleared her throat. "Let's get back to the chimes, shall we?"

"Yes, of course," Rue said. "I try to use found items. Sea glass. Seashell. Bits and pieces of driftwood. Feathers. Bones that I find."

*Whew,* Cora thought.

"But, a few years ago I experimented using semi-precious stones, like amethyst, moonstones, and so on. People seem to like them," she said.

"Sometimes these stones have a folklore behind them," Jane said. Cora could have kicked her. She didn't want the conversation to veer in that direction at all. "Are you creating them with that in mind?"

"Oh, yes," Rue said. "I only use gems that attract the light."

"I wonder why you're not teaching at the retreat this week," Cora said. "You are gifted. Your chimes are an art."

Rue flushed. "Thank you," she said. "I've been asked a few times, but I have other obligations."

"Oh?" Cora said.

"Yes, well, I try not to charge too much for my chimes. Only what I need. It's a part of my belief system, you see. I have plenty," she said, and gestured with her hand.

It was true, mused Cora. The smallish house, simply decorated, held an aura of plenty. "We don't need much in this world. We're only passing through," she said.

"What does that have to do with the retreat?" Jane asked.

"They charge too much," Rue said. "For everything. And I can't be a part of it."

"How well do you know Mathilde and, what's his name . . . Hank?" Cora said.

She grunted and said, "Too well."

*Well, that answers one question*, Cora thought.

"I'd like to take you into my little studio," Rue said. "I've got a couple pieces in progress."

"Oh, yes, I'd love to see your studio," Cora said.

They followed her into the small but tidy room, where there was a long table filled with small boxes brimming with stones, beads, glass, and so on. A window allowed plenty of light into the room. Several chimes were in front of it and the light played against the opposite wall—reflections of gold, red, sea-green, and orange.

"Those are my love chimes," Rue said, laughing. She placed her hands on the table. Cora snapped photos.

"I've been working with copper wire now for some time. I like it," Rue said.

A doorbell interrupted Rue. "Excuse me," she said, and left the room.

"Well, we're aware she knows Hank," Jane said.

"And we understand how she feels about the craft retreat. That's all we know," Cora said. "But this is going to make a great story for the blog."

"Agreed," Jane said. "But don't you think we need to wrap it up soon? We've gotten what we came for."

Cora nodded. "I suppose. It's so lovely here. So warm and welcoming. I kind of hate to leave."

She heard an odd noise out in the living room— was Rue okay? It was a crashing noise, Cora realized. She and Jane ran out into the living room to find Rue lying on the floor and a man standing over her. Cora recognized him.

"Step away from her," Cora said.

"Now hold on," he said. "I'm a police officer. I'm trying to help."

Cora's attention focused on Rue, who seemed faint. But she nodded. "I'm okay, sweetie."

The officer helped her to her feet.

"I'm sorry," Rue said to them, and turned back to the police officer. "Adrian Brisbane is not your man."

Cora's heart lurched in her chest. "What?"

"I sometimes consult with the local police. I'm a psychic," she said matter-of-factly.

"Brisbane is the only one we have anything on," the officer said.

"Keep digging," she said. "As I told you, I keep seeing a large woman."

Mathilde was a large, top heavy woman with big bones. Tall. Heavy.

Maybe they were all barking up the wrong tree. The police. Cora. Cashel. Everybody. Maybe Mathilde *was* the killer.

Cora swallowed. "I'm sorry. We need to head back to the retreat. I'll be in touch about the post."

"Are you sure you don't want to stay?" Rue said.

"I'd love to. I like it here. It's so comforting. But I need to head back to the retreat, unfortunately," Cora said. So ironic. This place felt more like a retreat than the retreat.

# Chapter 41

The ride back to the resort felt longer than ever and the sound of the tires, along with the movement of the car, lulled Cora into almost falling asleep.

"It's late," Cora said, when they entered the resort. "I'm exhausted and going to bed."

"Okay," Jane said. "I'm going to have a drink."

Cora lifted her eyebrows. "Don't be too late. Your class is early."

"Yes, Mother," Jane said, and smiled. "I'm so keyed up. A glass of wine might do the trick. Join me?"

Jane understood Cora's weakness was wine. Well, one of her many, many weaknesses.

"Okay," Cora said. "One drink."

They both were surprised to see Hank still sitting at the bar. Had he been here all this time?

The two of them waved to him and sat in a booth. Jane recognized a few of the craft retreaters hanging around in clusters. A group laughed over in the corner. It was much too dark to see them, as they were too distant. A pianist played in the other corner. Something soft and bluesy.

"We'd like some wine," Jane said to the server as she came up to their table.

"Here's our list," she said, and handed them a small menu.

"We'll take the Moscato," Jane said.

"Sounds good," she said.

Cora was wilting. She was quiet and her eyelids were heavy. One glass of wine and she'd be ready for bed.

"So what do you think of Rue?" Jane asked.

"I liked her," Cora said.

"That's not what I asked. What about all that psychic business?"

"Well, you know how I feel about all that. Most of the time it's nonsense."

"Most of the time?"

"I've met a few real psychics," Cora said. "Most of them keep to themselves."

"Yes, but she's trying to help. She told the officer that Adrian wasn't their guy. That it was a large woman," Jane said.

"I thought about that," Cora said.

"Mathilde," Jane said. The server came up and sat the glasses of wine on the small table. "Thank you," Jane said.

"Or Rue is trying to point us in another direction to sidetrack us," Cora said. She sighed. "All I understand is Adrian didn't do it."

"You two haven't . . ."

"Absolutely not," Cora said. "When has there been time? Besides we are—"

"Taking your time," Jane said, and rolled her eyes.

She took a sip of the wine. "Don't look now. But you-know-who is heading our way."

"Hey, ladies," Hank said as he sidled up to the table.

"Hi, Hank. I'm surprised to see you here," Jane said.

"Why's that?" Hank said.

"Because you were fired or quit or whatever," Jane said.

"True, but I live here," he said. "This is my home."

He slurred his words. He was a man who'd been drinking most of the evening. He was on the edge of being drunk. Jane thought she might take advantage of that.

"Please sit down with us," Jane said. "You live here at the resort?"

"Yes," he said. "Part of my employment package, you see. Of course, most of the time . . . I didn't stay in my place. I stayed with . . . Mathilde. But that's over. Way over."

"You mean . . . ?" Cora leaned across the table. "You mean you were more than her assistant?"

He nodded. "I never should have let it happen."

*Not gay then.*

Jane took a drink of her wine. Sweet. Delicious. Sort of like the news just now delivered. If Mathilde and Hank were together, it added a whole new layer of possibilities.

"But I did. We did. And now what a mess," he said.

"This was all over one disagreement?" Cora said. "Maybe it's not over." Cora was now her counselor self. Jane recognized it.

"Oh, it was more than that, actually," he said. "We'd been spatting about the tiara and then the murders happened and it became too intense. I'm not as tough as she is. I suppose that's why she's so successful."

"Spatting about the tiara?" Jane said, grinning. She noted Cora had brightened a bit since Hank sat down.

"Oh yes," he said, slurring his S's. "That damned tiara. Designed for Marcy. Worth a mint."

"What was there to fight about?" Cora said.

"Well, I gave it to Marcy," he said. "Mathilde was furious. I thought because Marcy was famous in some circles and well connected, seeing it on her head would elevate the design part of the business."

"And Mathilde wanted to charge her," Jane said.

He nodded. "But I was in charge of marketing and PR and I thought it was my decision to make. Evidently not," he said.

Jane didn't know how she felt about that. She understood what he was saying—giving away items sometimes had far-reaching effects that you couldn't put a price tag on. But as an artist herself, Jane needed the money for her own products she had put time, energy, and money into.

"How entangled are you with her?" Cora asked. "Did you sign a contract?"

"I'll receive a severance package. Plus, I imagine I'll take over the Drunken Mermaid," he said. "She has hardly anything to do with that, as it is. But we're both owners."

Jane's eyes met Cora's.

"We've heard there's a lot that goes on there," Jane said.

"What have you heard?" he asked.

The server came up to the table. "Can I offer anybody another drink?"

They all shook their heads no.

When she left, Jane leaned in closer to him. "Drugs. That kind of thing."

His face reddened. "Well, you have that in any beach bar. But we've tried to keep it at bay."

"Our friend Cashel was drugged there earlier today," Cora piped up. "What do you know about that?"

He coughed on his drink. "What? You must be mistaken." He stammered and hit his chest.

"I don't think so," Jane said. "He was at the hospital most of the day."

"Must be some kind of mistake," he said, again.

"It's not a mistake, Hank. Cashel was drugged at the Drunken Mermaid today, after researching the Marcy Grimm case for his client, my boyfriend Adrian Brisbane," Cora said.

Hank squirmed in his seat. "Well, obviously, I need to check into this. The police haven't come to me yet. Maybe they've contacted Mathilde."

"We saw you there earlier," Jane said.

"And? I don't like what you're implying, Jane," he said. He stood up. "And if I were you—both of you—I'd mind my own business."

# Chapter 42

That night Cora dreamed of her cat Luna, spirit chimes, and mermaids. She awoke early with mermaids on the brain. She made herself coffee and found her way to her laptop, where she prepared to write a blog post about spirit chimes. She downloaded the photos she'd snapped of Rue and her craft room. The photos were gorgeous and Cora thought that the blog post would be more of a photo essay.

Rue was a gorgeous, formidable woman and her craft suited her. Cora looked over photos of boxes of colorful sea glass, wires, threads, and so on, with Rue's long, delicate fingers resting near them or holding them. A cluster of sea glass and beads twisted into a macramé necklace hung from a shell behind Rue in one photo. She hadn't noticed it before. Cora zoomed in to it—it resembled a necklace designed by Zooey.

Nothing odd about that, was there? Rue was a creative, stylish woman and it wasn't a long stretch of the imagination to think she owned some of Zooey's macramé jewelry. She choked back the initial sense of dread she felt when she spotted it. Of course she felt dread. Poor Zooey, or Susan, or whoever she was, she was now dead, her body placed in a macramé bag in a last twist of a sick gesture, as if the killer was trying to be ironic.

Zooey, the gifted macramé artist, killed and shoved into a macramé bag. Who could have done such a thing? Who would want to make such a statement? True, Zooey was taken with herself and Cora was not overly fond of the woman, but how could she have made such a vicious enemy? Why? Because she'd changed her name and found success—a rare success among crafters? Had she gotten above herself? Was someone from her past pissed enough and jealous enough to kill her?

A pang of sadness tore through Cora. She herself was certain people from her past despised her for her success. But did anybody hate her enough to kill her? She hoped not. She hoped that people could be happy for her success—but she understood that wasn't always the case.

She mulled over Zooey. It wasn't as if she were a movie star who everybody recognized when she went out on the streets. No, she was only easily recognized among crafters. So if the killer was not someone from her past, maybe he or she was a jealous, vindictive person—possibly another macramé artist. Several macramé artists were at the retreat. Several who had been taking her class.

Cora tried to focus on writing her blog post and Rue's story—how she grew up making the spirit chimes, how she used to sit with her mother and aunts as they made the chimes, how it became such a part of her culture, and how she moved the craft into something more: art. Cora loved stories like this. Crafting was about more than making pretty and/or useful things. It could be about maintaining connections with your culture, as Rue was doing.

Cora was certain Rue could have moved out of her tiny swamp home, but she chose not to. She was one of the people their guide was referencing when he said, "Some of the people have more money than God, but they choose to live here."

Home was home and sometimes money wasn't enough to tear a person away from home.

Images of Kildare House played in Cora's mind. The stained glass window of Brigid, the Celtic goddess of crafts and poetry. Her window seat in her attic apartment. Jane's darling carriage house. The backyard flower garden. Ruby's herb garden. A sinking feeling came over Cora. Was she homesick?

She zoomed in on the macramé necklace in the photo. She was still uncertain if it was one of Zooey's pieces. But it was intricate enough to be one of hers. Macramé was an interesting craft, Cora mused. It was one in which the different knots went through historic phases. In the seventies, excessive knotting was popular. Now, macramé usually was a simplified, streamlined craft—of course depending on the artist. Some of the knots could be quite intricate. She wondered if that was always the case.

It was certainly going through a phase of popularity again—but a woman like Zooey must have been doing it since she was a child. Wait. Cora wondered if she knew Rue as well. She must—it was such a small community. So that was one thing both Marcy and Zooey had in common besides being cousins: knowing Rue.

Could Rue possibly have something to do with the killing of these two young women?

A chill moved up Cora's spine. Shame crept along with the fear. Of course Rue would not kill anybody. What a horrible, awful thought that was! But Cora was often surprised about who actually did commit murder. It could be any of them: Rue, Mathilde, Hank. She couldn't say which. But Adrian was innocent. She felt it deep down in her bones.

After she wrote her blog post, she wandered into Jane's room, surprised to hear London's voice. Then as she opened the door, Jane motioned for her to come in.

"How much longer will you be?" London asked Jane over the computer.

"One more day," Jane said. "What's wrong? Don't you like staying with Luna and Ms. Zora?"

"I do. We're having fun. We're going to make a cake today," London said. "There are no more bad things at the beach, are there?"

"No, it's fine," Jane said. "I miss you."

She was an artist and worked at home, and London was always there. She'd hired sitters to help from time to time, but usually, the sitters and London were always close by. Now London was in school, and she loved it, but once in a while, the child expressed how much she missed Jane. Were they too close? Did Jane hover too much? She didn't know. All she realized is she wanted her daughter near.

"I miss you, too. I'll be fine, Mama. I'll save you and Cora some cake."

London blew a kiss to Jane and went off with Zora, waving, before the screen went blank.

Gone from view now, Jane sighed. One of these days, her daughter would leave her. That was the way of things. But it seemed a long way off. She'd enjoy every moment of her until then.

Not that there weren't times she could use a break from her.

"Are you ready for breakfast?" Jane turned and asked Cora.

"No, I need to get my shower. Just thought I'd pop over and see if you finally connected with London," Cora replied.

Jane was freshly showered, dressed, and ready to go. "We'll see you later then."

"Yes," Cora said, and exited the room, while Jane closed her laptop, then reached for her bag.

Jane took an almost empty elevator downstairs and walked toward the bistro. She needed coffee and a croissant. That was all she had time for. She walked into the bistro at the same time Hank did.

"Well, hello, Jane," he said, sweeping his eyes up and down her person. "Lovely outfit."

"Thanks," Jane said, thinking she wasn't wearing anything special, a pair of jeans with a peasant shirt. She was planning on doing a lot of pottery today and needed the freedom of movement. What was he up to?

"Care to join me?" he asked.

"Um, well, I don't have much time," she said.

"Just a quick cup of coffee?" he asked.

She'd like to sit with him and pump him for more information—if she could. But he left yesterday with a warning to them. Was he trustworthy? A twinge of hesitation and fear lurked in her. But as she glanced around, she saw that there were plenty of other people nearby. He couldn't do any harm while they were in such a public space.

"Well, okay," she said, following him to the table.

A server came behind them. "I want a cup of coffee and a croissant," she said.

"That sounds delicious," he said. "I'll have that, too. Make that two croissants." He paused. "I'm a big boy."

It was an odd thing for a grown man to say. Even odder that he was still here, Jane mused. If she had been fired, she'd hightail it out of there. Why was he still here?

"I've got some business to wrap up today," he said. "Otherwise, I'd be nowhere around. Can I tell you something?"

Jane nodded as the server came by and filled her cup with steaming black coffee. Oh God. She sucked in the scent of it. She needed that coffee.

"Certainly," she said, pouring cream into the coffee, stirring it.

He sat back as the server poured his coffee, waited until she left. "I've never felt better. I mean, I feel so unburdened. I didn't realize how much . . . everything had been weighing on me." He let out a singsong sigh. "I mean, it's been a huge relief in my life."

He smiled. He was pretty, as Ruby had said. Jane was like Ruby in that she was not a fan of "pretty" men. His teeth were straight and white. He barely had a line on his well-shaven face. His brown eyes were clear and bright, framed in long eyelashes. Very pretty.

"Was it that bad?" Jane said, and sipped her coffee. Dark and rich, the roasted flavors played in her mouth.

"I didn't realize how bad it was," he said. "But last night I was talking to Tom. You know Tom? He was Zooey's assistant. He couldn't believe some of the things Mathilde made me do. The way she treated me. Zooey treated Tom like gold."

"Really?" Jane said. "That's so hard to believe. Mathilde has always been so kind to us and she has a great reputation."

"Of course she does," he said. "I saw to it. But now she's on her own and it's going to be interesting to see what happens."

"Won't she hire someone else?" Jane said, as the coffee kicked in.

He sighed a long and frustrated exhale. "She'll have to, I suppose."

The server brought their croissants, their smell filling Jane's nose. The divine scent of the freshly baked pastry set her mouth watering.

"They have the best croissants," he said. "They make them right here."

The server smiled. "We do."

"I have breakfast here a lot. My apartment is here at the resort. That's something else that's going to change. I've no idea where I'll go, but it will be off this island, far away from Mathilde and her shenanigans," he said.

"Well, you have the world at your feet," Jane said. "You've got experience. I'm sure something great will happen for you."

"I feel like turning over all our partnerships to Mathilde," he said. "You know, sign them away. I just want out of it all."

"That would be foolish," Jane said. "You've put a lot into it, I'm sure." It was almost like Mathilde and Hank were going through a divorce.

"Yes, I'm sure it would be foolish," he said.

Jane downed another drink of coffee, and bit into the most heavenly pastry she'd ever eaten. "Oh my God, you weren't kidding. This is delicious." She took another bite, allowing the flakey, airy, and buttery treat to mingle in her mouth before taking another drink of coffee. She glanced up at the clock. "Dang, I need to leave in a few minutes."

"Oh, I'm sorry to hear that," he said. "But before you go, I kind of wanted to apologize for yesterday. I'm a bit embarrassed about the condition of the Drunken Mermaid. We never meant for it to harbor the island's problems. I've been trying to spend a lot more time there to keep an eye on things. But it's so entrenched. The drugs," he said, and paused. "But it won't be my problem much longer. I'll happily let Mathilde buy me out of that one."

"What does Mathilde plan to do with it?" Jane said.

"Between you and me, I think she plans to let it ride. She couldn't care less if it's the place to go for drugs. Just as long as it's making her money," he said.

"Surely not, Hank," Jane said.

He nodded his head as he shoved two bites of croissant in his mouth. "Hmm-mmm," he said. "If you don't believe me, ask around. She's all about the money."

Jane downed the remainder of her coffee and took the last two bites of her croissant. Something told her that every word Hank said was true.

# Chapter 43

Had breakfast with Hank. He had some interesting things to say. Do you think Mathilde is "all about the money"? Jane asked in a text message when Cora was on her way to her class.

She considered it. She would not have thought that before this retreat. But, as she thought over the fights she heard between Mathilde and Hank, Cora thought it was probably true that she was money hungry. But the question was: why? She was successful and had plenty of money, didn't she? Why did she need to be so grubby?

Probably true, Cora texted back.

She walked into her full classroom. The crafters were ready for her to divulge her many secrets about craft blogging. She almost laughed at the thought of secrets. Blogging was plenty of hard work. She owed much of her success to luck.

She had no formula for successful blogging. She had no idea why her blog took off the way it had—except that it filled a niche at a time when the niche needed filling. Of course her blog was unique—but there were many others out there.

"Have the police found the killer yet?" Katy asked.

"What?" Cora took a moment to switch from blogger brain to the murders.

"The killer?" Katy said.

"Oh, I don't know. I'd have no way of knowing about that," she said.

"I hope they find the killer soon," Katy said with a quiver in her voice. "Linda is not coming out of her room."

"What?" Cora said. "I thought she was a nurse and had seen so much in her life she would be okay."

Katy shook her head. "None of us are okay." The other crafters were all settling into the classroom. "But she is too afraid to leave her room. She keeps saying something was off about the knots on the bag. Something that freaked her out. But she hasn't been able to figure it out."

"The knots?" Cora said.

Katy frowned. "I wanted to stay with her, but she insisted we all come to class this morning."

"I see," Cora said. "Well, take notes for her." Dread came over her—poor Linda, afraid to leave her room. She wondered how many others had been affected by the murder of Zooey right in the same resort where their craft retreat was being held. Cora glanced around the room. Most of her students had come back this morning. Of course, that didn't mean that they weren't frightened. Hell, she was frightened herself. Something strange was going on here: all the people involved were natives. That was pretty strange, considering the island's small population. And Zooey kept that bit a secret—Cora had read about her and hadn't come across anything that said she was from this island, let alone that she had another name. Had something gone on years ago that someone was seeking revenge for? Or did the murders have something to do with the newly proposed development that had recently been stopped? Or were they acts of passion?

As she readied her laptop, she thought about what she knew about murder—too much, she feared. Most murders in the US circled back to drugs. That thought led her straight back to the Drunken Mermaid.

The other leading cause of murder? Love. Unrequited. Or twisted. Love gone wrong.

Was Zooey involved with someone? Cora hadn't thought of asking that question before.

Marcy, of course, had just been married. It didn't seem likely she was involved with someone else. It didn't seem likely her spouse would off her on their wedding night. But stranger things have happened.

The person who killed Marcy understood the severity of her allergy to jellyfish stings.

The person who killed Zooey, brutally strangling her and stuffing her into a macramé bag, seemed to be making a statement about . . . what? Macramé? Zooey? Or was it the retreat?

Did someone have it in for Mathilde and her successful retreat? What better way to insure nobody would want to come to the retreat than to murder one of its famous headliners?

*Get a grip, Cora*, she thought to herself. *Your imagination is in overdrive.* But as she took in her students and gauged the mood, it was somber. She saw fear in many eyes. How many of them were fighting the impulse to go home? How many of them were putting on a brave face?

"Good morning," Cora said, trying to sound bright and cheery. "I realize many of you must not want to be here now."

A hush fell over the room.

"But I'm glad you're still here," she said. "Rest assured, we are safer than ever now. You've noted all the officers posted everywhere. And I can assure you the local police are doing everything they can to find the person who committed this hideous crime."

All eyes were on her.

"I think the best we can do now is move forward. Does anybody have any questions about the class, blogging, before I go on?" she asked.

One woman raised her hand.

"Yes?"

"I wonder if you can talk a little bit about the difference between the different platforms. I'm still trying to make up my mind between Blogger and WordPress."

Cora breathed a deep sigh of psychic relief. A question that she could answer.

After class, while Cora was gathering up her things, she remembered the conversation with Katy about the knots on the macramé bag that held Zooey's body. What could freak someone out about knots? What was so odd about them? She saw Katy slip out of the room. Cora quickly gathered her things to follow her. She wanted to talk with Linda.

"Katy!" she said, scrambling out the door.

"Yes?" Katy turned around.

"I was wondering if it would be okay for me to go and see Linda?"

Katy softened and blinked. "I guess she wouldn't mind you visiting. Let me text her."

They stood in the hall and waited for the answer, which came quickly.

I'd love to see Cora. Are you kidding? Send her right up.

"There you have it. She's in room 319," Katy said. "A word of warning . . . She is messed up over this." Her face spoke volumes about her worry about her friend.

"Okay, I'll be gentle with her," Cora said. "Don't worry. I used to be a counselor. Maybe I can help."

After all, helping was Cora's thing. She had the disease to please. And that wasn't always a bad instinct.

# Chapter 44

Cora followed Linda on to her balcony, where she was eating a large breakfast.

"Please have a seat," Linda said.

She moved plates of food around on the table and finally found the biscuit she wanted and spread butter on it. "I can't eat enough food," she said.

"I understand," Cora said. "I've seen that a lot among women, especially. Sometimes food is comfort."

"What do you mean you've seen it a lot?" she asked.

"I used to be a counselor in a women's shelter," Cora said.

"Is that why you're here? Did my friends send you to counsel me?"

"No, not per se," Cora said. "Is that a Bloody Mary?"

Linda nodded. "It sure is. There's a whole pitcher. I don't usually imbibe so early in the day. I need to get a grip. I realize I'm missing out on the retreat. But . . ."

"You're a nurse?" Cora said.

She nodded. "I've seen some stuff, but never someone who's been murdered." Her voice cracked.

"I know what you mean," Cora said, remembering the time she literally stumbled on a murder victim in Indigo Gap. She had passed out. And it took months for her to stop dreaming about it, remembering the image.

"Do you?"

"Yes, it's happened to me," Cora said. She paused. "Come to think of it, I will have a Bloody Mary."

"Oh, great," Linda said, and she rose from the table to fetch a glass. She poured the red, thick liquid into a large glass.

Cora took a drink. "Wow, that is one delicious Bloody Mary," she said. It had been a few years since she drank one. She was mostly a wine girl.

"I know, right?" Linda's eyes were covered by her sunglasses, but Cora still saw the lines of worry on the edges.

"It's going to take time, you know," Cora said. "I had bad dreams for weeks."

Linda merely grunted.

"And then something would happen and it would remind me of . . . the shape of his foot. And I'd freak out," she said.

"Yes, exactly." She paused and took a long drink. "You do understand, don't you?"

"Some people get over it quicker than others, or they think they do. Your friends are pushing through, but in the months to come, it might sneak up on them," Cora said.

"I was thinking that, too. Although I don't think any of them got the close-up view of her that I did. It was the bag, you see," Linda said. "The bag was beautiful. Now, I don't even think I can look at macramé."

"What was it about the bag that disturbs you? Katy told me," Cora said.

Linda sipped from her Bloody Mary. "I can't quite figure it out. It was off—that's all I can say about it. It wasn't quite right. I keep thinking about it. Thinking about those knots. What was it that was wrong with them?"

"If you can remember, let me know," Cora said.

"Why? Why are you so concerned?"

"Well, first, I'm concerned about you working through that image. Once you figure it out, you'll start to feel better. And secondly, my boyfriend is a suspect for the murder of Marcy Grimm. He has an alibi for Zooey's murder. But his lawyer and all the rest of us think that two murders in three days . . . Well, they have to be linked."

"You're hoping if you find Zooey's killer, he'll also be Marcy's killer and your boyfriend will be off the hook," Linda said.

Cora nodded.

"How very Jessica Fletcher of you," Linda said.

"Excuse me? Jessica Fletcher?" Cora said.

"You know. *Murder, She Wrote*," Linda said.

"Oh yes, I've heard of it," Cora said.

A breeze came across the balcony. The tablecloth fluttered. Cora grabbed her napkin before it was carried off by the wind.

"I wonder if it's going to rain," Linda said. "The sky's a little dark over that way, see?"

"I don't think they are calling for rain," Cora said. "But you never know."

"How did the class go this morning?" Linda said.

"Oh, here—I brought you the handouts," Cora said, and reached into her bag.

"Oh, thanks. That was so kind of you," Linda said.

"Your friends will bring you up to date, too. What an awesome group of women," Cora said with a smile.

"Oh yes. We've been scrapbooking together for over twenty years," Linda said. "They are like my sisters."

Cora beamed. She loved stories about women crafting together and forming deep friendships. "I'd like to feature your group on my blog. I think it would make a great story."

"How fabulous," Linda said, clapping her hands together. A smile spread across her face. It was the first time she'd smiled since Cora had been there.

"But in the meantime, you're aware how much your friends care about you. Don't shut them out," Cora said, with a soothing note in her voice.

"Oh, I won't," Linda said. "I need to work through this alone for some reason."

"May I make a suggestion?" Cora said.

"Sure."

"Do you knit? Crochet?"

"Well, I do now," Linda said.

"Sit with your yarn and needles. Make something. I've seen it help time and time again," Cora said.

Linda's head tilted toward her and her brows knit. "You know, you may be on to something there."

Cora finished her Bloody Mary. "I've got to go. But here's my card. If you can remember anything that might help us find the killer, let me know. Text me. Call me. Whatever."

"Sure thing," Linda said, taking Cora's card. "I'll stay in touch."

# Chapter 45

Cora and Jane had agreed to meet for Ruby's class on making beach sand candles. Even though Cora was not in the mood to sit in another class, she realized she had not attended any of Jane's classes and only one of Ruby's, and felt it was her obligation. But her mind was on Linda in her room mulling over the knots on that macramé bag, as well as on Adrian, who didn't even appear to be up and out of bed yet at 11 A.M.

He always texted her when he arose. She wondered where Cashel was—poor guy had been drugged and was trying to find justice in this crazy situation.

Jane glanced at her. "This class should be fun. Making candles out of sand? Interesting."

Cora nodded. It was an interesting idea, but she was feeling pulled elsewhere.

Mathilde slipped in at the last moment before class officially opened and sat next to Cora. She smiled and nodded a hello.

"Well, I'm glad to see so many of you here," Ruby said. "This project is a lot of fun. If you like the appearance of sandy, gritty texture, you're going to love these candles."

She held up a tray with three cranberry-colored candles that appeared as if they were dipped in sand. Cora imagined the candles would suit a beach house or a home that had a beach theme. But she certainly didn't want sandy candles in her home. First, would the sand start to peel away? It would end up being like the glitter she loved years ago and stopped using because it was so hard to control. It truth, she would still sometimes find glitter in her socks or towels. It was a mystery.

"The sand sticks well to the candles because it clings to wax and is sort of melted on it through the heating process," Ruby said. "I used to make these candles right on the beach with my son Cashel. These candles make a fun family project. But we're making them inside today. And you'll see you each have small tubs of damp sand. It's up to you what shape you want to make into the sand. This will be your candle mold. Just don't make it too delicate."

At the mention of Cashel's name, Cora thought to text him, to see how he was. How horrible to be drugged like that.

How are you? she texted.

Chattering sounds filled the room as the women played in the sand.

"It's been a few years since I played in the sand," Cora heard someone say.

"I used to love making sand castles," another voice said.

Fine, Cashel responded. Was that it? Cora bit her lip. Men!

Cora stuck her hands in the sand. A memory

tickled her mind. A beach memory. Had she ever vacationed on the beach as a child? She didn't think so. She hadn't seen the ocean until she was twenty-one years old. But there was sand, the feeling of sand, deep in her memory.

"Remember Sandy Beach?" Jane said.

Just outside the city of Pittsburgh, there was a small river and a developer had brought sand in to fabricate an ocean scene.

"Yes," Cora said. "I remember it."

"I love the beach," Mathilde chimed in, and she sunk her hands into the bucket. "I can't imagine living anywhere without a beach."

"Did you grow up here?" Jane asked.

Mathilde nodded. "Yes, we moved here when I was about ten. My daddy was a fisherman. We lived over near the area they call the swamp hoods these days. But not quite in the neighborhood. The place still stands over there."

Cora watched Mathilde turning the tub around and leading with her left hand, which was awkward for her.

"Are you a lefty?" Cora asked.

"No," Mathilde replied. "Well, I'm sort of both. I was born a lefty, but my parents forced me to be right-handed."

"That's awful," Jane said. "My daughter is a lefty. I'd never do that to her."

"Well, back then they thought it would be easier for me," Mathilde said. "But not all parents were like that. Hank is left-handed. He's only a few years younger than me. His parents—and teachers—were fine with it."

"The wax is almost melted." Ruby's voice rang over

the chatter. "It's plain white, but I have some dyes here if you want to color yours."

"I want sky-blue," Jane said. "For some reason, I think it should be blue."

"Also I have some objects here, seashells, tiny pieces of driftwood, and so on," Ruby said. "If you want to embed them into your sand, theoretically, they should come out as part of your candle," Ruby said. "It works most of the time."

Several crafters laughed over that.

Katy walked over to Cora and Jane. "Hey, ladies," she said. "Did you go and see Linda?"

"Yes, I did," Cora said. "I think she's going to be fine."

"What's wrong with her?" Mathilde said.

"She's the person who discovered Zooey," Cora said, with a lowered voice. "She's having a bit of a rough time."

"No doubt," Mathilde said. "I'm sure anybody would. Poor thing. Well, if she's not going to make it to the rest of the retreat, we'll refund part of her registration."

"I'm sure she'd appreciate it," Katy said. "I'm worried that she'll never heal from this."

"I think she will," Cora said. "It's going to take some time. You don't forget something like that easily. You just don't."

"You sound like an expert," Mathilde said.

Cora started to respond but Jane interrupted.

"She used to be a counselor. She's seen everything. Believe me," Jane said.

"Oh, that's right. I remember that being part of your story. You used crafts as part of your practice, launched your blog and, voilà, here you are," Mathilde said, wiping her hands on a paper towel.

Cora wanted to say that helping others was one thing, but trying to forget stumbling on a murder victim yourself was quite another thing. But Jane clearly did not want Cora to mention it to Mathilde. Maybe she was right. Jane did have a better "PR" sense than Cora. It was better not to mention the murders in Indigo Gap—nor that Cora was involved with them in any way. Jane had her back. Cora warmed.

She waited until the lines trickled down, then she wandered over to the stoves where the melted wax was on the burners. What a great classroom, complete with stoves and so on. And Jane's room offered its own kiln. This part of the resort was built for crafting.

But Cora preferred her own retreat house. Victorian and homey. And soon they'd have a new kitchen—just as soon as she could figure out how to pay for it.

Her heart sank. She couldn't believe how homesick she was.

She poured wax into her cup, dropped some pink dye into it, and took it over to her sand mold. She poured the wax in. A pink, sandy candle. Thoughts of a lit pink candle on a gorgeous laid-out table, Adrian sitting on the other side, holding her hand, played in her mind.

A ping went off, alerting her to a text message.

I can't find Adrian. Is he with you? Cashel wrote.

Her heart nearly jumped from her chest.

No, she texted back, her hands slightly trembling. I'll check out the restaurant.

That's where I am, he wrote. I've looked everywhere.

Cora dropped her phone, gathered her things, and took off for the restaurant.

"Cora!" Jane said, following.

"What's going on?" Mathilde said, following Jane.

"It's Adrian," Cora managed to say, while moving for the restaurant. "He's missing."

# Chapter 46

Several minutes later, Cora and Jane found Cashel in the crowded resort restaurant.

"Missing?" Jane said.

"I'm not saying he's missing. I'm saying I can't find him," Cashel clarified.

Cora's chest felt as if one thousand elephants were pressing on it.

Jane's arm went around her. "Do you have your medicine?"

Cora nodded, as Jane led her to a chair.

"Can I get you something?" A server came up to them.

"Water," Jane said.

Cora closed her eyes, tried to breathe, but the pressing sensation in her chest was too much.

Cashel, across the table from her, shot Jane a quizzical glance.

"She's having a panic attack," Jane said. "She'll be fine. Just give us a moment."

Fine? Who was going to be fine? Thoughts rushed through Cora's mind. She downed a whole pill. Adrian missing. Zooey/Susan dead. Poor Marcy, also dead. Newly married. Dead. And an ex-girlfriend of Adrian's. Mathilde and Hank and all their fighting. Cashel drugged. What the heck was going on here?

"He can't be missing," Jane said in a soothing voice. "Let's think about this. He has one of those bands on, right? If we can't find him, we call the police and they will tell us where he is. They can track him."

Cora's chest lightened. She opened her eyes and looked at Jane's soulful eyes, nodding. "You're right."

These damn panic attacks. They were not nearly as bad as when she lived in Pittsburgh. Then, it was almost every day. It had gotten so bad it damaged her heart. It left her with a weakness. Cora felt this attack slipping off. This one was quickly dealt with. Once she had had an attack that lasted two hours.

"I hate to call the cops," Cashel said. "But we might have to."

"Why don't you want to call them?" Jane asked.

"I don't want them to think he's tried to escape," Cashel said. "I don't think he'd do that. And yet . . . I can't find him."

"Looks to me like he's gone," Mathilde said. She'd been standing there quietly, looking about as uncomfortable as a penguin in the jungle.

"How long should we wait?" Jane said. "I think it's more likely that he's in trouble than he escaped, given what happened to you."

"What happened to you?" Mathilde said.

"I was drugged yesterday," Cashel said. "After I had been doing some research into Adrian's case."

"Surely not," Mathilde said, and paled.

"Yep," Cashel said. "I've deduced that someone

at the Drunken Mermaid slipped me a Mickey, as they say."

"Mathilde, I realize you have a reputation to protect and a craft retreat to run, but if you know anything about who could have harmed Cashel or who might have Adrian, now is the time," Jane said.

"Me? Why would I know anything? Believe me, the retreat has been a nightmare, yes, but it's kept me incredibly busy. I don't know anything," Mathilde said.

"I saw that you are on the board of Adair," Cashel said.

"Yes, that's true," she said. "But what does that have to do with anything? I'm for the new resort. It will bring hundreds of jobs to this island. I've made no bones about where I stand."

She stood tall, shoulders slightly back, but her chin quivered. Her pink lipstick was fading. Beads of sweat formed on her forehead.

"I'd appreciate it if you sat down and told us what's going on," Cashel said. "We've got several lives hanging in the balance. Two women are dead. We need to find some justice here."

She heaved a deep sigh and sat down. "What do you want to learn? Besides the tension on the island about the resort, I don't know of anything I can add."

"And it's been decided it won't go forward, correct?" Cashel said, his piercing blue eyes lit up.

"That's not been made public yet," Mathilde said.

"Why not?" Jane asked.

"I asked that they wait until after the retreat to make the announcement. I didn't want anything to take away from the retreat," she said, and guffawed. "I wasn't expecting not just one but two murders."

Cora chilled. What would she do if this happened at one of her retreats? She felt for Mathilde. Even though she didn't understand a lot of her attitude about things, she understood how the woman was trying to protect the successful retreat she had built from the ground up.

"This retreat is my whole life," Mathilde said. "I've been accused of being a money-hungry monster on more than one occasion. But this retreat makes the island thousands in revenue. I love the island. I love the retreat. And money is central to its success. As is crafting. I see women leave here feeling empowered through crafting. Rested. More energized. It's a win-win situation for everybody."

On Cora's imaginary checklist of suspects, she crossed Mathilde off. She was trying to make tough decisions. Cora could relate. Though she was not as brash as Mathilde and preferred to manage in a different way, Cora realized they ultimately wanted the same thing.

"Who would have tried to drug Cashel, if not you, for finding out about this?" Jane leveled.

"Oh, my dear," Mathilde said, flashing her eyes. "I could come up with a list of about a million people. But the question is, who knew what Cashel was doing that day? Who knew he was at the courthouse and library and knew what he was researching?"

"That narrows it down from a million, I'm sure," Cashel said wryly.

"Let's give that some thought," Mathilde said.

"In the meantime, where is Adrian? Can we please give that some thought, as well?" Cora said.

# Chapter 47

They spread out to search for Adrian. If they didn't find him soon, they'd have to call the police. The good news was if he had gone far, the alarms would have gone off and the cops would also be searching for him. Which meant he was here, somewhere on the resort—maybe on the beach.

Jane said she'd searched the restaurants and cafés. Mathilde decided to search the beach, Cashel the gym and spa, and Cora was going into the classrooms. The plan was to meet in twenty minutes and regroup.

Jane entered the first café, which was nearly empty. It was easy enough to see that Adrian was not there. The place had taken on a menacing quality. Was it the lighting? Her mood? She suddenly hated it there and wanted to escape from this restaurant, this resort, and island.

"Excuse me," she said to the cashier. "I'm searching for a friend of mine. Was he here?"

She showed him a photo of Adrian on her phone.

"I saw him in here yesterday, I think. Was it yesterday? Hmmm. Either yesterday or the day before.

Definitely not today," she said. "I'd remember him. Those eyes! And he's such a great tipper."

That didn't surprise Jane. Adrian was a class act. Which was one reason she got Cora and him together and was thrilled they'd gotten along so well.

Jane smiled. "Well, thanks." Off to the next restaurant, which was jam-packed with people getting up and eating the brunch buffet. The scent of eggs, bacon, biscuits, and coffee wafted as Jane searched for Adrian. Nothing.

"Can I help you?" A server came toward her.

"I'm looking for this guy," Jane said.

"Hmmm. I don't think I've seen him. It's been crazy this morning, though. He could've been here," she said. "Do you want to take a seat and eat?"

"No," Jane said. "I ate breakfast hours ago. But thanks."

She walked out of the restaurant into the hallway and turned the corner toward the mermaid fountain. One more restaurant to visit, since the others weren't open until later.

But as she got closer to the fountain, Cora and Cashel came into view. And they were speaking to a police officer. Uh-oh, what was going on? Cora's face was pale and her blue eyes were as wide as saucers.

"Jane," she said, reaching for her. Jane's arm went around Cora.

"What's going on?"

"We've been searching for Adrian," the officer told her. "The signal on his bracelet weakened, which alerted us." He held up a mangled bracelet. "This is what's left of the bracelet."

Jane stood, dumbfounded. "So, someone has him? Someone destroyed his bracelet?"

"That's what I think," Cora said.

"That's what I know," Cashel said. Cool, calm, collected. Cashel the attorney was taking over. "My client would not have removed that. He's a law-abiding citizen—a librarian, for God's sake. He's innocent of all the charges. I suggest you drop them and you find him immediately."

"You realize it doesn't work like that?" the officer said. "But I assure you we're doing everything we can to find him."

Adrian was missing. He was in trouble. He never would have escaped. He was an upstanding guy. Waves of panic surged through Jane. Cora was calm—she had just taken a pill. But Jane's knees wobbled. Whoa, that had never happened to her before. Where was she standing? The floor rippled.

"Jane?" Cora said, trying to hold her up.

"Furthermore," Cashel continued, "I'd like to know what is going on on this island. I was drugged the other day, Cora and Adrian were attacked at the Drunken Mermaid, and so on. It seems like we've stepped into a quagmire. Unless you'd like a few lawsuits and the publicity that goes with it, I suggest you and your cohorts tell us what's going on here."

Jane blinked. Cora was still trying to keep her awake. But her legs felt like mush and she wanted to close her eyes.

"Jane!" Cora said, and smacked her face—not hard, but hard enough.

"Hey!" Jane squealed.

"What's going on?" Mathilde said as she entered their circle. Cora explained what had happened.

"I think Jane needs to sit down and might need some water," Cora said, leading Jane to a chair.

"I'll get some water," Mathilde said.

Jane watched as she asked a man behind the counter for water. He reached underneath and handed her a cold bottle of water. At that moment, Jane wanted nothing more than that water. She wanted to yell out to Mathilde to hurry, hurry, please!

Cora sat next to Jane on the love seat and said, "Take some deep breaths for me. I've never seen you pass out, girl."

"I didn't pass out," Jane said. "I feel woozy."

"You almost passed out," Cora said.

"I did?" Jane said.

"It's a bit much, isn't it?" Cora said. "Everything that's happened, and now Adrian is missing." Her voice cracked.

"Hey, I'm supposed to be the strong one," Jane said. "I can't be passing out."

Cora grinned. "Sometimes we don't get a choice."

Mathilde was there and handed Jane the bottle of water.

"Thank God," Jane said. "I need this water. Maybe I'm dehydrated." She opened the bottle and swigged.

"You've had quite a shock, dear," Mathilde said.

"We all have," Cora said. "How are you?"

Mathilde flung her arms around. "I give up," she said. "I give up even trying to salvage this retreat. I think moving through it as best we can is the thing to do."

Cora nodded. "It might not be as bad as you think. I mean from the guests' perspective. We had an incident during our last retreat and the guests viewed it all in a different way than we did."

Cashel and the police officer were joined by two plainclothes men, as Jane drank her water. Passing out was not in the program. No, indeed. She must find Adrian. That's all there was to it. Poor guy. Came to this craft retreat to spend more time with Cora. How many men would attend a craft retreat to be close to their girlfriend?

"Well, I guess I can see that," Mathilde said. "Oh God, I hope you're right."

Where could Adrian be?

Cora swallowed. She closed her eyes. *Please, Adrian, be okay.* She whispered a prayer to the universe and a thought poked at her.

"Let's go see Rue. Just in case she can help us," she said.

"Rue?" Jane said. "That psychic?"

"Yes, the woman who makes the spirit chimes."

"I thought you didn't believe in psychics," Jane said.

Mathilde sighed loudly. "She's been right too many times, I'm afraid. I'm suspicious of her."

"I believe in psychics," Cora said. "Or rather, I believe some people have a kind of a gift. But I also think there are those who want attention and money."

"What about Rue?" Jane asked. "Which kind is she?"

Cora thought a moment. "I don't know, but she has an impeccable record with helping the police. And she's a gifted crafter."

"I'd agree to that," Mathilde said. "Oddly enough, she'll have nothing to do with the retreat."

"She thinks you charge too much money," Cora said.

"Another reason to like her," Jane said, and grinned.

Mathilde's face fell. "Do I? Do I charge too much money?"

"How would I know?" Cora said. "You're paying me well. Better than any other retreat, and that's a plus."

"Yeah, I've found in order to attract the best teachers you've got to pay them well," she said.

"Ladies," Cashel said, walking up to them, "I hate to break up this little circle, but the police have asked that we go into a conference room, where we can chat a little more." The two detectives were on his heels.

"I'd rather go and see Rue," Jane said.

"Rue?" one of the detectives said.

Jane nodded. "Maybe she can help us find Adrian. We're not getting anywhere. We've searched high and low."

"Please," Cashel said. "Let's do what the officers are asking."

"Actually we recognize Rue. It's not a bad idea to visit her," the sandy-haired detective at the computer said, standing. "I'll go with you."

"Okay, Mr. O'Malley, you come with me, and you"—the other detecive said and pointed toward Mathilde—"let's go into the conference room."

"I'm Detective Andrews," he said, and reached his hand out to Cora. She took it. His hands were large and strong and now that she saw him closer his hair was more gray than sandy.

She'd seen him before. He was the man who talked with Mathilde about the first murder when they were having breakfast.

"Cora," she said.

"Jane," Jane said as she shook his hand.

"Well, shall we go? I don't place a lot of stock in

psychics, but you never know," he said. "She's got a pretty accurate record of working with the police. It won't hurt to stop in and check with her, while the crews are out searching for Mr. Brisbane."

"You have crews out?" Cora's heart skipped a few beats. This meant they considered him a missing person.

"Sure," Detective Andrews said. "At this point, he's an escapee."

"Escapee?" Jane said. "He'd never do that."

He opened his car door to Jane. "So you say," he said, and tilted his head as a motion for her to enter the car.

"I don't think I like you," Jane said, sliding into the car.

"I'm not here to be your friend," he replied, and shut the car door.

He opened the other door for Cora, smiling at her. "Madam," he said, with a sarcastic note.

Cora laughed and slid into the car.

No matter how she tried to sit still during the car ride, Cora found herself twisting her hair, then her skirt, and wriggling around in the seat until Jane placed her hand on her leg. "Chill," she mouthed.


When they entered Rue's house, something appeared to be off. Whereas the energy had been all fuzzy and warm when Cora was here the day before, it felt entirely different now.

There was someone else here.

It was Rue's son—the grieving widower. He sat in a

chair in the living room, brooding, staring off, as the others entered the room.

"I'm sorry," Rue said. "This is my son. He lost his wife."

"I'm sorry for your loss," Cora said.

His eyes met hers. They were nearly vacant. He blinked. "Thanks," he said.

Did he recognize her? Realize that she was the one who'd defended herself and Adrian from him at the Drunken Mermaid? It didn't appear so.

"Unfortunately we're here today on police business, again," Detective Andrews said.

"Oh dear," Rue said. "What can I help you with?"

Rue was distracted by her son—as any mother would be. He was obviously bereft. But Cora suspected it was more than that. He was disturbed. He'd probably been imbalanced before his new wife was killed.

"Adrian Brisbane is missing," the detective said.

"The suspect?" Rue asked.

"Yes," he replied. "The very man."

"I don't think the man had anything to do with anybody's murder, but don't you have him under surveillance?" Rue said with an accusing tone.

"Yes, ma'am, we did," he replied. "But his bracelet has been removed."

Her hand clutched at her chest. Her eyes searched around the room, as if she didn't know where to begin.

"We wondered if you've seen him," Jane said.

"Or maybe if you can tell us . . . something. You know, with your psychic abilities," Cora said.

Rue guffawed. "Yes, my blessing and my curse, believe me."

Interesting. A blessing and a curse. Could she be the real thing? Could Cora allow herself a sliver of hope? Could Rue tell them where Adrian was?

"Do you need something personal of his? To get his vibes? Or something?" Cora asked.

"No. I don't work like that," Rue said.

"Mother, you aren't going to help Marcy's killer, are you?" Josh said.

"He's not a killer," Cora said. "Whatever Adrian Brisbane is, he's not someone who could have killed Marcy. He loved her at one point. She broke his heart. But he did not kill her."

"The text message. The needles," Josh said. He was grasping, trying to make sense.

His mother interrupted. "I don't think he killed Marcy either, but someone did. The police still have him listed as a suspect, so it's in our best interest to find him." She turned toward her son. "Please drink some more water. You need it."

He smiled a twitchy smile and lifted the glass to his lips.

Rue sat quietly, closed her eyes. "I'm trying to feel him, feel something about Adrian Brisbane."

They all sat quietly. And Cora's phone beeped.

Embarrassed, she reached for it quickly, noting that Rue's meditative stance had not changed. It was a text message from Linda:

I realize what was odd about that bag. It was almost completely backward, as if it were crafted by someone who was, I don't know, either joking, disturbed, or maybe, left-handed.

Left-handed? Cora sifted through the several people she'd met this weekend who were left-handed. Mathilde was ambidextrous. Hank was left-handed. Mathilde didn't kill anybody—that was for sure. Hank? Could Hank have been the person who made the bag, killed Zooey, and stuffed her inside? What possible motive could he have?

He had been fired. But that was after this incident.

Had he wanted to destroy Mathilde and the retreat all along? Even before their argument?

This was her best working theory. And if Hank was the killer, he might have Adrian. He would have approached him, and Adrian, in his innocence, would have thought nothing of it. Cora's heart raced and a bead of sweat formed on her forehead.

It must be Hank. Hank must have killed both Marcy and Zooey and tried to frame Adrian. He must have Adrian.

"I'm sorry. I can't get a handle on it," Rue said. "I think I'm distracted. Sorry."

"Me too," Cora said, standing. "Well, it's time to go."

"Wait, there is one thing you should know," Rue said, following Cora's lead and standing.

"What's that?"

"Adrian must still be alive," she said. "If he was dead, I'm sure I'd be aware."

"Good to know," Jane said wryly.

"And you are sure you haven't seen him?" Detective Andrews asked, as he stood.

"No" she said. "I've not see him."

"Me either," said Josh, and lifted his water to his mouth. With his left hand.

# Chapter 48

Cora could not ignore the fact that Josh was left-handed. So she pieced her theory together in the backseat of the detective's car.

"Sorry that didn't work out," he said as he drove away. "I know you were hoping for answers."

"Well, if you believe that kind of stuff, she did say that he is alive. And that's a good thing," Jane said.

"Yes, I thought the same thing," Cora said. She thought about the man sitting in his mother's living room. So disturbed. Was it the loss of his new wife? Or was it, as she had first thought, that he had problems anyway? Could he have killed his wife and Zooey? Why?

What would prompt a newly married man to kill his wife? Or Zooey? Cora mulled over that possibility. Since Zooey was Susan, who had at one point worked for Marcy, and was her cousin, Josh and Zooey probably knew one another. But what would the motive for killing be?

But if Hank was the killer, Cora could see in a

twisted way why he'd want to ruin Mathilde and how Zooey's murder resulted. But what about Marcy?

Maybe the two killings had nothing to do with one another and there were two killers on the island. Cora shuddered.

"What's wrong?" Jane said. "Are you okay?"

"I'm fine," Cora said. "But Linda texted me this." She showed the text to Jane.

"Don't you think we should tell the detective?" Jane asked. "Maybe this would help to find Adrian."

The detective pulled the car into the parking lot of the resort motel and turned around to look at Jane. "Tell the detective what?"

Cora explained what she found out.

He considered what she said. "That's great detective work," he said. "But both of the guys you've mentioned have rock solid alibis for both of the murders, unfortunately."

Cora's chest felt heavy. "Are there any other lefties on the island?"

The detective laughed a little. "We don't keep a file of left-handed Sea Glass Island folks."

"I realize that," Cora said. "I didn't know if you had any other suspects that were left-handed."

"I'll check into it," he said. "It could be, of course, that the murderer didn't make the bag. That someone else made the bag. Did that occur to you?"

"No," Cora said, feeling a little foolish.

"Look, I realize you're trying to help," Detective Andrews said. "But we're doing our best to find the killer and find Adrian."

"Please contact me the moment you find Adrian," Cora said, and offered him her card.

"In the meantime, what should we do? How can we help?" Jane said.

"I think the best thing for you two is to go about your daily life," he said.

*Well, that isn't an option,* Cora mused. Her boyfriend was missing. Two women had been killed—one of whom Adrian was still suspected of killing. Going about her daily life? Not going to happen. She wasn't going to sit in craft class while poor Adrian was out there somewhere possibly hurt—or worse.

Jane and Cora exchanged glances, while the detective opened the car door for them.

They were back at the resort. Maybe there was news about Adrian. Cora's eyes scanned the lobby hopefully. A typical day ensued around them. People moving around the expansive lobby. Desk clerks. The concierges. Smartly dressed managers. Bellhops. Luggage. It all looked normal on the surface.

But in a conference room somewhere Cashel and Mathilde were with the police talking about Adrian's disappearance.

And within these fancy walls and marbled floors a dead body was found folded into a macramé bag crafted by a left-handed person. Detective Andrews could be correct. Maybe someone other than the killer made the bag.

But the killer would have at least had access to the bag. If Cora found out who made the bag, it could lead her to the killer—and possibly to Adrian. Time was of the essence.

She followed the detective into the conference-turned-situation room, Jane by her side.

"Do we have any news?" Detective Andrews asked.

"None," the other answered. "We were hoping you had some."

"None," he said, and took a seat.

"Excuse me," Cora said. "I have a working theory. You can help, Mathilde."

Mathilde seemed shocked that Cora would think she could help. "Me? Well, certainly. I'm not sure what I can add. I know as much as you do."

"I know a little more," Cora said.

"Oh?"

Cora explained what Linda told them and what she surmised about the bag.

"That's interesting," the other detective said. "It might lead us somewhere. Great work."

Cora beamed.

"So, Mathilde, do you have any ideas about the bag? Who could have made it?"

"I'd have to examine the bag. I don't think I checked it out at all. I mean, I was so horrified," she said.

"We'll have someone bring the bag here," Detective Andrews said. "Johnson?" He said to a uniformed officer.

"On it, sir," he said, and left the room.

"So let me understand this," Cashel said. "You think the person who made the bag is a lefty, based on the way it was constructed?"

Cora nodded. "Well, it's not me. It's Linda's theory. She's more acquainted. She's the person who discovered the body. She's taking it hard and has been holed up in her room. I went to talk with her and she mentioned the macramé knots—that something was disturbing about them, but she couldn't figure out what."

"And then Cora got this text while we were at Rue's," Jane said.

"We know Hank is a lefty and we know Josh is a lefty," Cora said. "But what we don't know is if the person who crafted the bag is the actual killer."

"You act as though there's only one killer," Mathilde said. "Zooey's killer could have been a different person."

"Highly unlikely," one of the detectives said.

"What about Adrian in all this?" Jane piped up. "If the killer has him, time is of the essence. What are we doing to find him?"

The group had searched everywhere on the resort.

"We have search crews out, but so far, I have to say, it looks like he left the island," Detective Andrews replied. "They're searching for him on the coast, now, as well."

Cora felt her heart drop to her feet.

"He wouldn't have left the island without Cora," Jane said, after a few moments. "At least not willingly."

The room silenced.

"I have to agree," Cashel said softly. "The man is crazy about her."

Something about Cashel's tone reached out to Cora. He understood and recognized Adrian was crazy about her—but he wasn't happy about it.

# Chapter 49

Where the hell is everybody? Ruby texted to Cora.

Cora grimaced. Did they want to involve her? Ruby was doing what she came here to do. Teach. Mingle. Retreat. Did Cora want to inform her about Adrian?

"What?" Cashel said, catching her grimace.

"Your mom. Should I tell her what's going on? I mean, she's out there, probably having a fabulous time," Cora said.

"I understand your hesitation," Cashel said. "But she will be pissed if she finds out and thinks we've kept it from her. Mark my word."

"You're right," Jane said. "I'd want to know."

"Okay," Cora said, and texted her back.

The room was buzzing with police officers, both uniformed and not. Some were on their phones, some were on their laptops.

"Look at this," one of them said to another one. Cora stood and moved to a better place, where she could view what the officer was pointing to.

"This link is tracing somewhere," he said. "Watch it."

"What's the link to?" Cora asked.

Both looked up at her.

"This is the link to Mr. O'Malley's research at the courthouse. You were right. Someone was watching him," the man said.

"But who?" Cashel said.

"It's a sophisticated hack," the officer said. "It's going to take some time for this to run."

"What the hell is going on?" a feminine voice said from behind them. It was Ruby. "Where is Adrian?"

"We don't know," Jane said. "We're trying to find him."

"Well, sitting in a room in the middle of the resort ain't finding nobody," she said.

"We've searched the premises and teams are hunting the island for him," Cashel said. "You were in class. We didn't want to disturb you."

"What's this?" she asked, pointing to the computer.

"This is the proof that someone was watching me when I was researching Adrian's case. Probably the same person who drugged me and might have Adrian," Cashel said.

"Lordy bee," Ruby said, obviously amazed at the technology.

Suddenly the screen flashed. "Okay," the man said. "I think I've got it."

"What? What is it?" Ruby said.

"It links to a computer at the courthouse. A public one. One that anybody could be using," the man said with a note of disappointment.

"But wait," Cora said. "Don't people have to sign in to use them?"

"Not anymore," he responded. "But we could pull the tapes from the security cameras. Jacobs?"

"On it, sir," he said.

"So we're trying to find a left-handed person who was using the computers Saturday afternoon?" Jane asked.

"I don't think many people use those computers," the officer said. "It's a small island and most people have their own computer these days. This will be easy."

"Let's hope we're right about it," Cashel said. "And that it leads us to the person who can tell us where Adrian is. If they drugged me, God only knows what they've done to him."

"But why?" Ruby said. "Why would people bother with you two? I don't understand. It makes no sense."

"I know, right?" Jane said.

The officers quieted.

"Well, the answer is, as ridiculous as it sounds, Adrian is a murder suspect, and Cashel his attorney. That more than connects them to this island and puts them in the public eye," Jane said.

"Yes, but we know Adrian couldn't harm a fly. And Cashel was doing his job," Ruby said, then paused. "Someone is setting up Adrian."

"No," Cora said. "I don't think so. He texted Marcy. He was an ex-boyfriend. Then she turns up dead, poisoned by someone who obviously knew about her allergy. It does look suspicious. The police have to check everybody out."

"But he didn't do it," Ruby said. "We know that. The police should realize that by now."

"He does have an alibi for the second murder," one officer said.

"Doesn't that let him off the first one?" Ruby persisted.

"Not necessarily," the officer said.

"Do you mean there could be two killers on this island?" Jane said.

The officer shrugged. "We don't know now."

"We're doing our best," another one said.

A cell phone rang. One of the detectives picked up and walked to another part of the room.

"Well, are you hungry, Cashel? I can bring you something. It's getting late," Ruby said.

"No, Mom, I'm not hungry," he said. "Thanks for offering."

The officer who left the group came back, face fallen in confusion. "I've gotten some disturbing news."

Cora reached for Jane's hand and gripped it firmly. "Adrian? Is he . . . ?"

He shook his head. "No. Nothing about Adrian."

"Then what is it, man?" Ruby said.

"The person who was using the computer at the courthouse was Zooey," he said. "Our second victim. She was there about a few hours before . . . she was killed."

The room silenced. One officer in the corner stopped keyboarding. Another one walked over to the circle.

"Well, that puts a whole new spin on things, doesn't it?" he said.

"So, what was she hiding?" Cashel said. "What didn't she want me to find out? And who was working with her?"

"What do you mean? I don't follow," Jane said.

"She was not at the Drunken Mermaid. I'm certain I would have remembered. Someone there drugged me."

"Just because you didn't see her doesn't mean she wasn't there," Cora said.

# Chapter 50

"Okay, so you all are aware Zooey was Susan, who used to work for Marcy, right?" Cora said.

"Of course we know that," Detective Andrews said.

"Maybe Marcy was not a good employer," Jane said. "Maybe this was all about a disgruntled employee."

"Well, hold on. Just because she messed with Cashel doesn't mean she killed Marcy," Ruby said.

"Thank you very much," the detective chimed in. "Now, I think it would be fine for you to all leave."

"I'm not going anywhere until you find my client," Cashel said.

The room silenced again.

"Suit yourself," Detective Andrews responded.

"So back to Zooey, or Susan, or whoever she was," Jane said. "How long ago was she employed by Marcy? It must have been quite a while ago. Because I've known her work as Zooey for a long time."

"It's been at least eight years," Cora said.

"She was holding a grudge that long and decided

to off her ex-boss on her wedding night?" Ruby said, incredulous.

"Stranger things have happened, Mother," Cashel said. "But I agree we shouldn't jump to conclusions. I'm not interested in solving the murder. I'm interested in finding Adrian and having those charges dropped."

"But maybe finding the killer will lead us to Adrian," Cora said.

"I doubt it," Ruby said. "You've been watching too many *CSI*'s or something. Jesus."

"What's *CSI*?" Cora asked.

"A TV show," Ruby said.

"I don't watch TV," Cora said. "Sorry."

Ruby rolled her eyes. "Okay, whatever. I'm just saying things in real life often don't work like they do in books and movies."

"Here's something," one of the officers said. He was sitting at a laptop in the corner of the room. The group gathered around. "I searched for Susan and this came up. She was engaged to our boy, Josh Dupres."

"Back when she worked for Marcy," Cora said.

"Now, taking someone's man? That's cause for murder," Ruby said.

Everybody turned their attention toward her.

"I mean, nothing is cause for murder, but for a disturbed person, it's plenty," Ruby said.

"Okay, so we have a working theory. Let's say Zooey did kill Marcy," Jane said. "Then who killed Zooey?"

"I'd say, if your zany theory is correct, the next person to investigate is Josh, and he is left-handed," Cora said. "Whoever made that macramé bag was left-handed." A chill crept into Cora's bones as she remembered the vacant stare.

"If he's the killer, he must know where Adrian is," Cora said.

"We have no real proof of anything. We need to be careful here and get our ducks in a row," said the detective.

"We have proof of Zooey messing with Cashel's computer, but that's it," one officer said.

"And we're aware of the past between them all," Jane said.

"I think we can get a search warrant for the Drunken Mermaid," Detective Andrews said.

"I agree," Cashel said. "That's the place to start."

"What about bringing Josh in for questioning?" Cora said.

"In due time," the officer said. "We need to have a reason to bring him in. Your love triangle theory is a theory. It's a viable one. Don't misunderstand me. But still. We need to proceed with caution."

"Why? A man's life might be hanging in the balance," Cora said.

"We have to consider everybody's rights here. We can't accuse people of crimes until we have more proof."

"That's true," Cashel said. "Cora, you need to calm down."

"It's just that when we were at Rue's earlier, the man seemed disturbed and I kind of know what I'm talking about. I've seen that vacant stare before. It frightened me," she said.

"I say we need to make one more visit to Rue's place. He might still be there. We can go and ask for her help once again and check out the situation.

But I don't want to alert him. Not yet," Detective Andrews said.

Cora's stomach settled. At least someone intended to do something. She felt a sudden urge to leave the room.

"I need to take a walk," she said.

"Don't go too far," Cashel replied.

"No," she said. "I'm just going out on the resort beach. I need some air."

"I'll come with you," Jane said.

The room had gotten heated, even though the air-conditioning was running. It was a small room. Maybe there were too many people. Cora needed to leave.

She and Jane walked down the corridor and into the lobby.

Cora stopped dead in her tracks when she saw Tom, Zooey's assistant. It was the second time today she'd seen him. He seemed awfully cool and collected for a man who'd lost his boss to a gruesome murder.

"What's wrong?" Jane said.

"Tom, Zooey's assistant, over there. I don't like him," Cora said.

"That's not like you," Jane said.

"Look at him. Look how slick and cool he is. He's so fake. Something is not right about him," Cora said.

"It's likely he's not an emotional guy," Jane said, pulling Cora along to the door. "You're overwrought. Let's take in some fresh air and a glass of wine."

"Okay," Cora said. "Air is exactly what I need." But she couldn't shake her feeling about the slick man she'd left behind in the lobby.

# Chapter 51

Jane hated to leave the action in the situation room. But she felt like Cora needed to get out of there. Now that they were on the beach, Jane was glad they took the time to step out.

She sighed as she took in the sea. "It's so gorgeous here," she said.

"I wish I could enjoy it," Cora said. Her voice was taut. She was stressed. Worried about Adrian.

"I think he's going to be fine. He's a tough guy," Jane said.

"What? Adrian? No, he's not," Cora said.

"What I mean is, he's resilient."

Cora nodded. "Yes," she said. "That's a perfect word for him."

As they walked along, Jane spotted a cluster of sea glass and reached down for a handful. The glass shone the sea-green jewel tone against her skin.

"Gorgeous," Cora said. "The island is certainly gifted with glass and shells and all things beachy."

As they walked further down the shoreline, the sound of the ocean took over from the sound of people, laughing, chatting, children squealing. The roaring hush of the sea filled their ears.

"What will we do if something happens to him?" Cora said.

"Let's not go there," Jane said.

"Okay. What should we talk about? The price of rice in China?" Cora said.

"Let's talk about Zooey or Susan or whoever she was," Jane said.

"I never liked her," Cora said. "I found her to be fake."

"You don't like her assistant either. That's interesting. But I recognize what you mean about Zooey," Jane said. "I thought she was off-putting. But she was a gifted macramé artist."

"True," Cora said. "Proving yet again that just because you're talented, that does not make you a nice person."

"So, let's say Zooey did kill Marcy Grimm," Jane said. "Say she was pissed they were getting married."

"After all that time, to be harboring a resentment like that?"

"Maybe it's what fueled her success," Jane said. "She was so ambitious."

"Ambitious enough to change her name and get a nose job, apparently," Cora said with a sarcastic edge.

Jane wondered where her own ambition came from. As she mulled it over, she concluded she wasn't ambitious at all. She just wanted to do pottery, just be able to make a living from her art. She didn't care to be famous at all—although she was in some circles. What about Cora? Was she ambitious? She thought that over as they walked along the beach. Cora had certainly changed—and was still changing.

She'd grown from the anxiety-riddled counselor into a business owner who occasionally had bouts of anxiety. But man, as Jane thought it over, Cora had come a long way.

Indigo Gap had helped her. Escaping from Pittsburgh worked wonders. Nothing wrong with the city—it was her job and the memories there that were sucking Cora under. What was her friend's ambition? Was it to continue to help people, but in a different way? Or was there more to it?

"I miss my little carriage house," Jane said.

"I miss Indigo Gap," Cora said. "It has become home, hasn't it?"

"We've been there less than a year," Jane said.

"With any luck, we'll be there for many more years to come," Cora said.

"When we get back, we can talk about revamping the kitchen, okay?" Jane said. "It'd be so much fun to have baking and food crafting classes. Don't you think?"

Cora nodded. "I'm not sure we're there yet, but we'll know soon enough."

"I guess we should head back," Jane said. They turned back toward the resort.

"That room," Cora said. "I felt kind of claustrophobic."

Jane noted Cora's coloring was back. In fact, she was starting to redden.

"You might be starting to burn. We better get inside," Jane said. Cora was extremely fair—and Jane was not. They looked like quite the opposite people from the outside. Jane was tall, and voluptuous. Cora was a waif. Jane smiled—she always thought of a fairy-warrior princess when she thought of Cora, with her red curls and vintage clothes. Jane was all about jeans and T-shirts and wore her long, straight, brown hair in a ponytail.

"But other than the pink, your coloring is back. I'm glad you left the room when you did," Jane said. "It's stressful."

"Yes, but at the same time, I want to help. Adrian is my boyfriend. I care about him. But it's so frustrating. We've looked everywhere. The police are searching. He certainly didn't disappear into thin air. Where could he be?"

"I was wondering the same thing. I mean, the island is so small. How could you hide someone?"

"Are there caves? Underground caverns?" Cora asked. "Something like that?"

"I doubt it. But we can find out. More likely, someone has Adrian in a house or a basement," Jane said.

"That thought doesn't soothe me at all," Cora said.

"I know," Jane said. "But the reality is someone has him. He could be anywhere. We have to trust the local officials are searching the island thoroughly."

# Chapter 52

Entering the lobby of the hotel was like a cool, crisp splash of water to the face. Cora felt much better. Until Tom came her way.

"Hello, Cora," he said, turning on the charm. "How are you today?"

"Fine, Tom," she said. "How are you?"

"I've been better," he said. "Listen, I'd like to have a chat with you. Do you mind?"

"Sure," she said. What could he possibly have to talk with her about? They had barely spoken two words to one another the whole retreat.

"I'll meet you in the situation room," Jane said, moving forward.

"Actually," he said with his voice lower, as he grabbed Cora by the elbow and pushed her toward the elevator. "I'd like you to come to my room."

She planted herself. "I'm not going to your room, Tom."

His face reddened. "Look, I have something I want to show you."

She crossed her arms. "I've heard that one before and I can assure you you've got nothing I want to see!"

"Hold on," he said, and dug into his pocket and pulled out a slip of paper. He handed it to her. She recognized the neat, slanted handwriting. It was a note from Adrian. It read: "Cora, trust him. Go to his room with him. Love, Adrian."

Her heart raced. "Is this some kind of ruse? If you know where Adrian is, you better tell me and the police now."

"Please," he said, and pushed her around the corner of the corridor.

A woman who walked by glanced at them. He smiled and stroked Cora's hair.

She smacked his hand away.

"Cora," he whispered. "Adrian is in my room. I'm with the FBI. You need to come with me."

"But I—" she started to say.

He gestured for her to follow and this time she did so.

FBI? What was going on here? She'd always felt something wasn't right about Tom. If he truly was an FBI agent, why was he here?

She slipped into the elevator behind him, then leaned against the elevator wall as he pushed the buttons. All the way to the top. Were they going to one of the penthouse rooms?

"You better not be lying to me," she said. She still didn't like him. What if he had kidnapped Adrian and was the killer?

As they exited the elevator, she stood firm again.

They were the only two in the hallway. "I need to see some ID before I go any further with you."

He dug into his pocket again. "He said you were going to be a problem," Tom said, grinning.

"Who?" Cora said, taking the identification he handed her. It seemed official, but what did she know?

But if Adrian was with him, and Adrian had written the note, there was the possibility this guy was legit. "Thanks," she said, and handed it back to him.

She followed him down the hallway and, when he opened the last door, there stood Adrian, calm, cool, and collected, quite like the school librarian he was. She wanted to strangle him—but only after she hugged him.

She fell into his arms.

"What's going on?" she managed to say after what seemed like an eternal hug. She wanted answers.

"You better sit down," Adrian said. "It's quite a story. And it's not over yet."

"Why are you here? We've been searching for you everywhere!"

"He's here for his own protection," Tom said, motioning for her to take a seat.

Cora felt her jaw stiffen. She still didn't like Tom, no matter if he was an FBI agent or a circus clown.

"Protection from whom?" Cora said as she sat down.

"I've stepped into a bit of a quagmire, Cora," Adrian said.

"Yeah, well, I realize you set yourself up for them to investigate you as a murder suspect with all your texting," she said.

"If that was the only issue, I'd be okay," he said. "I didn't kill Marcy and I believe in the justice system enough to think my innocence will save me."

Cora blinked. She believed the same thing. Was it too optimistic? She'd seen it fail time and again. But for the most part, the way the system worked benefited everybody.

"I know you didn't kill her," she said. "Everybody knows that."

"Both Marcy and Zooey were being blackmailed," Tom said.

"We've figured out that Zooey killed Marcy," Cora said. "We saw her on the security tapes; she was spying on Cashel as he did his research."

"She didn't kill Marcy," Adrian said. "I can see how you might think that, though."

"We're getting close to solving this case. We're watching the police and the retreat carefully, but something has gone wrong," Tom said. And for the first time the superslick-looking Tom gave a human impression. "There's a major drug operation here on the island."

"Does it operate out of the Drunken Mermaid?" Cora asked.

"I guess you could say a part of it does," Tom said. "But it has long tentacles throughout the island and parts of the mainland," he said, then paused. "We're talking about a major crime syndicate. We've gathered enough information to realize Adrian was in trouble. So we took him in."

"Why Adrian?" Cora asked.

"He's gotten a bit too close to everything. And as a murder suspect who is trying to fight these charges, he's drawn a lot of attention to himself, the island, and the law enforcement here," he said with a level tone.

"The law enforcement?" Cora said weakly. Jane had gone back into the situation room. Cashel was there. Ruby was there. And maybe Mathilde.

"We're not sure how deep the corruption goes," Tom said. "But at least two detectives have strong ties to the drug lords we're honing in on. In fact, one might be in charge of the ring."

"Drug lords? On this island?" Cora said.

He frowned. "They are everywhere, unfortunately."

"Good God," Cora said.

"Marcy had quite the habit. It was one of the things that tore us apart," Adrian said. "I couldn't stand it. When you're young and experimenting, it's one thing. But it became a huge part of her adult life."

Cora mulled the information over. "What about her new husband?"

"He was right there with her. Quite the user," Adrian said.

It made sense, thought Cora, thinking of Josh's vacant stare.

"But you said Marcy and Zooey were being black-mailed," Cora said.

Tom nodded. "Both of them invested in the proposed resort, even though the rest of Marcy's family was against it. One of the locals didn't like it. Someone who was aware of their expensive drug habits. They were paying this person to keep his or her mouth shut. Zooey and Marcy decided to stop paying."

A chill swept over Cora. Their murders were professionally committed.

"And I was the perfect dupe," Adrian said. "I still am, evidently."

"You weren't Zooey's real assistant," Cora said to Tom.

"No. I'm undercover," he said. "She knew what I was doing. She was pleased about it. Marcy had been killed and Zooey was so scared she was next." He looked off into the distance. "After this retreat, she planned to get clean. She planned to go to a rehab facility." He gulped. "I was supposed to be protecting her. . . ."

"Oh," Cora said. And he now was protecting Adrian. She wasn't sure she liked this. Not at all. Her eyes met Adrian's. Was he thinking the same thoughts?

"So now what?" Cora asked.

"Now, we're hoping you can help," Tom said.

"Me?"

"Adrian says you've got a bit of experience," Tom said.

"Not much. I—"

"All we need you to do is wear a wire for us and go about your search for Adrian," he said. "You need to pretend you don't know Adrian is safe."

"Why?" Cora said. "I don't understand."

"Because the investigation going on downstairs may lead us to the killers of Marcy and Zooey."

"But you said they were professional killings."

"Exactly. How many professional killers could be here? Professional killers who are not trained police officers?"

Cora's heart ached. Most police were such great guys—but every once in a while a good cop went bad. She sucked in air and glanced at Adrian, who nodded slightly.

"I'll do anything I can to help," she said, ignoring the beads of sweat forming on her forehead.

# Chapter 53

When Cora entered the situation room, she was surprised to see how the groups of people clustered together. A group of three men were on their laptops. Another group of five were at a table. A third group—some police, but mostly her people—were at yet another table. Ruby's, Jane's, and Mathilde's hands were moving in rhythm. They were knitting. Knitting?

She approached the table, with her handy listening device in her purse. To an innocent bystander, the device looked like a cell phone. But it transmitted to the room where Adrian and Tom were listening.

"Cora!" Jane said. "What did Tom want?"

Cora's mouth dropped. Right away, she was flummoxed. What did Tom want? What should she say?

"Um. You know, he had some questions about our retreat. He had heard about it and wondered about working for us," Cora said. Brilliant, she thought.

"He seems like a nice enough guy," Mathilde said. "But he's not much of a crafter. I think Zooey hired him for other reasons. You know, he was organized, an expert at the computer. She didn't want to have to deal with any of that stuff."

"Who does, right?" Jane said, and smiled.

"You're knitting?" Cora said, as she sat down next to Jane.

"Sure, I've been learning," she said. "It does have a meditative effect."

"So I hear," Cora said, eyeing her best friend. The two of them used to poke fun at the knitters— good-naturedly, of course. Knitters always knit. They always found each other, sat together, and barely spoke to one another, but seemed to prefer it.

Cora had mulled over the many studies done on the therapeutic effects of knitting. Cora respected knitters now. But when she was younger, she didn't understand.

She had read about how the rhythmic, repetitive movements of knitting or crocheting kept people focused on the present by distracting them from thinking about past events or feeling fearful about the future. The therapeutic nature of knitting actually helped to bring down blood pressure, heart rate, and prevent anxiety-related illnesses.

Cora had tried to pick up knitting and couldn't seem to catch the knack. But she found embroidering helped lift her mood.

"So, is there any news?" Cora said.

"The police sent a crew to the Drunken Mermaid," Ruby said, looking at Cora over her glasses, which were perched on the end of her nose. "We're waiting to hear if they find anything there."

"Is that all they are doing?" Cora said.

One officer who was sitting at their table focused his attention toward them. "We're still searching the island," he said. "But for now the efforts are focused on the Drunken Mermaid."

"Isn't that the place our cabbie mentioned has a drug problem?" Cora said casually to Jane. Maybe too casually. She was not a good enough actress.

Jane cocked an eyebrow. "Um, yeah," she said, with a note of sarcasm, as if underneath she were saying, "You knew that, c'mon."

"It's had some problems, but believe me, there are other places on this island with similar issues," the officer said, and went back to his coffee.

"It's such a small island," Cora said. "What other places are there?"

"Well, here, for one," he said. "The place you're sitting. This resort brings a lot of money to the island, both kinds of money, if you know what I mean."

"Now, now, it's not that bad. You're giving them a bad impression," Mathilde chided.

He cocked his head in deference. "Whatever," he said.

"You want some coffee?" Ruby asked Cora.

"Nah, I better not," Cora said. She tapped her fingers on the table. "I'm a bit wound up. I don't need caffeine."

"A confession?" an officer on his cell phone said loudly from the group huddled over their computers.

They all turned toward him. "He confessed? I'm shocked!" the officer exclaimed.

"Who?" Ruby asked what everybody was thinking.

He held up his finger, trying to listen on the cell phone while the others were flinging questions at him.

The room silenced, and then he said: "Josh Dupres? I can't believe it."

Cora's heart skipped a beat. She believed it. Josh gave her the chills. Even if he didn't kill his wife, he could have certainly killed Zooey, if he thought Zooey had killed Marcy.

"Both murders?" the officer said.

"He's confessed to both murders," Cora said. "His wife and Zooey. Incredible!"

The officer who was sitting at the table slammed his hand down. "You're damn right it is. I've known Josh Dupres my whole life. I don't think he's capable of killing."

"But he confessed!" Ruby said.

He stood up. "There's all kinds of reasons people confess. Many times it has nothing to do with guilt."

Ruby harrumphed.

"I don't understand at all," Jane said.

"What reason would he have to confess to murder if he didn't do it?" Ruby said, placing her knitting into the bag. "I'm hungry. I need something to eat."

Cora pondered the reasons Josh might confess even if he was innocent. Was he stoned out of his mind? Scared? Was he being blackmailed, too? Or was he protecting someone else?

"Well, as far as I'm concerned the murder case is solved," the detective said as he ambled up to their table. "Why don't you all move along with Ruby here and find food while we try to clarify what our boy knows about Adrian."

Cora considered her position. Adrian was safe upstairs, but this cop didn't know she was aware of it. He himself didn't know Adrian's whereabouts. "I'm staying until there's word about Adrian," she said, and gave him the most charming smile she could muster. "I hope you don't mind."

# Chapter 54

"Any word yet on Brisbane?" a cop said from across the room. It had been at least an hour of sitting, waiting, watching others knit, click on their keyboards, and drink coffee.

Cora didn't know if Tom and Adrian had gotten what they needed yet. She simply had no way of knowing.

"No word," another replied.

"What? The police know nothing about where Adrian is? I find that hard to believe," Ruby said.

"Calm down, Mother," Cashel replied. "Let the officers do their work." He'd just joined them and seemed to have regained his health.

"Josh is our best hope of finding him," Jane said.

"Josh has confessed. Why hasn't he told us where Adrian is?" Cora said.

"I don't know," the officer said.

"Are you still searching for Adrian?" Ruby said.

"Yes, of course," the officer said.

"Such a small island. I'd think you'd have found

him by now," Cora said, realizing she was pushing it. But she felt compelled.

"It's a small island, yes," the officer said. "But there's forest, caves, beaches, plus homes and businesses. He could be anywhere."

"Maybe he's not here anymore," Cora said. "Maybe he's off the island."

"We've alerted the coast guard and authorities on the mainland," another officer said. He glared at Cora. "We told you that already."

"Yes," Cora said. "That's right. I'm sorry. It's so difficult. Not knowing where he is. If he's okay. I'm just not thinking clearly."

Jane reached for her hand. "I'm certain he's okay. He'll be fine."

Cashel frowned. "You know, I like him. I hope he's okay."

"You say that as if it surprises you," Cora said.

He eyeballed her pointedly. "It does."

Cora lurched back and raised an eyebrow. "I don't know what you ever had against him. He's a great guy."

But the truth was staring right at Cora in the way Cashel gazed at her. Jane had been right. Cashel had feelings for her. Why hadn't she seen it before?

She was sorry about that. She didn't reciprocate his feelings at all. Sure, he was handsome and had the bluest eyes she'd ever seen. But he was a pain in the ass. When she first met him, she did feel a spark of attraction, but nipped it in the bud because of her business relationship with his mother—and as she grew to know him and his mother, the small spark of attraction vanished.

She was certain she'd done nothing to lead him on.

She glanced around the room, not quite knowing where to fix her gaze.

Jane sat her knitting down. "I can't sit here anymore. I need to eat. And I'd like to call London."

"I'm not leaving until they find Adrian," Cora said.

"Yes, you are," Jane said, standing, hands on her hips. "I don't think you've eaten since breakfast."

"Okay," Cora said. "You're right. I better eat." She turned to the detective who seemed to be in charge. "Please inform us the minute you know something."

He nodded. "Either I will or your lawyer will."

Cora reached for her bag and slid it over her shoulder. A wave of weariness overcame her. She knew Adrian was safe, but what she wasn't aware of was if Tom had gotten enough information to make a bust. She was still nervous and wondering if she'd done her part—had she done enough to help?

As she and Jane made their way to the eatery, Cora couldn't believe she was keeping secrets from her best friend. As she approached the place, she told herself that there was no way to tell Jane until it was over. She was so grateful Adrian was okay. She wanted to tell Jane, but she swore she wouldn't—and of course the FBI was listening to her every word.

Cora felt someone watching her as she and Jane slipped into their booth at the restaurant. She kept her eyes focused on the menu for a moment, blinked, and took in the scene.

Hank. Hank was sitting right next to them. He waved weakly and winked. She smiled and waved back.

He kept turning up everywhere—like a bad penny.

Jane smiled and waved.

"Poor guy," she said, with a lowered voice. "He needs to find a job, I imagine. I wouldn't want to be looking for work now. It's tough out there."

His back was to them, and it stayed toward them as he left his table.

"He's going to be okay," Cora said. "Remember? He has a severance package. He lives on the resort. He's not paying for it. Besides, he'll find something."

"I hope so. I wish him the best," Jane said.

The server came up to them and took their orders. Once she'd left, Cora said, "It's been quite a day."

"Yep," Jane replied. "It ain't over yet."

Once again, Cora wanted to tell her about Adrian. He was hidden upstairs with an FBI agent and they were listening to all her conversations. But of course she couldn't. Her friends were going to be furious with her when they found out. But there was nothing she could do about it now. Nothing at all.

As she looked away from Jane sitting across the table from her and glanced out the window on the beach, she noticed Hank walking next to Rue.

"Well, look at that," she said to Jane. "Hank and Rue walking together along the beach. How strange."

"I'd say very strange," Jane said, as the server brought their food. "But right now I'm all about this plate of spaghetti. Bring on the carbs and the wine, please."

Cora laughed. "I hear you."

After dinner and one bottle of wine, both Cora and Jane were feeling much better.

"You know what's weird about seeing Rue and Hank?" Cora said.

"I don't want to even imagine those two together," Jane said. Her eyelids were drooping.

"Well, yeah," Cora said. "If my son were being questioned at the police station, I think I'd be there and not walking along the beach with someone."

# Chapter 55

Cora made her way back to the situation room, while Jane headed for her own room. Jane wanted to turn in for the night, so Cora was on her own. Well, on her own with Cashel, Ruby, and Mathilde, along with the crew of local police and detectives. Not to mention whoever was listening on the other end of the device.

"Any news?" she said as she approached a group of detectives.

"I'm afraid we've no news of Adrian," one replied. "Sorry."

Which sounded like there might be news of another kind.

Cashel pulled her aside. "You won't believe this," he said. "They've already let Dupres go."

"What? He confessed, didn't he?" Now it made sense as to why Rue was walking on the beach earlier with Hank. Well, at least somewhat.

Cashel nodded. "Something smells fishy to me."

"What do you mean?"

"Something is not right here; that's what I mean."

"You've said that before, but I'm afraid you're going to have to be more specific," Cora said.

"I mean the detective over there, Andrews . . . He's hiding something. He's nervous. Very nervous. I'm betting we've stepped into something bigger than Adrian's case."

"Yes, but what?" Cora said.

"The only other time I've seen something like this . . . well, let me see. . . . It was when I was working on a case another authority was already working. Things weren't adding up and information was being withheld because of the secret nature of the investigation," he said.

Cashel was in the right church, but sitting in the wrong pew. "Do you think that's what's going on here?" Cora asked.

"I'd bet my life on it."

"You kind of already have," Cora said.

"Yeah, I've never been drugged because of a case before," he said.

"If Adrian wasn't missing, I swear I'd leave now," she said. She meant it. Forget the retreat. Forget it all. She wanted to go home. Realizing he was safe was the only saving grace to the moment. But she couldn't tell Cashel. His frustration was showing on his face.

"Josh must have had a hell of a lawyer," he said.

"A local, I'm sure," Cora said.

"He confessed to murder. Claimed he doesn't know anything about Adrian and he's off scot-free."

It occurred to Cora that Josh must be in on the FBI operation. They must have gotten him off. So if he was in on it, who killed Marcy and Zooey?

"You said he confessed, but was his confession inadmissible for some reason?" Cora said.

"Possibly, but it takes a judge to determine that."

"Could they have gotten one on a Sunday evening?"

"Certainly," he replied. "Especially here. I think there are two judges on the island. They probably all golf together."

"What would make his confession inadmissible?" Cora asked.

"If it was involuntary," Cashel said. "Or if they couldn't corroborate it or if he was not mentally stable."

"That may be it. I mentioned to you about his vacant stare, that I got this weird feeling," Cora said.

Cora's phone buzzed. She turned away from Cashel to read her message. It was from Adrian:

They are lying to you. He's still in custody. For his protection.

Why are they lying? Cora typed back. I don't understand.

Because they want to suss out the real killer. He knows who murdered Marcy and he knows who murdered Zooey. His life is in danger.

Who? Who is the killer?

No response came right away. Then, a few seconds later: They are not telling me. I have no idea. Be careful tonight.

A chill traveled through Cora. The killer was still at large. It wasn't Mathilde. It wasn't Josh. It certainly wasn't Adrian. The killer could be anywhere on this island. Anywhere . . . even in this room.

"Who was that? Are you okay?" Cashel said.

"I need to sit down. It was Jane."

"I'll bring you a bottle of water. Take a seat," he said.

Were the police lying to them intentionally? Or were they being lied to by the people who had Josh?

Cora glanced around the room and realized, aside from the people she knew, she had no idea whom to trust in this room.

"Here," Cashel said as he handed her a bottle of water from a machine. "This has been difficult for you," he said, sitting back down beside her.

She nodded, twisting the lid off the bottle. "Adrian is missing, still. We thought we were getting a confession and closer to finding him."

"I don't know what to say anymore," Cashel said.

The water was cold and refreshing; exactly what she needed. "So I've been formulating suspects in my mind."

"I'm not surprised to hear this," Cashel said.

"I wondered about Mathilde, then crossed her off the list," she said. "Then I wondered about Zooey killing Marcy and someone else killing Zooey in turn, offing Tom, her assistant."

"Nah, he checks out," Cashel said. "I've run checks on everybody."

"I wasn't aware of that. Then I thought Josh killed Marcy and Zooey," she said.

"I did, too," Cashel said. "He's got a record. Drugs, mainly."

"Drugs?" Cora said, remembering this was the exact reason the FBI was here investigating.

"Yes, cocaine mainly, but also heroin," he said. "He's been in and out of rehab and jail. Kind of makes you wonder what someone like Marcy Grimm would see in him."

"She's got a few skeletons in her closet, too," Cora said. "According to Adrian, she loved her drugs."

"Ah," Cashel said. "Makes sense. I've seen it so many times."

She'd seen it, too. Addicts attracted one another. They were the worst thing for each other. She'd never seen two addicts make a go of it. It always fell apart.

She nodded as her phone buzzed again.

**Make sure you aren't followed, but please come and see me,** Adrian texted her.

She read the text and grinned.

"What are you two up to in this corner?" Ruby said as she walked up to them.

"Just trying to make sense of things," Cora said.

"Any luck?"

"Not at all," Cashel said.

"Oh, I can't believe this!" Mathilde said as she flung her phone across the table.

"What?" Ruby said, turning around to face Mathilde.

"They are flaunting it," Mathilde said. "Rue and Hank have been sneaking around behind my back. Now they are walking along the beach together. A friend just sent me pictures!"

"Rue and Hank?" Cashel said. "She's way older than him, isn't she? Besides, she's married, right?"

"What does that matter?" Ruby said, poking him. "The age thing, I mean. The marriage thing is another situation."

"But her son was just in the police station confessing to murder. I thought it was strange earlier when I saw them. You'd think she'd be with him. Or, I don't know, at least be concerned," Cora said.

"Unless she knew he didn't do it," Cashel said quietly.

The room silenced.

"Don't jump to conclusions," an officer said. "Remember, he was let go."

"After he confessed? C'mon, officer. What's going on here?" Cashel said.

"You're aware of everything I am," he said with a perplexed expression on his face. "I'm sorry to say," he added under his breath.

Cora realized the FBI was definitely on to something. This officer felt something wasn't right. She wondered how many others felt the same thing. The problem was in the police department. And might be in this room. With that thought, Cora decided to take her leave.

# Chapter 56

After she swung by to see Adrian—a short visit with one hug and a couple kisses—Cora took her newly refreshed device and headed to her room. It was going to be a long night, she figured.

She cracked open her laptop, noting many responses to her post about Rue and her spirit chimes. She wrote back to a few of them, feeling awful she hadn't replied earlier. It was one thing she prided herself on—responding to her readers quickly.

She planned on another post tonight about her class today. But she didn't have a clear enough head to write anything.

She kicked off her shoes. Her feet ached. Her back ached. She needed a bath. No, she needed sleep. Or to lie on the bed, watch a little TV to unwind, get ready for bed. She tamped down a momentary longing for her own quilt-covered bed and Luna.

Cora reached for the chocolate on her pillow. She didn't remember there being one on her pillow previously, but perhaps the resort only did it every so often. In any case, she appreciated the gesture. She tore off the wrapper and popped it into her mouth.

Plopping onto the bed, Cora grabbed the remote and switched the TV on, clicking from channel to channel. Eighty-two channels. Who needed eighty-two channels? Was there anything decent to watch on any of those channels?

*Click, click, click.*

She warmed as she thought of Adrian and her watching TV together. She didn't own a TV, but he did. She wished he were here now. She was so grateful he was okay. She mulled over what she had learned about him during this retreat. He had a past. But then again, who didn't?

But he had been deeply in love with Marcy. And hadn't seen anybody else until Cora.

She dropped the remote when she found a repeat of *Glee*, one of the early episodes, which she loved. Jane had told her it was worth watching, so it was one of the few TV shows she even knew about.

She lifted the remote from the bed to place it on the table.

She felt heavy all over. Maybe she was unwinding from the extremely stressful day. Finding out Adrian was missing, then finding out he wasn't . . .

She felt as if she were too heavy to move and get ready for bed. Just. Too. Heavy.

She was dreaming. Or was she awake? What was happening to her? Her eyes were closed. She couldn't open them. Her heart raced. Was she having some kind of attack?

She heard voices in the room. Was it the TV?

*Open your eyes.*

She was able to manage to lift one eyelid and she saw a hand move across her line of vision. A big hand. A masculine hand.

*Open your eyes!*

"I'm sure she's suspicious of us," a woman's voice said. "I saw her watching us."

"I say we just leave," a male voice said. It was familiar, but who was it? And why wasn't Cora able to open her eyes?

She wanted to shout out "Who are you? What do you want? Why are you in my room?" She opened her mouth and only a groan escaped.

"She's going to wake up soon," the woman said. "We need to move."

This voice was familiar, too.

"He's not going to be happy if we don't find anything," the male voice said.

"I know, but what can we do if there's nothing here to find?"

*Who are these people? What are they doing in my room?*

Cora heard the clicking of a keyboard. Was someone on her laptop?

A sharp pounding noise came from the door to the hall. *Bang, bang, bang!*

What was that? Was someone pounding on the wall?

"Cora Chevalier? Open up. Hotel Security!"

"Damn," the male voice whispered.

Cora heard frantic shuffling and the sliding glass door to the balcony open, but she still couldn't open her eyes or move. Next came the sound of the door to the hallway being knocked open.

"Quick," someone said. "They've escaped by the balcony."

"Cora!" a voice said. It was Adrian. His arms lifted her from the bed. "She's been drugged. Someone help her."

"Medics!" came a yell.

Drugged? No, she hadn't been drugged. It was Cashel. Cashel was the one who had been drugged because he was close to the truth. Whatever that was. She laughed at the thought of it. Cora Chevalier, drugged?

*That would never happen.*

Then everything went dark.


When Cora awoke, she was in a hospital room with a bag attached to her arm. She looked at the bag, looked at the nurse beside her bed, and went back to sleep.

# Chapter 57

"Yes?" Jane said into her cell phone. If this was another one of those sales calls, she planned to give them an earful.

"Jane, it's Cashel. Sorry to bother you at such an ungodly hour, but Cora has been hospitalized."

"What?" Jane said, tearing the blankets off her and standing up.

"She's fine," Cashel said. "I'm with her right now."

"What's going on?"

"It appears she was drugged," he said. "They are detoxing her now, but it's moved through her system fairly quickly."

"Why would someone drug her?"

"Someone was in her room," he said. "Two people, actually. The police think they've got them. But they need Cora to identify them."

"Two people were in her room? How horrifying!" Jane said, slipping off her nightshirt and searching for something decent to put on. "How did they get in?"

"I don't know," Cashel said.

"How did they find out about this? I mean, if she were poisoned . . . Did she call for help? What happened?" Jane was starting to panic. If this hotel wasn't secure, she needed to know. Out of habit she looked at the empty bed next to her, then remembered London was gone safely back to Indigo Gap.

"I'm not sure what happened, frankly. I received a call about an hour ago and here I am, at the hospital," he said with a sigh. An edge of weariness was in his voice. "I've called my mom. She'll be over to your room shortly to check on you. See if you need anything. I figure you'll want to come to the hospital."

"You're right," Jane said. "I'm livid. How could something like this happen? Someone broke into her room and drugged her?"

"I'm not sure how or when she was drugged," he said. "I imagine we'll find out shortly."

"Have they found the people?" Jane asked.

Cashel grunted a no.

She slipped on her jeans.

"They're still searching," he said.

Jane felt the rush of anger move through her. What the hell were people doing in Cora's room?

A light rapping came at her door. She peeked through the peephole at a disheveled Ruby.

"It's your mother. I've got to go," Jane said. "I'll be right over."

"I've called you a cab," he said. "See you soon."

Well, Cashel had thought of everything. His mother to check on her and a cab to take her to Cora at the hospital.

Jane opened the door.

"You look like the wrath of God," Ruby said.

"You don't look so great yourself, lady."

Ruby ambled over to the empty bed and plopped herself down. "I suppose she's going to be okay?"

"I hope so. She has a sensitive system," Jane said, gathering her purse and belongings. It might be a long night.

Ruby harrumphed. "Why doesn't that surprise me to hear?"

Jane glanced at her watch—it was 3:00 A.M. "You better go back to your room and catch some sleep. Thanks so much for coming over."

"Cashel gave me no choice."

"That son of yours . . . he's something else," Jane said.

"Yep. That's one way of putting it," Ruby said. "Please text me and let me know how she's doing." Jane liked to see how Ruby and Cora had grown to care for one another. They had some trouble at the start of their relationship, but things seemed to be going much better these days.

Jane ushered Ruby out to the hallway. "Pleasant dreams," she said before closing the door softly behind her.

The cab couldn't get Jane to the hospital fast enough. She was furious. Worried. Scared. Needed to lay her eyes on Cora.

When Jane entered the corridor outside Cora's hospital room, she saw Cashel there talking with the police and some others and he was asking the same questions she had been asking.

"It's completely unacceptable someone broke into

her room. What kind of security do you have if someone can do this?" Cashel asked.

"We're investigating this matter, sir. We're pulling security tapes, checking card key records, and so on. We're doing everything we can," one of the men standing there said.

"Those card keys easy to replicate?" one of the police officers asked.

"You have to know several passwords and be familiar with the system," the man said.

"Must be an insider," Cashel surmised. His attention was now on Jane as she approached.

"How is she? How is Cora?" Jane asked.

"She's going to be fine. She's sleeping now," he said. "She has a saline IV attached to flush out her system. But they had to put a sedative in it so she remains relaxed."

Relief flooded through Jane. They did not need Cora to have a full-blown panic attack. That was scary for Cora and for those around her as well. The last severe one she had was in Pittsburgh at the women's shelter. She hadn't had a bad one since. There'd been many mini-attacks, but not a full-blown one since they'd moved to Indigo Gap.

Indigo Gap. Jane felt a pang of longing for her little carriage house and the home they were creating there. The town, with all its shades of blue-named streets, quaint shops, and historic houses, was becoming her home. Roots. She and London finally had some roots. Jane embraced the sense of belonging she felt.

She walked into Cora's hospital room and sat down in the chair beside her bed.

All they needed to do was release Cora from the hospital, find Adrian, and go home.

There was one last event scheduled for the retreat—the closing party. Jane could not imagine attending it now as she sat viewing her best friend with tubes running in and out of her tiny body.

Jane pulled out her phone and texted Ruby. **She's fine, just sleeping. Like I hope you are, too.**

But even as Jane sent the text, she wondered what kind of hell was going to break loose when Cora awakened.

# Chapter 58

Cora felt like she was inside a cloud. Soft and misty.

Jarred awake by a nurse dropping a pen on the metal table near her bed, she sat up, clutching her chest. "What happened?"

"Sorry," the nurse said.

"Calm down," Jane said. Jane? She looked rumpled and half asleep.

"Okay, you tell me what's going on and I'll calm down," Cora said. "How's that sound?"

Jane smiled. "Relax, okay? You're fine now."

"I'm in a hospital room with tubes attached to me. It would appear I'm not fine," Cora said.

"Do you remember anything about last night?" Jane asked.

Cora sorted through her foggy memories. "I remember watching *Glee*. My arms feeling heavy, falling asleep. . . ."

"Is that it? What did you do last night?"

"Well, you know, we ate dinner together," Cora said.

"Did you eat anything in your room?"

"Chocolate," Cora said. "It was left on my pillow."

"That must have been it. I'm calling Cashel. The police need to find the wrapper and check it out," Jane said.

"What? Why?"

"You were drugged."

"I was?" Cora searched through an assortment of feelings and dreams. Were they not dreams? "Was someone in my room last night?" She gasped. "I thought I was dreaming!"

"Yes, but you're fine now, right? No need to panic," Jane said, dialing Cashel on her cell.

"Cashel, it was the chocolate. The trash needs to be searched for the wrapper. Maybe there are, I don't know, prints, or something?" Jane said.

Prints? Examining her trash? Who had been in her room? What did they want?

"'He's not going to be happy if we don't find anything,'" she remembered someone saying. She also remembered the sound of a keyboard.

"Hold on, Jane. Tell them to search my computer. I remember someone on my computer. God, I thought I was dreaming!" Cora said.

Jane repeated what Cora said into the phone. "I don't know," she said after listening to Cashel for a moment, then turned to Cora. "Are you ready to make a statement to the police?"

"Hell, yes," Cora said.

"You heard her?" Jane said, laughing. "Okay, later."

"I need to get this thing out of my arm and get out of here," Cora said to the nurse.

"You're not quite finished yet. We need to keep rehydrating you," she replied.

"I feel fine," Cora responded.

"You're not going anywhere yet," Jane said. "So relax."

"I have so much to do. A blog post to write. The retreat party. Adrian . . ." Cora said.

"No word yet about Adrian," Jane said.

Was that part of her dream as well? The part where Adrian held her, whispered to her it was going to be all right, rescued her? How did he know? The wire! He must have heard what was happening on it. She had forgotten to turn it off last night. Well, she may have remembered at some point—if she had not gotten drugged.

"What kind of drug did they give me?" Cora asked.

"The same one they gave Cashel—the date rape drug."

"Jesus," she said. "No wonder I couldn't move."

Adrian and Tom must have disappeared, once again, after hotel security and the police took over last night. She couldn't quite remember how it went down. But what she did remember warmed her. Adrian.

Something in her gave way. Was she starting to trust him? Were her feelings deepening? After everything she found out about him this weekend, all the half-truths, she realized they said more about her lack of trust than they did about him.

She bit the inside of her lip.

"What are you thinking about?"

"Adrian," she said. "I'm worried."

"I am, too. Where could he be?" Jane said.

A pang of guilt moved through Cora. How could she not tell her best friend what was going on? Her moment of angst was interrupted by a couple of detectives rapping on her door. Cora recognized them.

"Well, that was quick," Jane said.

"How are you feeling?" Detective Andrews said.

"Well enough to give you a statement," Cora said.

"Great," Detective Andrews said. "But we also wondered if you knew who was in your room. Could you identify them?"

"We realize you were drugged and might not have seen them. Did you hear anything? See anything at all?"

Cora was about to answer when Tom walked into the room.

"Tom?" Jane said. "What you doing here?"

"I came to see how Cora is," he said, leaning over to hug her. "Don't tell them anything," he whispered.

"What did you say?" Jane said. "What's going on here?"

"I just told her how well she's looking," Tom said, giving his million-dollar smile.

Jane shifted her eyes toward Cora, then back to him, confused.

"How are you feeling?" he asked Cora.

"To tell you the truth," she said, hesitating, "I was feeling okay, but now, I'm feeling a bit woozy."

"Woozy? Let me find a nurse," Jane said, walking out of the room.

"Water?" Tom said, nodding toward the pitcher.

"Sure," Cora said. Two detectives were standing there, in her room, and an undercover FBI agent had just whispered in her ear. She wasn't quite lying when she said she needed water—the situation was getting trickier by the minute.

One of the detectives cleared his throat. "We can come back later," he said.

Tom handed her a glass of water and smiled back at the detective. "I think it would be for the best."

He was so slick and fake—but, damn, he was good. The detectives decided to take their leave.

"My lawyer will be in touch with you," Cora called after them.

"What was that all about?" Jane said, entering as the detectives left the room. "What's going on here?"

Jane knew about Cora's strong dislike of Tom. Of course seeing him hug her had set off her radar.

"You're one smart lady," Tom said.

"We should tell her everything," Cora said. "Unless you want to be investigating another murder—mine."

# Chapter 59

"I can't believe you didn't tell me."

"I wanted to, believe me," Cora said.

"So you rescued Cora last night?" Jane said to Tom.

Tom nodded. "Yes, we were monitoring the situation."

"Why were people in her room?" Jane asked.

"They think she is on to them," he replied. "They were searching her computer files."

"And they found nothing," Cora replied. "I remember hearing that. And something else . . . a man was going to be angry with them if they didn't find anything."

Tom nodded. "Makes sense. One of the two guys who were just here has been behind this."

"You mean there was a killer in this room just now?" Jane said, in a rushed whisper.

"No, not necessarily," Tom said. "We think he was behind it all. He didn't necessarily commit the murders. He may have ordered them."

"Like, like . . . a mafia dude?" Jane said, her eyes wide.

"Precisely," Tom said. "Though we don't use that word. But there is definitely organized crime behind it all."

Jane's eyes shot back and forth between Cora and Tom. "We should tell Cashel. He's worried sick. He is Adrian's lawyer."

"The less people who know, the better," Tom said. "The more you know, the more at risk you are."

Cora understood, but she did think Cashel should be informed. He was haggard and blaming himself for much of what was happening. It didn't seem right to keep Adrian's whereabouts from him.

"So, both Cora and Cashel were drugged," Jane said out loud, but more to herself. "Cashel because he knew too much, or was getting too close to the truth, and Cora because the criminals suspected she knew something. Why? What did you do yesterday that would lead them to believe that?"

Cora thought for a moment. "I was in the situation room a lot yesterday. I was musing a bit about who the killers could be."

"What names did you mention?" Jane asked.

"We talked about Mathilde and crossed her off our list. We talked about Josh, Rue's son, and we talked about Hank and the fact that Rue and Hank seemed to be together or something," Cora said.

"The police are still rounding up suspects," Tom said. "They are going to ask you to identify them."

"I can do that," Cora said. "I know they were in my room. I recognized their voices."

"Who was it?" Tom asked.

"Rue and Hank," Cora replied.

"What?" Jane squealed and clutched her chest. "I can't believe it!"

"Excuse me," he said. "I need to call this in."

Cora and Jane sat quietly, letting it sink in that Rue and Hank had broken in to her room and in all likelihood had drugged her.

"But what happens to you if you identify them?" Jane asked, after a few moments. "I don't like this."

"If she says she can't identify them, we think she'll be safer," Tom said. "She's given the FBI what it needs. Right now, we are the only trusted law officers on this island."

"You think she'll be safer?" Jane said.

"But why would I not identify them to the local cops?" Cora asked. "They were in my room. They need to pay for what they've done. How dare they?"

"They were in your room searching for evidence for their boss," Tom said. "If you identify them, a number of things could happen."

"They could off you for knowing too much," Jane said, with her eyes wide.

"C'mon. How is that knowing too much?" Cora said. "I don't know who their boss is. I don't know anything. I know they broke into my room."

"How did they manage it?" Jane said, after a moment.

"Well, Hank lives there. He may have gotten hold of a key or something," Cora said.

"What happens if she doesn't identify them to the locals? How does it help the case? Or not?" Jane asked after a pause in the conversation.

"We then would watch them to see who they

contact, who they visit, and so on. They might lead us right to our guy," Tom said.

"I don't think I like this," Jane said.

"It's up to you what you tell the police, but I think it would be best to tell them you don't remember anything," Tom said, with a finality in his voice leading Cora to feel certain not to argue.

"I don't want to lie to the cops," she said. "That could come back on me."

"Don't worry. We've got you covered. We have an officer on the inside."

"Well, you've thought of everything, haven't you?" Cora said.

"We don't want them to know how you were rescued last night either. So, you should say, once again, you don't remember anything," Tom said.

Cora hated all this lying. But she had to trust someone—and this man was FBI. He had Adrian in his protection, and he had rescued her last night.

"So this is kind of a sting?" Cora said.

Tom laughed. "No. It's us doing our job."

"So you have a guy inside the local police force, so that means you think . . ."

"Our drug runner is a cop. But we need to make certain. It could get very messy. We're proceeding with caution, of course," Tom said.

Cora marveled at his friendly ease. He seemed like a different man than the one she first met as Zooey's assistant.

"I've lost Zooey and I don't want to lose another person," he said. "So caution is the order of the day."

Cora's head felt light and she drank more water. She felt hung over—she ached everywhere.

"As for you," Tom said to Jane, "we'd like you to go back and go about your business. We've got Cora."

"Oh no," Jane said. "I'm not leaving."

She crossed her arms and dug in. "Nope," she said one more time. "Cora is my best friend. I'm not leaving her alone."

"Then leave her with me," came a voice from the hallway. Cashel O'Malley walked in with a swagger. "Do you need to get back?"

"No," Jane said.

"How are you feeling?" Cashel asked, ignoring Tom's presence in the room.

"Like hell," Cora said.

"Cashel, this is Tom," Jane said.

Cashel turned to Tom. "I know who he is," he said. "I mean, what he is. Just took a bit of digging."

Tom cleared his throat. "I don't know what you think you know. . . ."

"I've a friend who used to work with you, so cut the drama," Cashel said. "I'd like to know what the FBI is doing on Sea Glass Island and what you know about my client's whereabouts. And I want to know that now or I will expose you immediately."

# Chapter 60

After Cashel and Tom stopped their bickering, Jane headed back to the resort to check on Ruby and the retreat. As she headed down to the café where they were eating, Mathilde came ambling up the hallway.

"How are you this morning?" she said. "How is Cora? The police informed me about her problem."

"Problem? She was drugged," Jane said. *By your ex-assistant,* she wanted to add, but didn't. No point in adding salt to Mathilde's wound or fuel to her fire or any other cliché Jane could think of.

"I know your students will appreciate you being here. I can't believe the retreat is almost over," Mathilde said. "It's been a rough one, to say the least."

"Next year will be better, I'm sure," Jane said. "This had to be a once in lifetime weird occurrence."

"A nightmare, if you ask me. Have they found Adrian?" Mathilde asked.

"No," Jane said. *Lies, lies, lies.* Oh, she hated the lies.

"I'm heading to the office," Mathilde said. "I have a few things to take care of before the party tonight."

Jane felt she should offer to help, but had plans to meet with some of her students. This last day of the event they had planned to spend together. It was "Retreat, Rewind, Relax Day," where all the crafters got together and worked on their crafts, ate, drank, and so on.

"I'm on my way to breakfast. I can help you later, if you like," Jane said.

"No need, dear. I've got it under control," Mathilde said, and walked away.

Jane stood there for a moment, gathering herself before moving on.

Something fluttered along the floor. Jane picked it up. It was a receipt with Mathilde's name and credit card number on it. Oh, brother. She turned in Mathilde's direction and hightailed it to try to find her. She saw her at a distance. She fought the impulse to yell and broke out into a run. She saw her up ahead. And then she didn't. What?

What happened to her?

Did she duck into one of the restaurants? A bathroom?

But when Jane got to the last spot she'd seen Mathilde, there was no café, restaurant, or bathroom. Just a service door, marked EXIT, EMPLOYEES ONLY. Could she have gone through that?

Deciding she must have, Jane cracked open the door, which led to a narrow hallway. She slipped through the door and calmed her nerves. Why was she so nervous? It was just a hallway. She had every reason to be here. Jane clutched Mathilde's receipt, determined to deliver it safely into her hands.

"Please," she heard someone say in a room—or was

it up ahead somewhere? "Please just take the tiara and leave us all alone!"

It was Mathilde's voice. Jane pressed herself against the wall.

She reached into her bag for her phone, carefully, trying not to make any noise.

"It's worth lot of money," she said. "Just take it. Please! Leave us all alone!"

A male voice was muttering.

Mathilde screamed.

Jane quickly texted Cora. Mathilde in trouble. In service hallway. Turning my GPS on. Send help.

Jane heard scuffling, grunting, sobbing. Her heart felt as if it would pound out of her chest. It pounded so loudly in her ears she wondered if anybody else could hear it. What should she do? Stay here?

No. She should get out of here.

*Feet, move.*

But they stayed planted.

*Feet, move.*

Exactly like all of her nightmares.

Danger lurked, but she froze.

A text came through. Get out of there. Help is right there. Might be behind you now.

Jane trembled from head to toe. But she couldn't move.

What was that man doing to Mathilde? Who was he? Was he their killer?

She felt frozen and had to will her back leg to move. Back up. One foot. Then the next.

*Reach for the door. Yes, there it is.* She opened it slowly. No noise, please.

The door opened, almost bumping into Cashel, along with Tom and several police officers.

When she saw Cashel, she leaned into him. His arms went around her, as the officer moved forward into the hallway. Her knees weakened and the room spun. Was she going to pass out? She'd never passed out in her life. She was a tough girl from the South Side of Pittsburgh.

But Cashel's arms felt warm, strong, and comfortable. The room spun, but Cashel held her firm.

# Chapter 61

Cora slipped her shoes on. Finally they were letting her out of this hospital. She intended to make the party tonight. And Adrian would be on her arm. Cashel would be on Jane's.

"We're friends, so don't get any ideas," Jane had said to Cora earlier, after she relayed what had happened to her.

Mathilde was going to be all right, but she would not be at the retreat party. She was not in any condition to party. Detective Andrews had been in the process of strangling her when the police found them. She was barely alive.

"I'm confused," Cora said, standing up and gathering her belongings. "Did Detective Andrews kill Marcy and Zooey?"

"No," Adrian said. "He ordered people to do it."

"People?"

"Hank," he said.

"Hank? Hank killed them both?"

Adrian nodded.

"But why? I don't understand."

"Hank had been dealing for him for quite some time. And Marcy, well, she owed them a lot of money."

"So they killed her? That's awful. And stupid. They'll never get their money now, will they?"

"No, but her husband stood to come into a lot of money. That's what they were counting on," he said.

"Rue's son," Cora said. "That's her connection."

"Yes, she was trying to untangle him from it," Adrian said, and opened the hospital door. "Let's get out of here, shall we?"

"You bet," Cora said, running her fingers through her hair, hoping she appeared presentable.

"Hey." Adrian turned to look at her. "You're gorgeous. You know that, right?"

She pressed herself into him. "You ain't so bad yourself, mister."

Their lips touched as Adrian ran his hand along her back, sending tingles through her.

When they pulled away, Adrian's jade eyes went smoky.

"Um," he said. "We better leave before I lose myself." He cleared his throat and pulled her by the hand.

Well, well, well, Cora mused.

They walked along the beach toward the resort. Cora had had enough lying around for one day and needed to move. The day was bright and sunny. The waves pounded the shore. The scent of warm sand and salty water filled her as she felt something unravel, a sigh, a whisper, an exhale. It was over. The island would be safe. It might take some time for the PR nightmare to subside, but ultimately, they would all be fine—except for Marcy and Zooey.

"What about Zooey? Why did he kill her?" Cora asked.

"Because she was the only person who could identify him. She knew exactly what was happening. Zooey and Marcy had remained friends. Did drugs together. Knew all the same people. If she didn't know exactly who did it, she would have soon," Adrian said, pushing his glasses back onto his nose. He needed to fix them. But then again, maybe not. It was such a sweet and geeky gesture and it made Cora's heart soar.

She loved geeks. She loved this geek.

She stopped walking.

"What?" Adrian said.

Could it be? Could she love Adrian? Could she be in love again? She never thought it would happen to her.

Was he ready to hear about her feelings? She gazed deep into those jade-green eyes of his and decided to wait.

"Never mind," she said.

He nodded and lifted one of his eyebrows. "Okay," he said, wrapping an arm around her as they walked along.

The resort was in eyeshot. A part of Cora did not want to return. She wanted to hang on to this moment, this feeling, alone with Adrian. But she realized she must venture forward to ready herself for the party. She promised Mathilde. Promises were meant to be kept.

Cora and Adrian stood for a moment and gazed over the beach.

"I need a shower and to prep for the party," she said.

"Me too," he said.

"What a retreat," she said. "Horrible things have happened." Her voice cracked.

"Hey," Adrian said, his finger under her chin to lift her face. He kissed her with a gentle, sweet kiss. "Good things have happened, too."

Her eyes met his and she smiled. He felt it, too. They were falling in love.

They would go back to Indigo Gap closer than before. She would go back to running Kildare House Craft Retreat, where she still had rooms left to be refurbished, and a possible new kitchen project ready to start so she could host a baking or food crafting class, and her cat Luna waited for her.

She missed it. She now had a place to call home. And a boyfriend she loved. Life was good.

As she thought back over everything that had happened here, and in her life, it seemed to her that it all brought her to this moment of understanding. Life was fragile. People were imperfect. Loss, hurt, and anger were a part of it. That's why moments like this were meant to be remembered, carried along with you like a security blanket.

She swallowed her fear. She'd not ask herself where she and Adrian were heading. She'd take it one day at a time and enjoy every moment.


Cora twirled in front of the mirror. She was wearing her doily skirt—the one her first group of crafters had made for her. She remembered them fondly— the manner in which they worked together and created something beautiful, something useful for her to wear out of a pile of old doilies gathering dust in a box in someone's attic.

She pulled her red curls into a sloppy bun, grabbed her purse, and made her way to the lobby to meet Adrian, Jane, and Ruby for the party.

"Well, look at you," Jane said. "The doily queen. Stunning."

"You look awesome," Cora said. And it was true. Her best friend was a gorgeous, voluptuous woman. Long strands of dark hair and beautiful doelike eyes—a smile as wide as the sky. She was dressed all in white, which set off her darker skin and eyes.

"You handsome devil, you," Cora said as she kissed Adrian and slipped her arm around him.

"My gorgeous girl," he said.

"Cashel," she said. "You're looking dapper."

"Yes. Now can we move this along? I don't feel like being here, partying with these people."

"But we got the bad guy," Ruby said. "What is your problem?"

Cora and Jane exchanged glances of acknowledgment. They knew what his problem was. He'd have to accept it.

Cora was in love with Adrian. His hand trailed down her back as they walked toward the party.

The room was filled with chimes, lanterns, and crafters galore. A jazz quartet played in the far corner. Groups of crafters were clustered at tables. All were dressed to the hilt.

"I'll grab drinks. What does everybody want?" Adrian asked, before he and Cashel went off to fetch drinks as the women sat down.

Katy and her friends came up to their table.

"I wanted to tell you your class was amazing," Katy

said to Cora. "I've already implemented some of your suggestions and, wow, the stats are skyrocketing. We should be able to start taking ads soon," Katy said.

"I'm so glad to hear that," Cora said, noticing Linda coming up beside her.

"How are you, Linda?"

"I'm feeling much better," she said. "Now that I know the killer has been caught."

"I hear ya!" Jane said.

"So am I to understand this all had to do with drugs and money and the mafia?" Katy said.

"Not the mafia," Cora said. "But a crime syndicate financed mainly by drugs." Cora didn't want to think of the lives she'd seen ruined by drugs. Marcy's and Zooey's lives taken because they owed too much money. Mathilde attacked and lying in a hospital room.

"I don't understand," Linda said. "Hank made the macramé bag? He killed Zooey and shoved her body inside? Hank did the killing because he was ordered to?"

"He was afraid for his life. He was desperate," Cora said. "Still, it's hard to fathom, isn't it? He made the bag, evidently trying to set up Josh, who was also left-handed."

"Nothing more than a hired thug," Ruby said. "Trash. The worst kind. If he knew all of this, he should have gone to the cops."

"But he couldn't," Jane said. "They had too much on him."

"And they probably would have killed him," Katy said. "And let's not forget there was a cop in on everything, from what you're saying."

"Can we please talk about something else tonight?"

Adrian said as he and Cashel walked up to the table with their drinks.

Katy's eyes moved from Adrian to Cora, and she grinned.

"Anyway, I just wanted to thank you," Katy said. "Your class was amazing and it's been wonderful getting to know you." She leaned over and hugged Cora. "Oh my. He's handsome," she whispered into her ear.

As Katy and her crew took their leave, the five of them remained, settling in.

"Good wine," Jane said.

"Agreed," Cora replied.

"A toast," Ruby said. "To us and to Mathilde, all fighting the good fight."

"With glue guns," Jane said with a laugh.

"Hear, hear!" Adrian said.

The only thing that would make the night more perfect would be to have Mathilde join them, but of course she couldn't. One of the paper crafters had fashioned a huge card for her, which was too big to be passed around, so crafters were standing in line to sign it. When the line died down Cora, Jane, and Ruby decided to take their turn.

The card was artfully done on lavender card stock, embellished with paper flowers and a doily. The signatures on the inside were all done in black Sharpie. Cora signed, then Jane, then Ruby.

The women who signed the card wrote personal notes about how much this time meant to them to explore and find new friends. Not one person mentioned the murders. Cora sighed. The beach retreat was ultimately a success, despite all the horrible things that had happened.

Cora's spirit lifted.

\* \* \*

Jane, Ruby, and Cashel stayed at the party, while Cora and Adrian left early.

"Come to my room tonight?" Adrian said as he reached for her in the elevator. They were the only two in the space, though Cora was certain it wouldn't matter if they weren't.

She hesitated.

"I don't know," she said.

"I won't push you," he said. "But, you know . . . I think we have something special and the next step is—"

"Shhhh," she said, and kissed him. She didn't want to hear about the next step. She was uneasy. Yet, she wanted to move ahead with their relationship, too. *C'mon, Cora,* she thought to herself. *You are no school-girl virgin.*

He held her hand firmly as they walked down the corridor to his room and stopped in front of the door.

His arms went around her. She tilted her chin upward and gazed at those jade-green eyes.

When he kissed her this time, she felt herself ignite.

"Maybe we should stay one more night?" he said as he opened the door to his room.

Cora nodded and shut the door behind them.

# CD and DVD Coasters

## Supplies

- CDs or DVDs you no longer want
- Sandpaper
- Micaceous iron oxide (any color). You can use any sort of acrylic color really, but this one struck my fancy.
- Paper Mod Podge
- Lacquer or acrylic sealing spray (optional)

## Directions

- Sand off the top shiny layer of the disc. The acrylic will stick to the surface better. You can do it lightly so the base still shows a complete shiny, reflective surface, or take the layer off completely to show the acrylic through the bottom. You can also etch the surface with a knife (carefully) to create patterns.
- Wash off the residue with water. Be careful, as some of the reflective layer could be in tiny splinters instead of dust.
- Spread the micaceous iron oxide acrylic over the surface of the disc in a thin layer. This stuff is thick enough that you can either do it smooth or texturize it. If desired, place paper graphics or other decoration on the acrylic before it dries (it acts as an adhesive as well).

- Let dry completely (the thinner the layer, the shorter the dry time).
- Once dry, coat with a thin layer of Mod Podge to seal. It goes on white and dries clear. You could use a clear acrylic spray instead.
- Another way you can do this is to use some lacquer or acrylic spray in the color of your choice. Use this outside or with good ventilation, and on top of newspaper/garbage bags. Apply a thin coat (according to spray can instructions) and let dry completely. It will adhere to the shiny layer and dry smooth, but where it is on the plastic itself it will dry in a cracked pattern. If you just use one coat, some of the original color of the CD/DVD will bleed through in the exposed plastic part.
- Try not to overspray, or some of it will leak underneath the disc.

# Simple Macramé
# Friendship Bracelets

**Supplies**
- Tape
- Ribbons/yarn/cording
- Beads/charms/buttons for embellishing

**Directions**
- Cut 4 pieces of 2-foot ribbon.
- Tie them together, leaving about 4-inches of ends (later you tie the bracelet onto your wrist with the ends . . . you don't want them to be too short!) Tape your ribbons down to your working surface.
- Separate the four ribbons and take the two in the center and anchor them down at the bottom of your work surface. You will make alternating knots with the two loose ribbons around the ones that are secured to the table.
- Starting with the left ribbon, cross it over the top of the center ones. (It looks like the number 4 at this point.) Slip the end UNDER the ribbons that are anchored and gently pull until the knot snugs up to the top.

- Now take the loose ribbon on the right side and lay it over the top of the center one. (It looks like a backward 4 at this point.) Slip its end UNDER the anchored ribbons. Snug it up next to your first knot.

- Continue alternately making these knots, working your way down the anchored ribbons. If you want your bracelet embellished, you can add beads, charms, or buttons to them by removing the tape of the anchored center ribbons. Thread a bead or charm up those center ribbons, then re-secure it to your work surface.

- Continue your macramé half-knots right around the embellishment.

- Work your way down to your desired length and tie off the ribbons with a knot.

- Trim ribbons at about 4 inches so you have enough ribbon left over to secure it to your wrist!

# Seashell Candles

Collect bits and pieces from old candles or buy new candles of wax for this fun project.

## Supplies

- Wax
- Any medium-size seashell with a large enough opening for a candle
- Candlewick

## Directions

- Put the wax in a microwave-proof bowl. Microwave the wax in 30-second to 1-minute intervals, gently swirling the wax in between heating. Use a pot holder to handle the bowl.
- In the meantime, prop the shells up/steady them. I use rice on a plate to support them so they don't tip over.
- Since the bottom of the shell is curved, you might need to bend the wick at an angle when you place it in the shell.

- Dip the bottom of the wick in the hot wax to anchor it in place and place on the shell. Then pour the wax into the shell.
- Let them sit and harden. Clean off/scrape away any wax that might have run onto the outside of the shell.

Be sure not to miss all of the books in
Mollie Cox Bryan's
Cora Crafts Mystery series, including

# NO CHARM INTENDED

Settling into her new life and career in small-town
Indigo Gap, North Carolina, Cora Chevalier is
preparing to host a "wildcrafting" retreat at her
Victorian home. But a specter hangs over the
venture when beloved local nanny Gracie Wyke
goes missing. Amidst leading their guests in
nature hikes, rock painting, and making clay
charms, Cora and her business partner, Jane,
team up with Gracie's boyfriend, Paul, to launch
their own investigation into her disappearance
when the local police prove unhelpful.

Cora and her crafters take Paul in, believing he is
in danger and not the suspect police have made
him out to be. However as they uncover new clues
and a body turns up at a local abandoned
amusement park, Cora and Jane begin to question
their decision. With more questions than answers
arising, is Cora crafty enough to untangle a knot
that could put an innocent in jail—and
permanently destroy her reputation?

Keep reading for a special excerpt.

A Kensington mass-market paperback
and e-book on sale now!

# Chapter 1

**I kidnapped her.**

Cora blinked and reread the message. It had been sent early this morning. She hadn't checked her phone all day. Between looking over supplies for the next craft retreat, making certain Kildare House was spotless and ready for the arrival of her teachers and crafters, and writing her next blog post, checking her own messages had slipped through the cracks of a very hectic day.

No name was attached to the text.

Her heart raced as she clicked and scrolled and tried to find out who sent such a message to her.

Could this have been an errant text? A complete mistake? Or, had one of her previous clients tracked her down in her new home?

Switching states and getting new phone numbers sometimes just wasn't enough. She had been warned. But she tried to sort through the Rolodex in her mind of clients this could possibly be—and didn't come up with a thing. Did anybody ever mention kidnapping to her?

Not in so many words. But parents often took children from other parents—this she knew. Cora remembered one case where a grandmother stepped in and took her grandson. The mother hadn't realized it for a few days—she'd been on a heroin binge. It was best for the child to be removed from her care, but the grandmother still had faced kidnapping charges. You had to follow the letter of the law when you took a child from his or her home—even if it was a bad home.

Cora sighed and vowed to break out the thumb drives where she stored all her ex-clients—as soon as she had a moment.

"Okay, calm down," she said out loud. Luna's ears twitched and she glanced at Cora as if to say, "Are you talking to me?" The cat blinked in disgust when she realized Cora wasn't speaking to her.

It was probably a wrong number. It probably was not an ex-client. It had been almost a year now since she held her post as a counselor at the Sunny Street Women's Shelter in Pittsburgh. Surely none of them would contact her at this point. Cora's life was now in Indigo Gap, North Carolina, in the craft retreat business. This was her new life.

Still, the text chilled her.

Kidnap?

Should she tell someone? The police?

And what would she say? "I've got this weird text message . . ." As if she hadn't already had a snootful of the local police.

No, she'd let it rest for now. It wasn't the first strange text message she'd ever gotten. Besides, she had enough to do to prepare for the Spring Fling Retreat. Her teachers were already here. The re-treaters were arriving tomorrow.

Cora glanced at her watch. She was already a little behind. She allowed herself one quick check in the mirror. Her 1970s blue minidress suited her more than she thought it would, and the white go-go boots were perfect. She smoothed her pink lipstick on her lips, ran a comb through her red curls, and she was ready for dinner with her guest teachers.

She opened her door and walked to the half flight of stairs to the third floor, where she almost bumped into Jane.

"What are you doing here?" Cora said.

"I have weird news." Jane's eyes were wide and she grabbed on to Cora's arm.

"What?" Cora said, thinking this retreat could not be any worse than the last one, where a teacher slept with her students and a murder happened right down the street. But the look in her best friend and business partner's eyes gave her pause.

"Remember Gracie?"

"Gracie who?" The name seemed familiar, but Cora wasn't making the connection.

"She babysat London a few times. She's her friend's nanny, remember?"

"Oh yes," Cora said. "We better get going. Can this wait?" she said, pulling away from Jane and walking down the hall.

"No," Jane said with urgency, grabbing her arm, stopping her. "You need to know this."

"What is it? Spill it. C'mon, woman," she said.

"She's missing," Jane said.

"Missing?" Cora's heart skipped a beat. "What do you mean?"

"She was supposed to babysit London tonight, so I called Jillie's mom because she never showed up," she said. "She's gone."

"Do you mean she took off?"

"Jillie's mom is calling the police. She says she's not been there all day. Her stuff is still there. Her car is still there. Everything. So I either have to bring London with us tonight or stay at home."

"I don't think London will be a problem—just bring her along," Cora said after a moment. She was the most well-behaved child Cora had ever known—a bit precocious, but manageable.

Cora stopped in her tracks, remembering the strange text. It wouldn't have anything to do with the missing girl, would it? She didn't even really know her. Why would someone send her a text?

"What's wrong?" Jane said.

"I just remembered this weird text I've gotten," Cora said.

"Hey, Cora. Hey, Jane. You about ready? We're starving!" Ruby said as she walked up the stairs toward them. Sitting in the foyer just below them was a group of crafting teachers. Cora took in the foyer of Kildare House, a large, old-fashioned room. The Victorians knew how to welcome guests, especially rich Victorians.

Cora smiled. "We're here. Everybody ready?"

London was also sitting in the foyer and peeked

up as they came toward her. She hopped up out of the chair and ran to Cora, who scooped her up in her arms. Jane's daughter had seen way too much change in her short life and yet seemed to have kept it together. Cora was in awe of her.

"Are you ready to eat?" Cora said.

"Yep," London replied, sliding out of Cora's arms. "I'm in the mood for pizza."

"You're always in the mood for pizza," Jane said.

"No pizza tonight," Cora said as she walked toward the door, the group following close behind her. When she opened the door, she gasped—Officer Glass was standing there, about ready to ring the doorbell. They'd gotten to know him very well during the last craft retreat, when he was investigating a local murder.

"Can I help you?" Cora asked. "We were just leaving."

"Hello, ladies," he said. "Cora, can we speak for a moment?"

"Is this important? As I said, we're leaving for dinner. We have reservations," she replied.

"It's about a text message," he said with a lowered voice.

"What? How did—"

"There were several sent today and the digital forensics team sent me over here to discuss it with you," he said.

Jane sighed. "Good Lord, what have you gotten yourself into?" she whispered.

"Nothing!"

"It's getting late," Jane said.

Cora took in the group. They were a famished, weary lot. "Why don't you all go ahead. I'll meet you there." Despite her own hunger pangs, she supposed it was the right thing to do—after all, she couldn't help wanting to help, even if it was the local police, who seemed to be always under her feet.

# Connect with Us

Visit us online at
**KensingtonBooks.com**
to read more from your favorite authors, see books
by series, view reading group guides, and more.

**Join us on social media**

for sneak peeks, chances to win books and prize packs,
and to share your thoughts with other readers.

facebook.com/kensingtonpublishing
twitter.com/kensingtonbooks

*Tell us what you think!*

To share your thoughts, submit a review,
or sign up for our eNewsletters, please visit:
**KensingtonBooks.com/TellUs.**